Ajeet Pratap Singh is a chocolatier with a passion for storytelling. He is an alumnus of HBTU Kanpur. Ajeet is an ardent admirer of high fantasy and wishes to create his own fantasy universe someday. In his free time, he likes to travel to places of historical importance and spend time with his family.

ARSENAL OF THE GODS

AJEET PRATAP SINGH

Om Books International

First published in 2025 by

Om Books International

Corporate & Editorial Office
A-12, Sector 64, Noida 201 301
Uttar Pradesh, India
Phone: +91 120 477 4100
Email: editorial@ombooks.com
Website: www.ombooksinternational.com

Sales Office
107, Ansari Road, Darya Ganj,
New Delhi 110 002, India
Phone: +91 11 4000 9000
Email: sales@ombooks.com
Website: www.ombooks.com

ISBN: 978-93-6395-223-2

Printed in India

10 9 8 7 6 5 4 3 2 1

To Papa

Contents

Prologue

So, what or who is truly running this world? Haven't we all pondered this? Some of us think about it more than others. Some say it is God or religion; some say it is science; some favour nature and its change in entropy. The most popular answer is money; some conspiracy theorists even say aliens, but we do not know, in fact.

We watch some unsung heroes saving mankind from extra-terrestrial threats, nuclear and biological warfare, from unthinkable and evil ideas of cynical geniuses in movies, but do such things really happen? Are those things happening around us while we are not even remotely aware?

On one fateful morning of September 2005, when a farmer in a small village in the state of Uttar Pradesh went to his field, he didn't know the turn of events that his daily levelling would start. He found some old clay potteries while doing his work. He thought his ancestors must have left buried treasure, so he dug deep in that area.

Soon, he began finding things made of bronze and copper. People working around him in their respective fields witnessed that, so they also started digging their fields. To their surprise, they also found valuables.

It was total madness until one farmer's hoe hit something in the ground, making a strange sound, as if he had broken something. He started rummaging by hand to ensure 'the thing' didn't get damaged anymore.

His hands touched something very smooth but hard. As soon as he dusted off that thing, he screamed, realising he was looking at a human skull. His scream was loud enough to attract the attention of people standing all around, and somebody from the crowd called the police and local media persons; people in other fields kept digging, unfazed.

Surprisingly, the police arrived within minutes, maybe the word 'treasure' was key here. The police stopped them from digging, but farmers violently opposed, so the police had to use force.

The next day, it became the lead story of the local newspaper. By 11 a.m., an insignificant village nobody knew of had luxury cars pouring in as it was only sixty-seven kilometres from the capital of the country, Delhi.

The village was Sinauli.

People wearing expensive suits and watches took over the fields. Some people who looked like scientists came to the site with big suitcases carrying modern equipment and started assembling them in the fields. It was total mayhem; farmers didn't want to give their land to these people and continued to protest.

The door of one of the cars opened, and a man who seemed significant started going towards the crowd of protesting farmers; two people who looked like bodyguards followed him. The intensity of the protest started dwindling upon seeing that person approaching. He reached the spot and said something to which most nodded assertively. One of the farmers shouted, but the person responded calmly.

There was no protest anymore.

The scientists started scanning the grounds and soon after locating the points, they marked the areas. The digging continued for months, and several graves and skeletons were found.

One evening, one of the youngest diggers came shouting to the site director, breathless, and informed him about what he thought he had found. The director received a phone call the same night. They filled up the whole area and left the very next day.

After twelve years, just a hundred meters from the previous site, a farmer unearthed some potteries again, the treasure hunt began, police came, it became the local newspaper headline and the ASI team again came to Sinauli, this time with another man at the helm. They cordoned off the area, marked the spots and started digging.

As soon as it began, the new director, who had been a part of the previous excavation, started sensing that this site was not the same as the previous one. This new area had coffins. In the 2005 excavation, no coffins were found; those had been simple graves. Ornaments made of precious metals were found on some of the skeletons, indicating they were royalty. These had intricate designs and weapons, which were very modern for that era. And then, they discovered the most important thing—a 5,000-year-old chariot.

A deep blue-coloured Mercedes-Benz G-class stopped at the site. A tall and fit person came out, wearing an Armani suit, shades and expensive red shoes. An officer came up to him and asked, "Sir, may I know who you are?"

"No. It's classified," the gentleman replied.

"Sir, can I at least see your identity card?" a visibly nervous officer asked, already knowing the answer.

"No," the man said without even looking at the officer. "Where is Hooda?"

"Umm… Director sir was admitted to the hospital in Delhi yesterday due to dehydration and food poisoning. I am the acting director here, my name is…"

The man interrupted, "So, Mr Acting Director, show me the progress so far. It would have been better to get answers from Hooda, but I will meet him in Delhi."

The officer started updating him timidly, but the man emphasised, "I said, show me." The officer obliged and took him to the site and explained everything.

As per schedule, the excavation stopped at 6 p.m. Everyone started preparing food for the night, but they could sense the stress in the atmosphere due to the gentleman's presence. Workers had dinner and went to their tents for a sound sleep after a hard day.

The next morning, when they woke up, the car was gone. People heaved a sigh of relief and went about their respective work. At lunch, some villagers approached the acting director.

"Good afternoon, sir," they greeted the officer. He wished them back.

"Sir, it's a village. When a dog barks here, people in nearby villages also wake up; many of us could not sleep last night due to the noise," one of them complained.

"Sorry, I don't follow you. What do you mean?" the perplexed officer asked.

"Sir, you people should do your work only during the day. Villagers are angry, but we came to you, expecting it was a one-night thing and would not happen again," he threatened the officer subtly.

"We stopped work as usual at 6 p.m. yesterday and slept early. Nobody was digging," explained the officer.

"Sir, we don't know and don't want to, either. Director sir is not here, and you are already struggling, so we don't wish to make a scene, but it must not repeat," said the leader of the farmers, pointing a finger at him, and the group left.

He scooted his lunch and rushed to the main grave with a coffin where the digging was in progress. He asked, collecting his breath, "How is it going?"

The young intern answered, "We have reached the bottom-most corner, sir, as you can see. I think the excavation work in this grave is over, sir, only some finishing needs to be done."

"OK, I can see that. You go for lunch," said the officer, looking at the freshly dug-up corner. The intern climbed out carefully and left the area.

The officer started inspecting and noticed a structure at one corner. He took out his spatula and brush and started removing soil from it. This structure was made of bronze and resembled a support.

"But if it is a support, there can't be only one. Where is the other one?" The officer muttered. He found a similar structure coming out some feet away from the first one. He resumed work, and his experienced hands realised the soil was loose. Now he was standing in the middle of the grave with two triangular supports in front of him, *But what were they supporting?*

"Hey, call the girl who was working here," he shouted.

Suman, the intern, was in front of him within a few seconds.

"When did you start digging this?" the officer asked frantically.

Suman answered apprehensively, "Sir, I started around 11 a.m."

"And you finished by 1?"

"Yes, sir," responded Suman.

"How was the soil here?"

"In comparison to yesterday, it was a little soft."

"Soft or loose?" the officer shouted.

Suman asked, panic-stricken, "Sir, what is the difference?"

"Do you think it had already been dug before and then covered up?" the officer asked, lowering his voice.

"I can't say with confidence, sir. This is my first project. But the soil was not that loose," answered Suman, expecting an outburst from the officer. But he shook his head in disbelief and waved at her to leave.

The next day, the director joined back and was apprised about the incident. He dismissed the officer and made a phone call.

"But, sir, lots of things are pending here."

"It is over, Hooda. Stop the work. I want everything from that site to be brought down to our museum. Work twenty-four hours, innovate, I know nothing of this scale has ever been done, but what we are going to witness has never happened either. I am sending security for you people." The phone disconnected. Hooda was standing in disbelief and thinking, *What the hell has happened here?*

Somewhere, two people were engaged in a heated conversation.

"How the hell could this happen, Amatya?"

"Emperor, we are not even sure whether anything has happened."

"But when did the digging start? Why were we not aware? Like last time, we could have stopped it."

"That is where we failed. All this took place without our knowledge. I assure you, O great Emperor, nobody in this world can locate it."

"There is always somebody. I can sense a shift in the balance of power. And if this happens, it will change the world or, who knows, destroy it."

Speculatively, is the balance of power running the world? Not power, balance of power. The unspoken understanding between the powerful or the fight between the ones who have and those who don't. As night balances day, evil balances good, cunning balances honesty, death balances everything a man desires, hate balances love; similarly, power balances power.

Some countries and people in this world are so powerful that they can do whatever they want, but they are restrained by another country or person balancing that power from the other side. When power is in the right hands, it improves the society; the problem is that these righteous people are not ruthless and they don't use wrong ways to achieve right. On the other hand, those balancing them, are ruthless and when they get the same power, they do not think twice before doing exactly that thing what caused them to not receive it.

So, what would happen when a power—so pure, so raw, so ancient—kept away from mankind for its own good, comes into the hands of the very people who only cause destruction? Over the last 5,000 years, the power was balanced, but now, it is time for chaos. A gust of wind has disturbed the pendulum.

1

Let's Meet

"Roll up the window, man. The air has become colder these days," requests Prashanna.

Rudra retorts, "I am feeling hot, and anyway, it's not that cold. It is Goa, not Delhi."

"It seems you leveraged the absence of Auntie quite nicely today. Rum or whiskey?" Prashanna winks at others in the cab.

"It's 26 January, genius. And yeah, that idiot Abhishek forgot to stock the bottles yesterday." Rudra closes the window, and the car rushes towards the factory with the night shift officers.

Yes, it has become quite cold in the last 2-3 days, and as it is close to midnight, it is even colder. The drive to the factory is only fifteen minutes from the town where they live, but during the night shift, this seems longer, since they won't be able to sleep that night.

"Why the hell does the demand increase during holidays? Nobody will die if we don't produce chocolate for a day," says Ravi. "Sometimes it seems like management thinks we are making rockets and would miss the launch date if we close for a day."

"Hi, sir, I am Amod. I joined last week. From today, I have been asked to come on the night shift for my training," a visibly excited young lad in his early twenties says.

Ravi barks, "For your training? What training? They sent you tonight to make you understand that you don't have a life anymore. The day the whole country celebrated Republic Day, we were sleeping, because we were on the night shift; and when people are going to sleep in their beds, we are going to work."

Amod says hesitantly, "Right, sir," and an awkward silence follows. He again asks after some time, but not to Ravi, "Sir, is our factory visible from this road?"

But again, Ravi replies, understanding that this boy didn't like his sarcastic reply. "Yes, in another 30-40 seconds, it will be visible from the road. Not the whole factory, but a small portion of it. Now, look there. Do you see that tall column-type edifice coming out of a huge structure below? That is our chocolate tower. The refining and mixing process takes place there, and it has four floors—the tallest in the factory. The rest are a maximum of two floors. You can even go to the factory roof from the second floor of the chocolate tower. Last time I went there was four years back."

"Who goes there anyway? Not that it's haunted or something. Yeah, but for your *training*, you can definitely go," says Prashanna, and all of them burst into laughter. "I hope you know the shift pattern of this factory."

Amod replies, "8 a.m. to 4 p.m. is morning shift, 4 p.m. to midnight is evening shift, and midnight to 8 a.m. is night shift. Right, sir?"

"Yes, right. So, a shift officer enters the factory and takes charge from the previous shift's officer after changing clothes and shoes. Handover is mainly about how the line is running, the plan for the next eight hours and turning over the shift's mobile phone. If it rings, it means there is some issue and somebody is calling for support, but when it doesn't ring, just don't assume everything is right; take a round and check the line condition yourself," explains Prashanna.

"Wow, beautiful night, isn't it?" Ravi says in awe, looking outside. The car crosses the old bridge on the way. The night indeed looks beautiful; fog has covered the mountain peaks on either side of the narrow river and is slowly spreading on its surface, which looks divine with the moonlight piercing through the fog.

Looking outside the window, Rudra thinks, *Finally, the last night shift before I go home.*

The car reaches the factory. It is a huge chocolate manufacturing unit spread over a hundred acres. They enter through the main gate and stop at the parking lot. These four young gentlemen—HR even refers to the night shift officers as supermen—punch in and go to the changing room. There is no uniform for Rudra on the shelf, which is not unusual. He goes to the laundry, takes an apron, changes his shoes and enters the process area.

Nikhil, the current shift superman, is waiting to hand over the phone to Rudra. He shakes his hand and asks, "So, last night shift, huh? You are leaving tomorrow, right?"

"Yes, bro, no tension for the next fifteen days. Don't call me even if there is a nuclear attack," chuckles Rudra.

"No tension for you, man, but nobody was ready to come on the night shift, so I will be doing back-to-back shifts for two consecutive weeks," says Nikhil. "But anything for you, brother. Your flight is in the morning, right? Leave on time or earlier if necessary; nothing will happen in a couple of hours." He gives the shift mobile phone to Rudra and starts leaving.

Rudra shouts, "You are also supposed to hand over the shift. Update on how the line is running, the plan and all."

Nikhil laughs, "Lines are running awesome." That's how his handover has been since he joined. No matter how pathetic the condition is of both manufacturing lines, even when machines are not running and the product is falling on the floor, it has always been, "Lines are running awesome."

Rudra starts his round and finds that both the manufacturing lines are running without any issue, and there is enough manpower. He goes to the chocolate tower but doesn't find any problem there either. He thanks God and Nikhil for a comfortable night shift before a hectic day of a long journey and returns to his office. After completing the necessary activities, he plans to solve a few question papers of an exam he has been preparing for. So, he calls the rest of the officers on shift, informs them he won't join in for tea, and starts solving the questions.

It is 3 a.m., and Rudra has not received any phone calls regarding any breakdown or other issues, so he leaves his office for another round. Everything is running perfectly. People are awake and doing their jobs. He walks towards Line-2. There is a massive hall between these two lines. He enters that hall. He is halfway through when suddenly, the noise of machines fades away, and he finds himself amidst utter silence and darkness.

It is as if he is dreaming but it is so real that he can even hear the mild babble of flowing water in the distance. It cannot be a dream, but how can there be such silence and darkness when lines are running and, most importantly, Rudra has never heard a river, ever, near the factory before.

"Rudra sir, sir, the electrician is not accepting my calls. The tank's pump is not running. Sir, sir!"

Rudra finds a technician shaking him, as if he is trying to wake him up from a deep slumber. There is light everywhere, and the hall is filled with the buzzing of machines again. Rudra mumbles something and then, controlling his senses, answers, "Yes, yes, tell me."

"Sir, what happened? Why were you not responding?" the technician asks.

"Oh, it was nothing. Just felt a bit light-headed. I will go to the first-aid centre after the round. Don't worry. Tell me what happened."

The technician replies, "Sir, the chocolate tank's pump is not working, and the electrician is not picking up my call."

Rudra responds, "I will call him, don't worry," and walks towards the second line.

"Light-headed for this long?" the technician mumbles and looks at Rudra in a confused way, but Rudra has already crossed the hall and entered the second line, pretending nothing has happened while thinking about the incident. *Was it really light-headedness or something else, and what about the sound of a flowing river?*

He enters the chocolate tower, which has the control room on the ground floor where operators sit. Generally, officers check the chocolate stocks on the control room screens, but Rudra starts ascending the stairs. Why? That too at this time of the night when nobody is on the upper floors.

Rudra finds himself on the roof outside the emergency exit of the tower's second floor, confused, without any knowledge of why and how he has reached there. It seems like a dream again, where he doesn't have control over his body or actions. Suddenly, he falls on his face, touching green grass. *Grass? On the chocolate tower roof, how the hell is it possible? It has always been concrete,* thinks Rudra, perplexed and tired, *and why the hell am I feeling so weary, like I haven't eaten anything or slept for days?*

He hears approaching footsteps. *But why do they sound so quaint?* Rudra tries to stand but cannot even move his head, which is when he realises, he is lying in mud. He spots a set of muddy army-style boots through the grass, closing in on him. Even after his best efforts, he is unable to keep his eyes open. Before passing out, he hears dogs barking incessantly. It is so violent that he is scared for his life now and shakes in utter panic, but ultimately, he loses consciousness.

2

Kshitip

The next shift officer, Kshitip, comes to the factory in the morning and enters the process area, expecting a handover from Rudra. He calls on his personal number, which rings continuously, but Rudra doesn't pick up. Kshitip goes to the office, but he doesn't find Rudra there.

He calls the shift mobile number, and it starts ringing. Kshitip hears a feeble ringtone; he opens the office desk drawers, and in one of them, he finds the phone. He opens the communication book and checks for any message, but the last entry is from 2 a.m. After that, nothing has been documented. He gets angry and says to the other officer there, "What irresponsible behaviour! Rudra left early without a handover and didn't even bother filling the book. How am I supposed to know what to do?"

The guy shakes his head and says, "Man, you have to stop being so negative about him all the time. He is going to his hometown today, and his flight is in the morning, so he must have left early."

Kshitip shoots back, "How would I know that he had a flight to catch?"

"You would not. You have to talk to people nicely to know about them," answers the guy without even looking at Kshitip.

Kshitip leaves the office in anger. Kshitip is not a very lovable character; he is short-tempered and doesn't get along with most of the people he meets. He has been transferred to the Goa factory from a smaller one in the north about two months ago to learn new things. Only God knows whether he is doing that or not, but he is known for his loathing towards Rudra.

Kshitip calls Rudra again after 3-4 hours, thinking he would have landed by then, but gets no answer. Generally, Rudra is not like this. Whenever he misses a call, he calls back as soon as he gets time. Kshitip redials around 2 p.m., and the same thing happens. He decides to inform their boss.

"Sir, Rudra left early today without a handover and is not picking up my calls either," Kshitip notifies.

The boss replies, "Guys, you should keep all this between yourselves. You don't have to come and inform if somebody doesn't give you a proper handover."

Kshitip gets defensive and says, "No, no, sir, that's not what I meant. Rudra has not picked up my calls for the last 5-6 hours. I hope everything is OK."

"He is travelling after the night shift; he must be tired. He will call you back; I suggest you don't bother him repeatedly. Let him enjoy his holidays. Is there anything urgent that you need him for?"

"No, sir. I was just worried."

"About what?"

"About him not calling back."

"Well, I don't think there is anything to be worried about."

He leaves the room silently and returns to his office. He doesn't talk about his hunch to anybody. Before the handover, he goes to the chocolate section around 3 p.m. to check and write down the stock of chocolate. A shift handover is considered good when the previous shift officer ensures a healthy stock of chocolate for the next one. So, before the end of their respective shifts, officers go to the chocolate section to write down the stock.

Kshitip goes directly to the control room. While writing down the stock, the operator opens the logbook to record Kshitip's entry time. As this section is sensitive, every person's entry and exit time is noted in a separate logbook. Kshitip glances at the notebook and notices Rudra's name. The entry time is 3 a.m., but the exit column is empty. He asks, "Who was the operator on the night shift? Why is this column blank?"

The operator retorts sharply, "Sir, how often have we asked to put cameras here? It becomes challenging to manually write everyone's entry and exit time while doing our regular work."

Kshitip controls his temper and asks gently, "I understand, Rajesh. Just check the log sheet and tell me the names of the operators on the night shift. I need to talk to them."

Rajesh checks and replies, "Inqalab, Vinay and Nitin."

Kshitip requests again, "Just tell me the operator's name from your logbook when Rudra was inside the tower."

Rajesh opens the logbook and says, "Inqalab was here then."

Kshitip takes out his mobile phone and dials Inqalab, but Rajesh objects, "Sir, he was on the night shift; he must be sleeping now." Kshitip ignores his words.

"Hello," a sleepy voice answers the call.

"Sheikh, I am sorry for calling you at this time, but I just needed to ask something," says Kshitip.

"No issues, sir. What do you want to know?" Sheikh replies politely.

"The logbook says Rudra was in the chocolate section last night..."

Before Kshitip can finish his sentence, Sheikh starts complaining, "Sir, the refiner is still not working properly. I have told each of you about this issue, but nobody is paying attention."

"OK, Sheikh, I will talk to the engineering team. First, answer my question."

"I am answering that, sir. I told Rudra the same thing. Later in the night, he went up to check the refiner," answers an irritated Sheikh.

"Why would he go and check the refiner on a night shift? It's a big task and should only be done during the day. Was there anyone else with him? Any mechanic or electrician or you?" a surprised Kshitip asks.

"I was also confused. Without entering the control room, he started ascending the stairs alone. He didn't even look around for anyone. I can't think of any other reason than checking the refiner," answers Sheikh.

"And when did he return?" Kshitip asks, his heart racing.

Sheikh replies, "I didn't see him coming down, sir. I went for a break after he went upstairs."

Kshitip knows where to go now. He thanks Sheikh and starts ascending the stairs. Kshitip searches all four floors, but doesn't find anything out of order. He starts coming down, looking for something unusual on every floor. Fourth floor, nothing. Third floor, nothing. After finding no clue on the second floor, he turns to go back and notices the emergency exit. He opens the door and steps out on the roof.

It's a huge roof, and he is clueless about what to look for. Kshitip came here about a month ago, when some maintenance work was in progress. He notices that the roof is much cleaner now. He remembers vividly how dusty it was back then. He turns back to find the walls of the chocolate tower dirtier as though all the dust from the roof has somehow shifted to the walls.

He walks around looking for anything atypical. The vast roof has smaller dividing walls for various sections. He hedges the small bund walls to go from one roof to another and searches almost the entire area, but finds nothing, so he decides to return. While going back, he notices something shining under a small heap of dirt at a corner near the emergency staircase, a few feet from the door. He removes the dust and finds a mobile phone that he recognises immediately. Rudra's mobile phone.

I knew it, he thinks.

Kshitip's phone rings. The caller ID reads: Boss. "The factory manager wants to meet you."

"OK, sir. I will go and meet him," says Kshitip, disconnecting the call.

Kshitip enters the factory manager's office.

"How are you, Kshitip?" the manager asks.

"I am doing well, sir," replies a nervous Kshitip, oblivious to why he has been summoned.

"I hope you learnt some good things in this factory?"

"Yes, sir, ours is a small factory, but here the practices and systems are much more robust," answers Kshitip, wondering, *Why did he say 'learnt'?*

"The manager of your factory called me a while back. They need you back there."

"Sir, when am I supposed to leave?"

"Today. One more shift officer has resigned from your factory. I apologise for not giving you sufficient time. You must travel today, and your luggage will be transferred later. I hope it is OK with you," the FM says while his desk phone starts ringing.

"Yes, sir, I don't have any problems," answers a surprised Kshitip.

"Good, meet your boss. He will share your ticket and other details." The FM shakes Kshitip's hand and picks up the ringing phone. Kshitip comes out, puzzled, trying to figure out whether what happened inside the FM's office was good or bad.

"Oh, good that I found you here. I am going for a meeting and wanted to give you the tickets myself. Best of luck! I hope that you learnt some valuable things here. Thanks for contributing to this department and factory in the last two months. You will have to leave right away; your flight is at 8 p.m., so you also have to pack. We will plan a grand farewell once you come for your luggage transfer," his boss says, finding him outside the FM's office. He shakes Kshitip's hand and leaves for his meeting.

There are people all around him in the admin area, working, talking, laughing, but he feels he is watching a silent movie. Standing alone with his flight booking details, he reckons what happened in the last 10-15 minutes.

On his way back, something comes to Kshitip's mind and he stops at the main gate to ask the security guards, "When people leave the office before their shift ends, you note down their name and out time, right?"

"Yes, sir," answers the security supervisor.

"Please show me today's entries," requests Kshitip. The guard hands over the register to Kshitip, who checks and finds no entries for the morning. "Is it possible that you people might have missed someone's name?"

The supervisor replies, "No, sir, we open the gate when staff go in or out. So, that's not possible."

Kshitip hands the register back to the guard, thinking, *Does it mean Rudra didn't leave the factory?*

He starts his bike when the supervisor shouts from behind, "Sometimes new recruits who don't know about the whole process don't do the entries. On the night shift yesterday, there were two new guys."

Now Kshitip doesn't know what to think. He leaves the factory.

While going back, he even visits the society where Rudra lives. A huge lock is hanging on Rudra's apartment door. He goes to his own apartment and starts packing for his flight.

3

Light-Headed

"He is trying to open his eyes," says the nurse. Rudra opens his eyes and is surprised to see himself in a hospital room with his mother.

"What was the need to bring me to a hospital? It was just light-headedness, and I fell due to dizziness. Oh! My head hurts, could you please switch off the light, sister?" Rudra whimpers.

"Light-headedness? Dizziness? What do you mean?" asks his mother, wiping her tears.

"Ma, stop crying, please. There is nothing serious. I couldn't eat anything yesterday after dropping you at the railway station. I came home, went to bed directly and woke up when the cab driver called me for my night shift. I left for the factory. Somehow, I was not feeling hungry either. But how come you are here; you should be in Allahabad. You took a flight, finally?"

"What are you saying, beta? We are in Allahabad," she says.

"Allahabad? Are you messing with me, Ma? I was in Goa last night and fainted in the factory due to weakness." But he notices that the nurse is speaking proper Hindi, not Goan Hindi. Their conversation stops due to the noise of hurried footsteps in the corridor. Somebody is walking towards his room recklessly. The sound becomes unbearable for Rudra due to his headache, and he starts feeling restless. The door of the room opens.

"Papa, you too? What is going on? Am I really in Allahabad? But it can't be," Rudra almost screams.

"Oh, thank god, you are awake," Rudra's father says while hugging him and asks, "Nandini, what happened?"

"He doesn't remember where he was. He says he fell in his factory yesterday due to dizziness," his mother starts crying again.

His father instructs, "Nurse, please inform the doctor about Rudra gaining consciousness and ask him to visit us."

"Ma, what do you mean by I don't remember where I was? I was on a night shift yesterday and went on the chocolate tower where I fell due to weakness, maybe..." Rudra recollects with a hand on his head, feeling a bit confused now.

"Oh god, it's OK, it's OK," mumbles his father with concern. He sits in the other chair in the room and says slowly, "So, what do you think the date is, today?"

"27 January, obviously," answers Rudra, without any doubt in his mind.

"No, it is not 27 January, beta," he says with a sunken heart, "It is 8 February, and yes, you are in Allahabad. You were found unconscious by some people in a field, and they admitted you to a hospital. Luckily, somehow the hospital found out about us and called me. We have been waiting for you to wake up. Your mother has not left your bedside. You have been unconscious since 11 a.m. yesterday, and it is almost 3 p.m."

Rudra's mouth opens in disbelief after listening to all this. He thinks, *But how come I don't have any memory of all these days?* His parents are looking at him expectantly, but Rudra has so many questions to ask that he doesn't know where to start. The terrible headache adds to his misery. He closes his eyes and groans, "Please call the doctor, I can't bear this pain."

Rudra's father rushes out of the room with those darn shoes again to call the doctor, and Rudra closes his eyes for some rest, but is unable to shake off the discomfort over losing his memory of almost a fortnight. He doesn't remember where he was, what he was doing, or who was with him. The cardiograph machine starts beeping loudly, his blood pressure is 100 bpm.

The doctor enters the room, running and checks his cardiograph. The reading has already crossed 130 bpm. Rudra's body is shaking badly, and it seems he is having a seizure. The doctor gives him a Hydralazine injection. Rudra's body is still shaking, and he closes his eyes as everything blurs out. The readings start going down in 30-40 seconds, and within a few minutes, they regain normalcy.

"What happened?" the doctor asks.

"He thinks it is 27 January, he doesn't remember anything about the last twelve days," his father answers softly, hoping Rudra doesn't hear.

"Oh, I see. He looks extremely weak and tired. Has he always been like this?"

"No, sir, he has been a healthy guy. He has gotten weak in these last twelve days," responds his mother, "I had left him a day before his disappearance, and he was perfectly fine."

"Sometimes people lose consciousness due to fatigue and malnutrition. You are unaware of where he was, but one thing is certain: he has been under extreme stress. Anyway, I have given him medication to relax and dilate his blood vessels. It will lower his blood pressure. It also treats hypertension. Let him rest for a few hours, and yes, please do not talk about his memory loss, at least for the next 5-7 days. It looks temporary. Sometimes such memories come back within a few days. Let's hope for the best," assures the doctor. "Nurse, ensure the drip is replaced on time, he is extremely dehydrated. I will leave now. See you tomorrow." The doctor leaves the room, and Rudra slips into deep slumber.

"Nandini, it is 9:00 p.m. already, go home. You need a sound sleep. It's already been more than thirty hours since you last slept. How will you care for him if you are not healthy?" Rudra's father says.

"I am perfectly fine, Santosh, I am not going to fall sick," Rudra's mother replies.

"Then at least sleep on this bed," Rudra's father says, pointing to the additional bed in the room.

"He looks so weak. He has not eaten anything for 2-3 days. Even after all these saline bottles, it appears he will not be able to sit".

"Ma, please switch off the light, it is hurting my eyes," mutters Rudra. It is evident how much effort he puts into opening his mouth, let alone the struggle in speaking. His mother switches off the only light in the room, but luckily, it is not entirely dark with a streetlight beaming through the window. Rudra tries to sit on the bed, but both parents try to stop him on an impulse.

Rudra says, "I want to sit for a few moments, my back is aching." Noticing his struggle, his father uses the lever beneath the bed to lift it onto his head. Rudra sits with stretched legs and looks at his parents with a wry smile on his face. "Ma, go home and take some rest. I am feeling much better now," he requests.

"Why are you both asking me to go home? I will sleep here only. I am not leaving this room," she says, not with anger but care, "And, anyway, I will not let anyone talk to you except the doctor."

"Okay, Ma, don't worry. I won't talk to anyone but..." says Rudra.

His mother cuts him short, "No ifs and buts, Rudra. Take rest, get well, and we will talk about everything at the right time. First, let's focus on your recovery."

"How is your headache?" his father asks.

"It is better now, Papa, but my eyelids seem very heavy and sleepy. Direct light to the eyes feels very painful. I am thirsty, please give me a glass of water," Rudra stretches his hand for the glass. His mother stands up, fills the glass and helps him drink the water.

"Yes, due to weakness, the light must be stinging. You have also been sleeping for almost a day and a half, such things happen. The injection the doctor gave might have some effects, too," says his mother.

His father suggests, "I think you should sleep now; your eyes look tired. We will talk tomorrow. I will straighten the bed."

"No, Papa, let it be. It feels better," requests Rudra.

"Ok, I will leave it like that. Sleep well. Good night, beta," he says, waving at his wife to come out of the room. He opens the door, and Nandini follows him. He closes the door behind him and says, "Now that you insist on staying here, don't punish yourself and have a good sleep. The doctor's visiting hours start at 08:00 a.m., right?"

"Yes, he came exactly at eight this morning," replies Nandini. Santosh leans and whispers something in her ear. She says, "Yes, good night. Drive carefully; it is pretty late now."

"Yes, I will," he winks at her and walks away.

4

One Day at a Time

At 08:10 a.m., Rudra and his mother are awake and waiting for the doctor.

"Where is your father? He told me he would be here by 8:00 a.m.," she says, sipping her tea.

"He is either stuck in traffic, Ma, or making his perfect sandwich. He will be here, don't worry," says Rudra, looking fresh.

"Why isn't he picking up my calls? I have tried twice since morning, but he didn't answer. It seems like he is still sleeping. I asked him to bring us breakfast. I hope the doctor allows you to have homemade food from today. Let me try his number again," his mother vents, visibly irritated now. The call goes unanswered again. She opens the door to look outside and finds that the doctor is two rooms away, so she looks in the corridor, but doesn't find Santosh. She closes the door and starts waiting for the doctor, shaking her legs.

"Everything is going to be fine, Ma. Why is Papa required for the doctor's visit? We will understand whatever the doctor suggests and later explain everything to Papa. You are unnecessarily worried, and if Papa is not buying himself, you gift him a new mobile. You know the condition of his eighteenth-century phone." Rudra tries to calm her down.

The door opens, and the doctor enters with a big smile and greets them, "Good morning, Rudra, it's good to see you awake."

"Good morning, sir. I am not just awake but feeling better, too. My head doesn't feel as heavy as yesterday, and I can tolerate the light now," answers Rudra, smiling.

The doctor asks, "Have you been able to stand, leave the bed, or are you still feeling weak?"

Rudra replies, "Sir, I woke up around six today and went to the toilet myself. I do not feel 100 per cent fit, but much better than yesterday. Yes, I have some back pain, so I'm unable to stand straight." Surprised, his mother looks at him as she didn't see him leaving the bed. The doctor asks him to stand on the floor. Rudra does the same. The doctor checks his tongue, eyes, hands and heartbeat, asks the nurse to put some sensors on his head at various points and then asks him to sit down. He checks the readings of various machines and nods his head, calculating something.

"So, you don't have a severe headache anymore, you say. Any progress on your memory front, flashes or anything else?"

"No, sir, I don't have any memory of those twelve days," answers Rudra.

"What is your last memory? Don't push hard, if you don't remember, it is okay," the doctor asks, calmly looking at the notepad without giving away the importance of the question.

"Sir, my last memory is from the night shift in my factory. I was sitting in my office, doing the regular activity."

"Where do you work?"

Rudra replies, "The Orion chocolate factory in Goa, sir."

"Oh, where in Goa?"

"It is in Palolem, sir."

"And where is this Palolem in Goa, exactly?"

"It is basically in the south of Goa."

"What is your education?"

"Sir, I have done my B.Tech from Trichy."

"Do you have any siblings?"

"No, I am the only child."

"So, Rudra, we did various check-ups when you were admitted. There is nothing wrong with your head. Your brain is functioning properly, and you have all your memories except for the last few days. I think it will come back; it is temporary. Don't push too hard, just follow your daily routine, eat properly, and start some physical activity. For the time being, you can start walking in the hospital. We have a very nice garden here. You can start having fruit juices and some light food like homemade khichdi," says the doctor. Then he turns to the nurse and says, "Stop the saline drips, let him have food." The nurse removes the drip from Rudra's wrist. The doctor continues, "So Nandini-ji, I am writing some medicines for your son, please ask Mr Singh to bring these now," and explains the dosage. "By the way, where is he, Nandini-ji?"

A worried Nandini replies, "We are also waiting for him, sir. He should be here any minute now; he is running a little late."

"OK, OK. Please bring these as soon as possible, as we have already removed the drip. He may start having headaches again." The doctor starts leaving the room.

Rudra's mother asks quietly, "So, doctor saab, when do you think he would be discharged?"

The doctor replies, "I do not see any major problems, Nandini-ji. Though his cardiograph readings are perfectly fine today, I would recommend that Rudra spends some more time under supervision, considering yesterday's panic attack. He is taking the memory loss thing quite maturely, but I don't want to take any chances," he says all this feebly, ensuring Rudra doesn't hear and leaves the room, saying he will visit again in the evening.

Where the hell is Santosh? He is thirty minutes late already, Nandini thinks, fuming. She turns to Rudra and says, "Everything is fine, you should be happy now."

"Oh yes, I am. At least I don't have that headache anymore. Ma, call Papa again and ask him to bring something. I'm feeling hungry now."

She dials him, and it starts ringing. *But why isn't he picking up?* She hopes everything is OK, but deep down she is very worried. Why wouldn't she be? Her son was missing for about two weeks and was found by some people in a secluded area, unconscious, without any memory. Now her husband has been incommunicado since last night.

The IVR starts with, "The customer you are calling…" and she disconnects. She starts panicking and says, "I am going to the medical store for your medicines. It may take some time." She takes her jacket and moves towards the door, but the door opens from the other side.

Santosh enters with earpieces plugged in, humming some song and greets them loudly, "Oh, how are you, beautiful? Hey, beta!" He removes his earpieces.

"Where the hell were you, Santosh? We were so worried. Why are you late? You were supposed to be here before eight. Where is your mobile?" Nandini shouts at him.

Santosh answers calmly, "You asked me to cook breakfast for three of us. I couldn't find most of the stuff in the kitchen and got late. I thought this was more important as you would not eat outside food, which won't be good for Rudra either."

"And the mobile, Santosh?"

"Oh, you called?" He checks his mobile and notices missed calls from Nandini. "Oh, I think I again set it on silent mode accidentally. Sorry, I should have checked"

"Why don't you buy a new mobile, Papa? I know your mobile automatically sets itself to silent mode, as it sometimes starts dialling numbers itself. Who uses a Walkman these days for listening to songs but you?" says a smiling Rudra, "Anyway, what have you cooked?"

"Khichdi for you."

"What, even in breakfast? I thought at least I would have something better for breakfast, and khichdi would be lunch or dinner."

"Ask your mother, man. She told me yesterday to prepare khichdi for you for breakfast, lunch and dinner. All three times."

"Oh, Ma, I am just twenty-seven years old."

5

And, the Sunshine

"It is the same hospital where your appendix operation was done, right, Ma?" asks Rudra, leaning on the first-floor railings of the hospital terrace.

"Yes, it is the same," replies Nandini, admiring the beautiful hospital lawn.

It is almost 9 a.m. and the duo is taking their morning walk after having their home-made breakfast. Rudra has started feeling better now and is walking quite normally. Surely, the weakness has its effects, and he stops every now and then. It is a beautiful February morning. The sun is hiding in clouds, a cold breeze is flowing, and people are still wearing sweaters.

"Let us take a walk in the garden area," says Rudra and starts walking again. They take the stairs to the ground floor. After crossing the reception area, Rudra swings the door, and they are out in the open.

There is a pathway on the right for walkers, heading to the garden, and another straight one goes to the parking area. They take the right one but stop hearing somebody call from behind,

"Good morning, Rudra." They both turn to see the same doctor waving at them. "Did Dr Batra visit you this morning?" he asks.

"Yes, doctor saab, he came in the morning today," replies Nandini.

"I came very early, as there was an accident and all those injured were brought here. So, I was busy in the operation theatre," Dr Patwardhan explains, "It's good that we met, I wanted to see your progress. Mrs Singh, I am going out for 10-15 minutes. If you don't mind, can I take Rudra with me? It has been three days already."

"Sure, doctor. I will wait in the room. Rudra, once you are back, come there directly," answers Rudra's mother. Rudra walks with Dr Patwardhan towards the parking area, and his mother goes towards the lift.

Dr Patwardhan starts his car and asks, "So Rudra, do you know how to drive a car?"

"No, sir."

"Do you do drugs?"

"No, no, sir." Rudra is taken aback.

"Don't worry; I am not going to tell your parents." He chuckles and stops the car at a roadside cigarette shop. "Do you smoke, Rudra?"

"Ah, yes, sir."

"Two Gold Flake Lights, please," the doctor hands fifty rupees to the shopkeeper. The shopkeeper gives him two cigarettes and some change. Rudra extends his hand, expecting one of the cigarettes from the doctor, but he puts one cigarette on his lips and the other in his pocket.

Noticing his extended hand, the doctor smiles and says, "I am your doctor, for god's sake. I should not even smoke in front of my patient, but you are an educated and mature person, so I thought, what's the issue? Do not smoke for at least fifteen days; your immune system needs to recover." Then he asks, "So, no luck with the memories of those days?"

Rudra answers, "Not at all, sir. It is not even blank. I feel more like I didn't live those twelve days."

"But do you have a headache or dizziness anymore?"

"No, sir, from yesterday evening, I have not had any headache or dizziness. But yes, I am feeling weak; better than yesterday, but not fully well."

"This weakness would not go overnight; it will take time. Are you taking the medicines on time?" Dr Patwardhan asks.

"Yes, sir."

"OK. I will ask the nurses to run some tests. We will plan your discharge based on the results. Let's go back now."

Dr Patwardhan drops him near the reception gate and says, "You act pretty cool about your memory. I hope you are not overthinking it; that will not help. Give your brain some rest. Your memory should start coming back, and even if it doesn't, I don't think the world will change," he winks and drives on towards the parking.

Rudra smiles and takes the lift to his room. He opens the door and finds his mother talking to his childhood friend Roshani.

"I have been waiting for you for the last hour. Even in this condition, you are roaming around like a dog," complains Roshani.

Rudra responds, "But I was gone for hardly twenty minutes."

"Whatever. I brought you something to eat." She opens her bag excitedly.

"Did you cook, or was it your mom?" Rudra teases.

"You want to eat or not? Anyway, Uncle is bringing your khichdi for lunch. This is for Auntie," she replies mischievously.

She unzips the bag and takes out Rudra's favourite dry potato, green peas and cauliflower sabji with crispy golden yellow parathas. Rudra looks at his Ma, she nods, and he attacks the parathas like a hungry lion feasting on its favourite prey.

"Auntie, you go home and freshen up if you want. I can stay for a few hours. I have brought my laptop, I can work from here," suggests Roshani.

"There is no point in driving thirty minutes. Santosh is managing things at home. You people talk, I will take a nap," answers Nandini and lies on the other bed.

"What a good friend you are! I am in the hospital, lying unconscious, and you come after three days," taunts Rudra.

"I got to know today itself. I hadn't seen Auntie for the past few days, so I asked Santosh uncle today, and he told me about you," answers Roshani.

"Oh, OK," says Rudra, wondering why his parents have not informed anyone.

"So, I heard, you lost your marbles. Is it true?"

"What did I lose?"

"I mean, have you gone bonkers? Offo, I mean, have you lost your memory, idiot?" she asks again. "Auntie and Uncle asked me not to talk to you about this, by the way."

"And which part of 'Auntie and Uncle asked me not to talk to you about this' you didn't understand?" Rudra teases her. He takes a pause and continues, "Yes, I don't remember about these last 11-12 days at all. I don't have the slightest idea about where I was or what I was doing. I remember vividly being in my office, doing my regular work. I was on the night shift, fell due to weakness and was admitted to the hospital."

"And what does the doctor say?" asks Roshani ominously.

"He says that I should start smoking after fifteen days," laughs Rudra quietly, keeping an eye on his mother. "He says there is no permanent damage, so it may or may not come back eventually."

Roshani gets very worried after hearing this but tries to look as cool as possible and chirps, "It will come back, bro, don't worry."

"Don't call me bro, you idiot," Rudra reacts sharply.

"Why not?" Roshani asks, laughing internally. Rudra changes the topic to talk about the performance of her blog page. Being the idiot she is, she plays along and makes him feel he successfully dodged that question.

"When did you come?" asks Nandini, waking up from her deep, refreshing sleep.

"Just five minutes back," replies Santosh.

"Oh, when did Roshani leave? Was I asleep too long?"

"Roshani left before lunch, and it is almost time for the doctor's visit. Finally, you slept calmly after days, Ma," answers Rudra, smiling.

The door opens and Dr Patwardhan enters with reports in his hands and says, "I checked your reports and everything is normal and..."

"Sorry, doctor saab, which reports are you talking about?" Rudra's mother asks, concerned.

"I had written some tests today which he has already undergone," answers Dr Patwardhan, a little surprised.

"Ma, you were sleeping like a baby after so long, I didn't want to disturb you. Roshani was here, so I went with her," assures Rudra.

"OK, OK," says his mother, "Yes, doctor saab, you were saying?"

The doctor continues, "So all his reports are fine, and we will discharge him tomorrow morning. We will write down some medicines which he will take and visit me after five days. I will not be able to meet you tomorrow. Just one piece of advice, Rudra: for the next week, focus on recovering your physical health and gaining strength. After a week, let's assess your situation. Do not focus on your memory. OK?"

"Yes, sir, I will keep in mind," answers a visibly happy Rudra, after hearing that he will be discharged the next day.

"OK, I will leave now. Best of luck to you! Mr and Mrs Singh, please do not be worried about all this," says the doctor while walking towards the door.

"Thanks a lot, doctor saab, for everything," says Nandini, getting emotional, and Santosh taps her shoulder, trying to console her.

The doctor leaves, waving at them, saying, "It is my duty, ma'am."

Santosh wipes Nandini's tears and hugs her. There is a smile on Rudra's face, seeing his parents happy after such a stressful time. "So, finally, I am going home tomorrow," he says, beaming with happiness. "Let's have dinner, I have to go for a walk too."

"Yes, yes, Forrest Gump. You want to walk all the time now," his mother teases.

Rudra asks, surprised, "You watched *Forrest Gump*, Ma? Good going."

"Even boredom becomes a habit if you don't explore. I have all the time in the world once you go to the office, so I started watching these movies," she replies with an unspoken pain and starts serving them dinner. Finally, it is not khichdi.

"How is the boy?" a deep, husky voice asks. The type that intimidates anybody who hears it. Authoritative, powerful, respectable, or even fearsome.

"He has lost his memory, but physically he is healthy, sir. He is being discharged tomorrow morning," answers another voice.

It is a massive hall without any windows. This hall doesn't look man-made but more like nature's work, like a cave, but is equipped with modern amenities like electricity and air conditioning. It has a magnificent chandelier on its uneven roof, so grand that it seems like some medieval Indian palace. And not just one chandelier, but four others at equal distance from each other, keeping the biggest one in the centre of a square. There are four more forming a bigger square enclosing all other chandeliers. Though these are smaller, they have no less grandeur.

Ten majestic chairs are arranged in a circle, one bigger than the other nine. Eight holograms of people are sitting on these chairs, but the larger chair, resembling a sinhaasana, and one other chair are empty. They are wearing peculiar full-body robes, and their faces are not visible, as the holograms are projected with blurred faces.

"And what about the findings?" the husky voice asks.

"They are with him, and he has already found a few pieces too," answers one of the holograms.

"Do you have a number?"

"Two, sir."

"And we could not find the pieces or the remaining leads?"

"No, sir."

"It has been an enormous mess. We need to clean it ourselves, right now."

"Our people are keeping an eye on him and his family. As soon as he regains his memory, we will ensure we have all the leads and pieces, sir."

"We don't have any other options. A lot is at stake here," a figure emerges from the background, speaking these words in a deep voice, wearing similar robes and a mask with a golden ring on his head and sits on the sinhaasana. He waves his hand, and all the holograms disappear, acknowledging the order.

6

Homecoming

Santosh stops the car, and Nandini gets out to open the gate of their house. She opens it, and Santosh parks the car in the narrow parking area.

"You converted my room into a parking area?" Rudra asks, surprised and disheartened.

"Since you were not here and we faced a lot of problems with parking space, we did this. But don't worry, you can stay in the TV room," explains his father.

They get out of the car. His mother opens the front door of their small house, and they enter. First comes the guest room, then there is a small open space, and then comes the lobby with five doors. The first one through which they entered, the second door to their left, opens in the parking area, which is locked most of the time. The third one is in the parents' bedroom, the fourth is more of a door frame for an open counter kitchen and the fifth, just opposite the guest room door, is the TV room, where Rudra will stay.

"There are many medicines that you have to take—just explaining, so that you remember, if we forget. Take these two tablets twice daily, after breakfast and dinner; the red syrup, all three times. Now, this small capsule is to be taken post-lunch and the bigger one after dinner," explains his father, carefully keeping the medicine box on the table beside the bed in his room.

Rudra thinks, *I have only forgotten those days, but I will not forget everything.*

For the next five days, his daily routine remains the same. Waking up around 6 a.m., going for an hour-long walk near the Yamuna bank, having breakfast around 8 a.m., and then watching TV. The problem with watching TV is that he mainly likes watching cricket, but now that the India v/s New Zealand series is over, he watches something random and falls asleep midway. Waking up again around 1 p.m., he takes a bath followed by lunch of his choice. Sitting on his roof for 15-20 minutes in the shade, he observes people. Coming back to his room, he switches on the TV, and falls asleep while it's on, again, to wake up around 5 p.m. Waiting for Roshani to join for tea, he stays excited to talk to her, or more like listen to her talk about their school and college days, until she returns before dark.

His father returns from the shop around 7 p.m., and then the family has teatime, followed by an evening walk to the Yamuna bank again, engaging in aarti at the temple. He comes back home, watches the news with his father, then has dinner with the TV on, and finally sleeps again around 11 p.m. Of course, a lot of medicines in between.

He spends five days with the same routine, and on the sixth morning, he goes to the hospital with his parents. Dr Patwardhan asks Rudra similar questions as last time, but notices that he doesn't show any signs of trauma.

The doctor says, "I have always believed that your memory loss is temporary, but how long it will take to recover cannot be quantified. I will suggest you resume your normal lifestyle and start at the office. Maybe that'll trigger your memory. I have a good friend who is practising in Goa. When you go back there, meet Dr K.C. Naik. I will talk to him and give you a referral letter too," and he starts writing on his letterhead.

"Is he fit to join work, sir? I mean in this condition." Rudra's mother enquires.

"Medically, he is healthy now, so he should join back. You cannot wait for his memory to resurface. There is a possibility that it may never happen," tells Dr Patwardhan firmly.

"I understand that, doctor, I will be in Allahabad next month too. So, I will meet you then. Thanks a lot for saving my life," Rudra says with gratitude and confidence in his voice, to move ahead from all this.

"You're welcome, Rudra, and best of luck." Dr Patwardhan hands over the letter to Rudra and shakes his hand firmly. His parents also bid adieu to the doctor, and they leave his office.

While getting inside the car, Rudra tells them, "Let us book tickets to Goa now. Ma, this time I will also come with you by train because, as usual, you won't take a flight, I know. My boss knows about my conditions but has been following up to resume work as another guy is on leave, and there aren't enough people to handle the shifts." He checks online and exclaims, "Luckily, tickets are available for the day after tomorrow. Ma, I am booking for both of us, and the train is in the morning."

While driving, his father says, "Book a ticket for me too, I would also like to spend some time in Goa."

"Who will manage the shop then, Papa? Don't worry, Ma and I will travel safely," says a surprised Rudra.

"No, he is right. Mahesh will manage the shop for some days," Nandini supports her husband.

"OK, so I am booking three tickets for the day after tomorrow morning and… it's booked," says Rudra, running his fingers on his father's laptop keyboard.

They reach home, and his father leaves for the shop to make the necessary arrangements for his absence period. As usual, Rudra switches on the TV, has his lunch and falls asleep while watching it. He wakes up in the evening and waits for Roshani to come, but she doesn't. It starts getting dark, so he stops expecting and instead helps his mother pack. They don't even realise the time until his father honks, asking to open the door, so Rudra goes out. He notices it's already 10 p.m. and his mother is too exhausted to cook, so Rudra prepares Maggi for dinner. They eat and fall asleep in a blink after the day's labour.

Rudra wakes up and waits for Roshani to show up, to tell her that they are leaving for Goa the next day. He takes his breakfast and lunch but skips all his naps in between, expecting Roshani. He doesn't have his mobile, so he picks up his mother's to call her, but before he can dial, the doorbell rings and Rudra knows it's her. He opens the door and returns to the lobby with Roshani, where his mother is still packing.

"Hi, Auntie, are you all going somewhere?" she asks innocently.

"Yes, beta, all three of us are going to Goa tomorrow morning," answers Nandini, still busy packing.

Roshani looks at Rudra with wide eyes that question: *And you didn't tell me?*

"The doctor said I would have better chances at regaining my memory if I get back to my normal lifestyle. So, today only we booked the tickets for tomorrow," says Rudra.

"No, beta, have you forgotten? We booked the tickets yesterday," says his mother, unknowingly exposing Rudra's lie.

Roshani gives him a glare, *You liar,* and Rudra just shakes his head at his mother's innocence.

"So, you are also going with him?" Roshani asks Nandini, turning away from Rudra in anger.

"Yes, all of us. His father will come back after spending some time. We will give you the keys, in case there is an emergency," answers Nandini.

"Why didn't you tell me yesterday?" Roshani asks Rudra quietly, realising there is no point being angry since he is leaving tomorrow.

Rudra answers immediately, "Yesterday, the doctor said that I should start my normal life, and tickets were available only for tomorrow. You also didn't visit me last evening."

"And you couldn't call me?" Roshani asks in anger, controlling her pitch.

"You know I don't have my mobile here," he says innocently.

"You have one in your hand right now!" She says, eyeing his mother's mobile in his hands.

He feels arguing won't help when he knows he is wrong, so he says, "Yes, I am sorry. I should have told you yesterday."

"It's OK. It happens," chuckles Roshani, like all she wants is to hear him apologise. "Let's go to the roof," she says, and they both go upstairs.

"What did the doctor say about your memory?" she asks caringly.

"He said it may or may not come, but resuming my normal life can help me regain it," Rudra answers blankly, looking at the sky.

"OK. Tell me the last thing you remember," she says, adjusting herself on the railing beside him.

"Now you are acting like a doctor. Anyway, I remember being on the night shift on 26 January, doing my regular work and then falling due to dizziness," he answers, still staring at the horizon.

"Rudra, I know you are tired of repeating it over and over again, but please tell me in detail. I mean, what makes you think this memory is of the same night, not from some other day? You do the same duty every night shift, right? Yes, you fell due to dizziness, but where? Do you recall anything specific to prove the date is 26 January?" she asks sincerely.

Her smart approach amuses Rudra, and he asks, "What are your blogs about, by the way?"

"I am a psychiatrist, Rudra. I know you disagree, but it is what it is. Now answer"

"Something specific?... Yes, there was a new guy on the night shift, ah, what was his name? Pramod… No, Amod. It was his first night shift, and he was asking a lot of questions about the company. I think Ravi whined that it was Republic Day," he gradually recounts.

"Good, then?" she asks with a plain face. Rudra's winning expression disappears.

"We were explaining the job to him, then we reached the office, and after changing my clothes, I entered the process area. Ah, no, I didn't change. My uniform was not on the shelf, so I wore an apron. I took the shift handover from Nikhil, checked the lines, sat in the office and started doing my work. I remember looking at the clock at 3 a.m. and going on another round. That's it," he stops.

"Excellent, Rudra, but you must focus and recall incidents beyond that. Close your eyes and try to picture it." She nudges him.

Rudra closes his eyes and says, "I am taking my round, I can see all the machines are running perfectly fine on Line-1, and now I am going to Line-2 through Africa."

"Africa?"

"Oh, there is a huge hall between these two lines where the temperature is generally high, so we call it Africa. I am crossing Africa, then suddenly it is dark." Rudra holds Roshani's right hand in fear. She gently frees her hand and places them on his temple, relaxing Rudra under her massaging fingers. He resumes speaking, "All of a sudden, it is dark and there is no machine noise. I can hear the flowing water. Then somebody comes and shakes me out of it. Oh, it is Prajot, my shift technician. There is light everywhere, and machines are running. It is surprising. I skipped going to Line-2. I am in the chocolate tower, ascending the stairs, but why? I have been on the upper floors only once or twice since I joined this factory. I am standing on the roof. The wind is howling, and I fall on grass and, and, and I hear…" he opens his eyes in horror.

"What did you hear, Rudra?" a terrified Roshani asks.

"I hear, I hear…" Rudra is horrified and starts shaking. Roshani is scared as hell because Nandini has told her about his panic attack in the hospital. Not knowing what to do, she wraps him in her arms tightly. He stops shaking in a few seconds, then she starts rubbing the back of his head.

"I hear, I hear…"

"Shh, shh, shh, shh…" Roshani tries to calm him down.

Within a few minutes, his wails become mumbling, and he calms down slowly. Sensing he is fine now, she loosens her hold to see his face, but Rudra doesn't let go. She tries to escape the tight hold, but he says, "Let it be for a few more minutes."

Roshani reminds, "We are on the roof, Rudra."

"I am leaving tomorrow," he responds, and she stops struggling. "We have an early morning train. You won't be able to see me off tomorrow. This is what we have left until next month."

She closes her eyes and just says, "Hmm."

After a few seconds, Rudra loosens his grip. She unwraps her arms and goes downstairs without even looking at him once, while he stands there all alone, surprised at his own act and smiling like a fool.

It is past midnight, but Rudra is unable to sleep, thinking, *Why didn't she look back? Was she angry? I shouldn't have done this. What was I thinking? Did I just lose my childhood friend?* He doesn't realise when he falls asleep and wakes up to his mother's voice at 4 a.m. He freshens up quickly and books an Ola cab to the railway station. Even while loading the bags, his mind goes back to his childhood friend, and he curses himself for that risky move.

Keeping all the bags in the cab, Rudra says, "Ma, aren't you forgetting about giving the keys to Roshani? Hand it to me, I will go give them."

His mother replies, "I already gave the spare keys to her when she was leaving yesterday." They sit in the car and close the door. It is 4:30 a.m. The driver starts the car. He looks at the window of Roshani's room when the car crosses her home, expecting to see her for the last time, knowing it's too early for her to be awake. The light in her room is off, but it switches on when he is about to turn his head towards the road. There she is, standing at the window in her white nightie, smiling, waving at him. Rudra waves subtly to avoid gaining his parents' attention. Only God knows whether she can see it or not. The car takes the first turn and zooms past her smile, face and window.

7

Back to Bedlam

"Yesterday, when we left Allahabad in the morning, it was freezing. In Goa, there is no trace of cold at all. You are lucky that you spend winters here. Ask me how difficult it is to survive winter in Allahabad," says a visibly delighted Santosh, while Nandini is opening the door.

"Hungry anyone? I will go buy something for lunch," says Rudra.

"I will make something, you don't need to go anywhere," shouts his mother.

Rudra retorts sharply, "There is no vegetable or other grocery. Don't you remember emptying the containers of rice and wheat flour before leaving for Allahabad?"

Picking up on the atmosphere, Santosh says calmly, "I will go and get lunch. We can do grocery shopping in the evening."

Rudra's mother nods and mumbles angrily, "He has become quick-tempered."

Santosh grabs the scooter keys and leaves. Rudra walks towards the bathroom, muttering an apology, "I am sorry."

Before he enters the bathroom, his mother shouts, "I heard it and I forgive you." Rudra closes the door, smiling.

Santosh comes back with packaged food, and they all have brunch together. The family spends the rest of the day watching TV, lifting groceries, and chatting idly. They go to bed early, tired from the long train journey.

Rudra wakes up at dawn with butterflies in his stomach. He cannot believe that he is excited about going to the office, a place he has a love-hate relationship with. He is thrilled about meeting his colleagues and boss. He has been asked to join the morning shift, so he will have to leave around 7:30 a.m. on his scooter, as the company doesn't provide a cab for this shift. He gets ready, has his breakfast, and leaves for the office.

He reaches the factory and enters the process area after changing into his uniform. He finds Nikhil sitting in the office, focusing seriously on something on the computer. So, he peeks in to find out that Nikhil is so engrossed playing solitaire that he doesn't even notice Rudra walking in and standing right beside him.

Rudra taps on his head gently and chuckles, "When will you change, man?"

Nikhil lifts his head and finds Rudra smiling at him. He stands up, startled and shakes hands with Rudra, then says, "Bro, perfection can't be improved. Anyway, finally, you are back. Where were you? You left for some ten days and are coming after a month."

Rudra replies, "Not after a month, after seventeen days. Something happened, so I had to extend my leave. Aren't you guys aware? I mean, wasn't there any gossip?"

Nikhil laughs, "Why? Were you kidnapped or something? Boss said you were not well. Oh, that reminds me, how are you?

You look fine to me, by the way," he says the last sentence without even looking at his face.

A confused Rudra answers, "Yes, yes, I am totally fine," thinking, *Why aren't they aware of my hospitalisation? Didn't my family bother to lodge a missing complaint?*

"What happened, bro? We all think that people would be worried about us when we are not there, but nobody has time to care about anyone other than themselves. That's the harsh truth." Nikhil is too blunt.

Rudra nods, but internally utters, *My case is different.* He asks, "So what's new in the factory?" changing the topic.

"Nothing much, we are still making chocolates as if we are building rockets and expanding GDP. And yes, Vishu sir from R&D has resigned, so his position is up for grabs. Everybody is eyeing the coveted position. We are all buttering up our bosses to get a recommendation. He was an assistant manager. Just assume if I get the position, there will be a minimum 50 per cent hike and the tag of R&D guy. You know how critical that can be for my career?"

"Vishu sir has resigned? You all are trying for his role to get a huge career boost?" queries a surprised and optimistic Rudra, "Do you think they will consider me?"

"You too? There is enough competition already, but yes, you can also throw your hat in the ring," says Nikhil, almost unfazed by Rudra's candidacy, as though knowing he won't be selected.

"At least I can try. Anyway, anything else?"

"Nah, the rest is the same. Oh, haan, that weird guy from another factory who came to learn the operations was sent back almost a couple of days after you went home. They didn't seem very happy about his training," recollects Nikhil, twitching his lips and eyes, "What was his name? He was here for almost a month, but people don't even remember his name."

"Kshitip. He was here for two months," says Rudra spontaneously.

"Yes, yes, Kshitip. You have a good memory indeed. He spent most of his time learning from me, still, I couldn't recall it." Nikhil winks at Rudra. "OK, I need to go to the shop floor and act like I am worried about the line output. Our boss will be here anytime," says Nikhil, and goes out of the office.

"Sure, I will wait for him here," responds Rudra, walking out with Nikhil.

Nikhil goes on the shop floor and starts shouting at people, directing them erratically. Rudra waits near the office for the boss. Their boss enters the area, sharp at 9:00, and notices Nikhil, instructing people, throwing his arms in all directions. He says to Rudra, "Such a sincere boy, he gets involved so deeply in operations sometimes that I get worried about his personal life. I hope everything is OK with him."

Rudra says, controlling his laugh, "He is very emotionally connected with his team and this company, sir. He is…"

His boss cuts him short and says, "I wish I had more people like him. Anyway, how are you? I heard you had some health-related issues, but if you are in any trouble, you should call me rather than your parents calling the factory manager directly. It looks awful when the FM knows more about my team than I do." He expresses his annoyance at Rudra.

"Sir, things were not in my control," justifies Rudra.

"Still, I should have been informed before the factory manager. He wants to meet you, check with his secretary, and make an appointment," says his boss, and leaves without going on lines, knowing Nikhil will handle it.

"May I come in, sir?" asks Rudra, opening the FM's office door.

"Oh, yes, please, Rudra," says the FM in his deep voice. The FM is a tall, well-built man in his late forties, known for being hardworking and soft-spoken. Whenever Rudra sees him, the first thing that comes to his mind is the FM's sea-facing huge bungalow situated on the poshest beach in Goa. The second thing is that he can buy an MG Hector with his monthly salary. The FM shakes Rudra's hand, tells him to sit down and asks, "How are you now?"

"I am doing well, sir," answers Rudra, willingly avoiding his memory loss thing, thinking there is no point in sharing it with somebody who cannot help and maybe doesn't care.

"Your mother called the office after your disappearance. She was very frantic and wanted to register an FIR. The call was transferred to me. So, we lodged a police complaint the next day, but kept it a secret to avoid panic. Police did their investigation, but they couldn't find any clues. You were seen leaving the factory next morning in the main gate CCTV footage, so it was clear that something had happened outside our premises, not inside."

Rudra listens to every word carefully and feels a little relieved that there is an FIR, but he thinks that the last thing he remembers is being on the chocolate tower in the middle of the night and falling. He doesn't recall anything about leaving the factory. The FM notices Rudra being perplexed, so he says, "So we informed the police when you were found, and your case was closed. Where were you, by the way?"

Rudra answers hesitantly, "Actually, sir, I don't have any idea about that duration, but the doctor says it is a temporary memory loss. I will recover eventually."

The FM nods, looking outside his office, contemplating something. "In my family, something similar happened a few years back … anyway," he abruptly stops and looks back at Rudra with a faint, sad smile. "You can call or meet me anytime, you know that, right?" the FM reassures.

Rudra replies, "Yes, sir. I will let you know if I need any help. Thank you." The FM gives him the same smile until he is out of the office.

"So, how was the day? Any luck remembering anything about that night?" his father asks.

Before Rudra can answer, his mother snaps, "You don't have to talk about his memory every day. He will let us know if he recalls anything. It is not that important."

Rudra wants to talk about the FIR and police findings, but he doesn't. He sits down on a chair in the hall, pretending to watch the news on the TV with his father. Santosh winks at him and passes a small gift packet. Rudra gets excited and asks, "What is it?" His father signals him to open it.

Rudra unwraps it to find a smartphone and a SIM. He says, "Thanks, Papa," smiling eye to eye.

His father comments, "Now you know how to waste your idle time."

Rudra goes back to his room and explores his new mobile phone. He shouts from his bed, "I have to go on B shift tomorrow, I mean, at 3 p.m. The cab will be here to pick me up. I will be back after midnight." Then, dials Roshani's mobile number.

8

Puzzle Starts

The next day, Rudra reaches the factory around 3:30 p.m., changes his uniform, enters the process area to take shift handover from Nikhil again and starts his routine. After about two hours, when everything is set and he ensures some time for himself, he goes to the office, does the necessary paperwork and decides to visit the chocolate tower rather than going for tea.

While crossing Africa, he pauses for a few seconds and closes his eyes, focusing on what he hears. His ears pick up the loud machine noise; no flowing water, not at all. He moves towards the chocolate tower, recalling his visions of that night.

He meets the operators sitting in the control room and checks the level of various tanks. Then he ascends the stairs to the second floor, which has the emergency exit door. He opens the door and steps out to the roof. It is a vast roof for a factory spread over one hundred acres.

While coming out of the emergency exit, he notices two pairs of shoe prints on the dust accumulated under the stairs. It is an area where people seldom go, but it's almost impossible to identify individuals by shoe pattern because everyone wears the same industrial shoes. He removes a pen from his pocket and measures the length of the prints with the shoes he is wearing currently.

One of the shoe prints matches his shoe size perfectly, but the other is an impression of a bigger shoe. *So, somebody else has been here after me. It could be a policeman searching for me.* He explores further but finds nothing. He clicks some pictures of the prints and returns to his office while thinking, *Was there somebody else with me on that roof that day? Or did someone go there looking for me and find something out?* He is busy with his thoughts when his shift mobile phone rings.

"Sir, the cooling tunnel's temperature has increased, so we are stopping production. I have already called the electrician. He will be here in five minutes," an operator informs on the phone. Rudra hangs up the call and walks towards the tunnel. The repair keeps him busy till the end of his shift, so he grabs his dinner from the factory canteen itself. At the end of the work, he hands over the shift mobile phone to the next officer, changes his clothes and reaches the parking area for his cab.

It is exactly 00:00. The rest of the officers assemble, and the cab starts. Rudra keeps thinking about the second shoe mark. It resembles the first one, so it must be some factory employee, not a policeman. He doesn't realise when fifteen minutes pass, and the car stops at his drop-off point. Rudra gets out of the car and walks to his flat. It is about 300-400 metres away, and he always walks that distance without any safety concerns since it's Goa.

He is plodding when he suddenly hears a faint howl of a dog. That road has a few stray dogs, but Rudra has never faced any trouble before tonight. After the first dog, a second one starts howling, and then a third. Their howls become barking in no time, and Rudra, who has never feared a dog, is terribly scared and starts walking briskly.

The dogs start following Rudra, barking even more loudly. When Rudra realises the distance between the dogs and him is reducing and they will bite him before he enters the lift, he starts running with the dogs now chasing him. They bark incessantly. Rudra runs for his life, reaches the lift, opens its door, and enters. He turns back to close the door, but one of the dogs leaps at him. Rudra manages to shut the door a fraction before it can enter. The dog rams into the lift door with a thump. Rudra plops down on the lift floor with his head curled between his knees, covering his ears with his palms. The dogs are still barking violently.

Everything starts fading into darkness in front of Rudra's eyes, and he finds himself standing in a gloomy, moonlit open area. A pleasant breeze is blowing across the place. There is a huge, black rock wall in front of him. He hears the flowing water of a mighty river behind him again, and then he snaps back to reality.

He hears some loud thuds by a tall figure, trying to scare the dogs away. The figure opens the lift and carries Rudra in his arms when he loses consciousness.

Rudra opens his eyes in his room. He walks through the door; the sun has come out. He finds his mother preparing breakfast, and his father is sitting on the balcony, looking outside. Rudra clears his throat to get their attention, and both quickly turn, happy to see him awake.

His mother says, caressing his face, "Go, freshen up. We will have breakfast."

Rudra expects his parents to ask him about last night, but after listening to his mother, he gets irritated and shouts, "Neglecting what happened isn't going to help me. We must talk about it. I also need some answers."

His father enters the hall from the balcony, puts his hand on Rudra's shoulder and says, "Yes, we should talk, but you get fresh first."

Rudra shakes his head in disbelief. Nandini looks straight at him in anger and scoffs, signing, *Go and get ready*. He leaves the hall, frustrated, goes to the bathroom and comes out after bathing. He sits on a chair and starts, "Should we?"

"Rudra, nobody is ignoring what happened. We also want answers you are looking for, but what options do we have except waiting for your memory?" his father says helplessly.

"Papa, we can discuss it. When I think deeply, sometimes I recollect a few things," answers Rudra.

"OK, what happened yesterday?" Santosh asks, leaning towards Rudra.

"I think I had a vision in the lift about those days. I saw myself standing in front of a huge ancient wall. I could feel I was standing there in that moment," replies Rudra, pressing on the word 'moment'.

"I am not a psychiatrist, Rudra, but normal people like us do not go on such adventures to some ancient palace and work so secretly that you lose your memory. This vision can be from some movie or documentary?" he reasons.

"But Papa, it was so strong that I could feel it in my bones. It cannot be from a movie, I was standing there," Rudra tries to convince his father, but noticing his frustrated face, he asks, "OK, what did the police say about my disappearance?" At this moment, his mother walks in with breakfast and hears Rudra's question.

Santosh turns his head to Nandini in confusion and opens his mouth to speak, but she interrupts, "They couldn't find any clues from the factory, as you were seen leaving the next morning. The neighbours also saw you unlocking and locking this flat and leaving with your bag. You boarded the flight from Goa to Lucknow. After this, the Goa police contacted the UP police, and they tried to locate you. After Lucknow airport, as there was no reservation, they could not track you. Their investigation was still in progress when you were found in that field." Her face becomes sad at the last sentence.

"So, I disappeared from Lucknow?" Rudra asks.

"As I said, they could not confirm that, but yes, you were in Lucknow for sure," answers his mother.

Rudra lies back on his chair, puzzled and starts thinking *Why is my last memory from the chocolate tower roof? Why don't I remember travelling?*

"We, too, want those answers, Rudra. We are your parents, but Dr Patwardhan had clearly said that you must not keep thinking about this; otherwise, what if you have another seizure?" says his mother, controlling her tears. But Rudra is not listening to her anymore. He thinks about that massive rock wall and tries to remember if he knows that place, but he can't recollect anything.

His phone rings. He is surprised because he has not shared this number with anyone. He checks his phone and finds it is Nikhil and remembers sharing his number the day before, and thinks, *I must stop overthinking.*

"I heard some stray dogs attacked you yesterday. I hope they didn't bite you," says Nikhil in a worried voice.

"No, no. I survived somehow," answers Rudra.

"So, when are you coming to the office?" asks Nikhil.

"In B shift, obviously."

"Aren't you coming early? The boss told me that the FM wants to meet you again."

"The FM wants to meet me again? Is everything OK?" Rudra asks, surprised and worried.

"I don't know, man, but I think it has something to do with the dogs' attack. Anyway, I have to go to a meeting. Please plan to come to the factory ASAP," suggests Nikhil, disconnecting the call.

"What happened? You look tense," asks Rudra's father.

Rudra says, "Give me breakfast, Ma, I need to go to the office. FM sir wants to meet me."

Rudra reaches the office on his scooter, and after changing his uniform, he meets the factory manager. After a thirty-minute meeting, he comes out and looks happy. Nikhil finds him outside the FM's office and asks his reason for delight. Rudra replies, "The FM asked me about yesterday's incidents, and when I told him about the dogs, he was not pleased. From today, the cabs will drop the shift officers at their doors."

"And this is why you have such a broad smile?" Nikhil asks sarcastically.

Rudra replies hesitantly, "I am moving to R&D to fill Vishu sir's role."

Nikhil doesn't expect this news. He gets shocked and sad too, as he also wanted to move to that position. It could have been a career-defining move, but he controls his emotions well and says, "So, you are going to become a general shift guy now. No shifts, huh? What do I have to do to come out of these freaking shifts? Plan an attack on me?" Nikhil winks at Rudra, who smiles wryly, noticing Nikhil's sadness. "Chill, don't worry about others' expressions, I am happy for you. It was a shock, but anyway, when are you moving to R&D?" says Nikhil, trying to cheer up Rudra.

Rudra replies, "From immediate effect, I mean from tomorrow."

9

It's a New Day

Rudra wakes up early the next day, excited and thanking God for giving him such a good opportunity. He gets ready, taking his time with the excitement of having his cubicle now. Rudra finishes breakfast quickly, but his stomach is already full of butterflies as he leaves for the office.

He reaches his office well before time due to his habit of arriving early for shifts. His new colleagues start coming one by one. There are a total of four people in this new team, excluding his boss, and there is one housekeeping guy, Naveen, responsible for cleaning the floor, bringing water, and couriers from the gate. Soon, Rudra realises it's the same factory and the same people. Nothing much has changed, and his handover starts.

After 2-3 days, Naveen comes with a letter and puts it on Rudra's table, "Sir, there is a letter for you." Rudra doesn't even look at the letter in the middle of his handover and keeps it aside. Vishvendra, the guy who is leaving the company and whose position Rudra is taking, is a peculiar person. Sometimes he is elated and teaches Rudra affectionately, and other times he becomes so rude and mean that he scolds Rudra in front of everyone. So, Rudra avoids infuriating him. At around 5:30 p.m., when their handover is over, Rudra starts packing his bag to leave.

"Oh, Imperial Bank of Switzerland? Do you have an account in IBS? I didn't know you were a big shot." Prakash, one of the colleagues, who sits in a neighbouring cubicle, pulls Rudra's leg while checking the envelope Salim gave earlier.

"I don't have an account in this bank. Naveen might have brought someone else's letter," says Rudra in a tired voice.

"It has your name on it, so it must be for you," says Prakash, handing the letter to Rudra.

He opens the envelope and finds an A4-sized paper inside. He unfolds the paper, and it is blank. He turns the paper, and only two lines are printed on that paper, in the middle:

Stop taking your medicines, especially that red syrup. I hope you want your memory back.

Don't trust anyone, nobody, except your visions.

Rudra reads the letter, and his eyes remain fixated on the sentence. 'Don't trust anyone, nobody, except your visions.' He thinks, *How come the sender knows about my visions? Knowing I am having a red syrup is not difficult, as I bring it to the factory for the post-lunch dose, but visions?* He once again checks the envelope for any address, but it doesn't have any except Rudra's.

"Are you coming, or do you have some work?" Prakash asks.

"Hmm? Yes, yes, I am coming," says Rudra, absent-mindedly. He folds the paper and puts it back in the envelope. He zones out, walking from his office to the changing room to the parking lot, thinking about the letter. He starts his scooter and leaves the factory premises. Prakash stops outside at a shop to buy something, but Rudra doesn't wait and keeps riding, spaced out.

Who sent that letter? How the hell does somebody know I am having visions? Should I really stop taking my medicines? What on earth was I doing in those days? Have I done something terribly wrong? Have I done something illegal? Rudra reaches his home, lost in his thoughts. He rings the doorbell, and his mother opens the door.

"Sit, I will bring water for you," says his mother, closing the door and going towards the kitchen. Rudra removes his shoes and sits on the chair beside his father in front of the TV.

Santosh asks, "So, how was your day? You look quite tired." Rudra looks at his father and shakes his head, gesturing that nothing is wrong, but his face gives it away. His mother brings a glass of water from the kitchen for Rudra. He drinks it and keeps the empty glass on the table next to him. Santosh notices Rudra's absent-mindedness and, to get his attention, lifts that empty glass and drops it on the floor, making a loud noise.

Rudra jumps in his seat, and his mother shouts, "Santosh, your kid has outgrown you. When the hell will you be mature?"

Santosh replies coolly, "His mind is still in the office. I just wanted to bring him back."

Nandini shoots back, "There are other ways, fifty-year-old kid," and returns to the kitchen to prepare tea.

"You are too much, Papa. Do you like getting scolded?" Rudra says, shaking his head with a smile on his face.

His father replies, "Your mother lives here with you. I get my family time when you guys visit Allahabad. Otherwise, I still live like a bachelor. I am leaving tomorrow morning, so until then, spend time with me. I know, your job profile has changed, and you are quite busy, but just don't come home out of your office, be here mentally too. Is your new job tough?"

Rudra answers hesitantly, "It is not like that, Papa, the new profile is okay. There is something else."

"What?"

Rudra opens the zip of his bag and puts his hand inside to search for the envelope, but a thought comes to his head: *The letter says not to trust anyone, and to stop taking my medicines. If it's right, I can start by discontinuing them in the office after lunch. It's not like anybody will notice it. And if the letter is fake, missing one dose will not change much, but if I share this with Ma and Papa, they will get concerned for no reason.*

He takes a bunch of papers from his bag and hands them to his father. "I got my promotion letter today."

His mother comes out of the kitchen, hearing this, hugs her son tightly, and says, "I am proud of you."

His father checks the papers and says, "Almost 45 per cent increase in package, great. Let's celebrate."

"Yes, let's go to the temple," Nandini cries in joy.

"That's not what I meant by celebration. It's Goa, not Allahabad, where you go to the Sangam to celebrate everything," Santosh complains.

"I know what you meant by celebration. You celebrate in your way," laughs Nandini.

Rudra's father exclaims like a child, "Really! Can I have whiskey?"

"No, beer. Whiskey turns you into a parrot," says Nandini from the other room.

"Wow, I am really proud of you," he winks at Rudra, "What about you, do you drink?"

Rudra stutters, "No, Papa, I don't."

"But you are an engineer. I have heard lots of things about life in engineering colleges."

"Yes, Papa, there are all kinds of guys," says Rudra, feigning innocence. "Some spoiled kids who weren't raised well used to drink. But not the kids with values, of course."

"It's not bad to have alcohol occasionally. But it's your choice, obviously."

"Ah, I tried beer in college once, but it was too bitter. I didn't like the taste."

"Not everyone likes the taste, but it is good that you don't drink," Santosh says, feeling proud of himself as a parent. They start getting dressed to go out.

A small detail Rudra hides from his father is that his college nickname is Bewda.

10

Separated Again

"Wake up, Rudra, wash your face and let's drop your father at the railway station. It's 4:00 a.m. already, the cab will be here anytime now," says Rudra's mother, softly waking him up.

"Ma, his train is at six. It takes only thirty minutes to reach the station. The cab will come after an hour," replies Rudra, annoyed and starts getting off the bed. They freshen up and sit in their usual seats in front of the TV.

"What is it with you people always taking a train over a flight? I can understand that Ma is afraid of flying, but you too? Unnecessarily, you will waste two days," says Rudra, to start a conversation before the tea comes. "And please don't lecture me about saving money."

"It means you already know my answer. You generally get 10-15 days leave, so each day is important. In our case, it is not, so why should we waste money? It's illogical," says his father, smiling.

Nandini comes with three cups of tea and a few sandwiches and sits in the empty chair. The room is filled with silence, occasionally broken by the slurping of tea. None of the men talk, aware of how emotional Nandini is. They finish their breakfast, and Nandini collects the cups and plates and goes back into the kitchen.

Santosh says, "I know you would be worried about your lost memory. Just hang on, and keep going. It will come back, and if it doesn't, who cares?"

Rudra nods without looking at his father and says softly, "That's OK, Papa, but what if I have done something terrible?"

"What makes you think that way? It's life, not some movie that you saved the world in those days, and somebody wiped out your memory," says Santosh plainly.

Rudra argues, "I know, Papa. It's not a movie, but what about the visions I have been having lately, doesn't it mean anything?"

"The brain is really complex; sometimes it makes up things on its own to fill the voids."

Rudra looks at him, surprised, as he never expected his old-fashioned father to know such things. Santosh responds to Rudra's unasked question. "I watched it on the Discovery Channel. Don't look at me as if I am illiterate. I am your father, and I am not even fifty-five." Rudra smiles at his answer, and Santosh returns it.

Rudra's mother steps out after changing her nightwear and says, "Let's go. The cab will be here soon."

The father-son duo looks at each other, and Santosh says, "It is still 4:45 a.m. The cab won't be here in another fifteen minutes. Sit down."

Nandini sits down, looking at the wall clock and shaking her head. Santosh starts narrating about her nature of always being before time. One story after another, the room gets filled with laughter.

Soon, the cab arrives, and they continue the story time there. They reach the railway station without realising how fast time passed. Once they get down, Rudra takes out the luggage from the cab's boot, and Santosh pays the driver. Nandini stops him, "We will return in the same cab, right? Why are you paying now?"

Santosh smiles and says, "Because I am your husband."

Nandini looks at him, overwhelmed with emotions. Santosh turns towards her after paying the driver and notices her eyes are filled with tears. He pats her back, the best thing he could do to show his love in a public place and signals her to start moving towards the entrance of the railway station. Rudra sees all this and thinks, *Ma and Papa don't get to live together because of me. Even at this age, Papa has to live a bachelor's life. I should ask Ma to go home. I can manage my chores. They look so happy together.*

Rudra doesn't catch up and walks behind them to give them space. He is surprised to see such emotions on his father's face. His mother still has tears in her eyes. They talk and look at each other. After a pause, one of them says something, and the other controls their tears. The train arrives, Rudra puts his father's luggage underneath the berth and returns to the platform, where his parents are still talking. It's a small station, so the train starts almost immediately. Santosh boards the train and waves at his son and wife.

Nandini starts crying again, so Santosh gives a flying kiss and laughs before disappearing in the morning fog. Nandini also laughs with teary eyes and then turns back to go home. They get in the cab; Rudra sits in the front, and Nandini sits alone in the back. The cab back home is extremely quiet, the opposite of their ride to the station.

11

Sleep Sugar

It has been ten days since Santosh left Goa. Rudra has been spending longer hours in the office learning his new role without any time to think about his lonely mother.

The door opens, and Rudra enters. Exhaling heavily, he removes his shoes and sits down in a chair. His mother comes from the kitchen, holding a glass of water and takes the adjacent chair. A tired and sweating Rudra finishes drinking the water, puts the glass on the table and again leans back on his chair, his eyes fixed on the ceiling fan.

His mother asks, "So, how was the day?" Rudra doesn't answer. She tries again, a bit louder, "Rudra, how was your day?" Rudra realises he's distracted and calmly says, "It was okay."

"Don't you think you are working too hard? Your previous role was better, working for eight hours and coming back home without any tension," says Nandini innocently.

Rudra responds, "I am promoted now, Ma. They are paying more than earlier, so obviously my work has increased, and anyhow, I don't have to go in shifts anymore."

"How much extra are they paying to double your pressure? Your peace of mind is also important. By the way, why are you sweating like a pig?"

"I don't know," he says indifferently while answering the question. "And yes, I have signed up for a one-hour swimming session every morning starting tomorrow. So, pack my breakfast, I will have it after the session and leave for the office."

"You are already out all the time. Now this swimming?" She asks, surprised.

"Need to do something to relieve my stress, or I will burst," Rudra replies, annoyed again.

Nandini notices his tone and leaves him alone for some time.

Rudra has suddenly started perspiring for the last couple of days. He doesn't care about it, but he conjectures after his mother's question. *I have always been that guy who never sweats much, even during the hottest days. Why is it happening now?* He googles and finds various difficult-to-pronounce diseases and scrolls down. *Blah, blah, medications' side effects, withdrawal symptoms, blah, blah.* He goes back up to withdrawal symptoms and thinks, *Is it because of the medicine dose that I have discontinued? It could be. I stopped taking it about ten days ago, and started sweating after that. What is that medicine for? Is it that strong?*

"Anyway, let's see for some more days," he mutters and stands up to go for a shower.

After having an early dinner, Rudra goes to his bed.

"Did you forget to take your medicines?" his mother asks from outside.

Rudra replies, "Yes, yes, I am coming." He leaves his bed and goes outside, where his mother is standing, holding a glass of water. He takes the glass, swallows his medicines and returns to his room. Rudra is extremely tired, but he is having problems sleeping. He keeps tossing and turning in his bed. It has been more than forty-five minutes, but Rudra is still awake. He removes his mobile from the charger and sends "Hi" to Roshani. Almost immediately, he gets "Hi" back.

How are you doing these days?

Nothing much, I was a little busy with a project. You seem busier, though—no messages or calls from more than a week.

Yeah, handover for the new role is in progress. The guy has asked for early relief. I am also going on leave again, so lots of things in a short time.

How many leaves does your company give you, man? You were on leave for a month, just fifteen days back.

Everybody is surprised that I am going on leave again, but it was planned before I went missing. Also, I am in a new department and have a medical issue, so nobody objected. And yes, I was on leave for seventeen days, not a month. ☺

You don't need to explain.

I am not explaining. Why do you have to be an idiot all the time?

Take a chill pill, angry young man.

Hmm.

So, how come you have time for me today?

With every passing day, I am having trouble sleeping. I've been in bed for the last hour.

How long is it going to be before you become normal? I mean, like before that incident.

I am tired of all this now—trouble sleeping, headaches, and so many medicines.

I understand.

OK, good night. I have to go to the office tomorrow.

Can I ask you something, Rudra?

Obviously. I don't have the luxury of saying no.

You remember when we were on your roof, and I was helping you recall?

Yes.

You became frantic, listening to something. What did you hear?

Honestly, I don't know. I don't remember now.

I can understand.

Why did you ask this now?

I have been thinking about it since that day, but I could never ask.

Hmm.

OK, I am sending you an MP3 file. Just download it and play. It will help you fall asleep.

Are you doing these things now?

I am a psychiatrist, Rudra.

Under training.

Whatever.

Rudra downloads the file and plays it. It's a soothing flute single. The music is helping Rudra calm down and sleep, but her question has stirred his thoughts.

It is 3:00 a.m. Rudra finds himself standing in front of an incredibly high stone wall, almost endless on either side. It's dark all around, and a cool breeze is blowing. In the background, he can hear the flowing water. The wall has guarding posts like medieval military forts. He closes his eyes, and when he opens them, he is now standing in a cramped room, feeling suffocated. *The room is not that small, so why am I feeling claustrophobic?* He looks around at the strange walls. Walls with square patches. He stretches his eyes to focus on those squares, but then does not close them, wary of waking up somewhere else the next time he opens them.

He tries to focus more on these patches, but cannot identify anything because of the claustrophobic feeling. He looks up and finds that the ceiling of a temple is just a few inches above his head. He sees snakes everywhere on it, some of them slithering, too. He hears some noise and turns his head in fear to see.

Rudra wakes up breathless and sweaty. He sits on his bed and tries to control his breathing to avoid waking his mother. After a few minutes, he goes to the kitchen to fetch a glass of water, drinks it, thinking *Is this also an effect of stopping the morning medicine?*

12

13 March

Rudra has the same visions for three nights in a row, each clearer than the previous night. He is tired all the time—sweating, hungry, and thirsty. He has also started feeling paranoid, as if every person around him is monitoring him, talking about him, or judging him. He zones out during the handover, keeps thinking about his visions and has reduced interactions with his team members. He even goes for lunch after everybody is back from the canteen.

At closing time, when everybody has already left, he locks his office to go home. He feels somebody is watching him throughout, while he puts his laptop in his bag, leaves the chair, takes the keys, switches off the lights, locks the door, and descends the stairs. It is an unsettling feeling. While returning from the factory, he gets terrified whenever another vehicle crosses him.

He goes home and has dinner after taking a shower. Then, he takes his medicine and goes to bed.

It is 3:00 a.m. Rudra finds himself standing in front of the stone wall again. A cool breeze is blowing. In the background, he hears the flowing water. He feels hardened sand below his feet and tries to walk towards the river, but the next moment, he finds himself in a not-so-small, cramped room with a feeling of suffocation.

He looks around the dimly lit room with strange walls. Walls with square patches. He focuses on one of the patches, and after a little struggle, he realises that they have, in fact, idols of gods carved inside them. He identifies idols of Laxmi, Shiva, Saraswati, but cannot recognise several others. He looks up and finds that the temple ceiling is a few inches above his head, and the roots of a huge tree are spread everywhere. Upon looking closely, he notices the roots also cover the walls, slithering like snakes. Then he hears a noise.

He turns his head in terror and finds somebody behind him, his back towards Rudra. He tries to speak, but even after multiple attempts, cannot utter a single word. That person somehow looks familiar. Suddenly, that man turns. It's Rudra himself, but he is not alone; somebody else is accompanying him.

Rudra wakes up sweating and huffing, petrified of his dream. He wants to reach out to the water bottle on the table, but his hands are shaking. He sits down on his bed and tries to compose himself. After several minutes, his shuddering finally stops. He drinks water and prays. *Please, God, I can't live like this. Please show me what I have done.*

13

Go Goa Gone

It's 15 March and Rudra is also travelling by train this time with his mother. It has been two days since that vision. He ponders, *Since the train started ten hours back, I have slept twice, but why does it seem like, except Ma and I, everybody is just acting to be reading a newspaper, book or magazine? They haven't slept even once. Are they watching us? Whenever I go to the toilet or buy something, somebody is always staring at me.*

Whether people watch him or not, Rudra is on the edge, thinking that something will happen anytime. He is unable to sleep now. It is an AC two-tier compartment. Rudra and his mother have lower berths, and all other berths have been occupied by four men of 35-45 years of age, two on the side berths and one each on the upper berths.

None of them seems to know each other, so there is no discussion in the compartment other than when Rudra and his mother talk. All four have been quiet, reading a book or newspaper, or sometimes watching movies on their phones. This makes Rudra uneasy. With darkness, his anxiety starts increasing.

Rudra opens his laptop bag and takes out a book to read. He puts his pillow on the window, leans on it, opens his book and pretends to read it. From the top of the book, he is keeping an eye on all four fellow passengers as well as anybody who enters the coach.

It is around midnight, and Rudra is still awake, observing everyone. The train starts to slow down in the middle of nowhere.

"We just crossed Manmad Junction, the next station is still hours away. Why is the train stopping here?" an agitated Rudra mutters.

"We reached Allahabad?" Nandini asks, waking up.

"No, no, Ma, sleep," Rudra assures her everything is OK, hiding his nervousness.

The train gradually comes to a halt, without any jerks, in an area with no sign of human habitation. Slowly, people start getting up and murmuring in the compartment, but Nandini stays asleep. People peer outside their fogged windows to see what is happening outside, but only find trees visible. Indians are a curious lot, so now passengers start snooping around. After ten minutes, some of them go to open the compartment gate. Rudra disapproves of the idea, but anyway, they open the door and find many people from other compartments already on the tracks. They see some of them coming from the engine side.

"A local woman committed suicide by jumping in front of our train. Police will be here shortly, and then the train will start. Don't worry," shouted one of them.

After staying forty-five minutes at that spot, the train restarts, but a paranoid Rudra doesn't leave his berth for even a second and continues pretending to read his book, thinking, *Where is the fourth guy? He went outside when the train stopped, but hasn't returned yet. Was it just a suicide or a murder to stop the train?*

Rudra fails to fall asleep while the three gentlemen and his mother sleep like the most peaceful people on the face of the earth.

Rudra's mother wakes up in the morning and asks, "Were you awake the whole night?"

"No, I slept in between but not properly," Rudra replies.

"We will reach Allahabad soon, sleep as much as you want there."

It's 1 p.m. when the train drags onto platform number three of Prayagraj Junction. While alighting, he sees the fourth guy sleeping on one of the berths near the door. He thinks, *What is wrong with me? I need to relax; I wasted the whole journey overthinking.*

"There he is," shouts Rudra after spotting his father standing some twenty metres away, and waves at him. He waves back and comes to them, and all three move towards their car.

"What's the plan for tomorrow?" Santosh asks.

"No plans, Papa. I am here to write an exam this time, not on holidays"

"Man, you have taken your life too seriously. Relax, you are just twenty-seven."

"I will relax, Papa, after 18 March, when my exam is over," says Rudra. Then, Santosh starts the car.

14

Was There a Question?

"How was your exam?" Roshani asks.

"Tsk," Rudra twitches his lips in response.

"You have been preparing for this exam for the last two years, right?" she asks absent-mindedly.

"Roshani, everything is not a joke. This exam could have changed my life, and I messed up. I am not in a good mood. Don't make fun of it," he retaliates angrily.

"Rudra, don't ever use this tone with me. You didn't prepare well, so you messed up. I have bunked my classes for your exam, and you are showing me attitude," retorts Roshani sharply.

Rudra has never seen her like this. She is always the one on the receiving end and never complains. He stands dumbstruck for a few seconds and says, "Sorry, I overreacted," expecting her to say OK with her trademark chuckles, but she sits on her scooter and doesn't even look at him. Rudra silently takes the back seat, and she starts with a sharp acceleration, nearly bumping into another bike. Rudra understands she is enraged.

Ten minutes into the ride, Rudra says, "I need some water, I am thirsty," but Roshani doesn't respond. After a while, he repeats, a bit louder, "Roshani, I am thirsty."

She stops the scooter suddenly and snaps, "Do you see any shops here, Rudra? Or do you expect me to dig a well for you?" Rudra is stunned at her response but starts laughing. She yells, "You are irritating me, Rudra, that's not funny."

Rudra replies, "Oh yes, it is. Or should I dig a well for you?" imitating Roshani. She shakes her head in disbelief and smiles. "Oh, finally, someone is smiling. You almost gave me a heart attack. I am sorry about my behaviour, I will never talk to you like that," Rudra apologises with his face down.

"It is not just about your tone, Rudra. Why do you get angry so easily?"

"You are saying as if I have always been like this. This memory thing is hard to handle, Roshani. I have not slept in days. I wake up early, and it becomes extremely difficult to fall asleep again. It's been more than two weeks, and I am sleep-deprived," Rudra explains his misery.

"I know I cannot understand what you are going through, I should have reacted maturely," says Roshani apologetically.

"Yes, you should have. You, heartless person," he fakes a sad face.

She hits his head, "You pig."

"We make an awesome couple."

Roshani replies, amazed, "We are not a couple, Rudra. We are just friends, childhood friends."

"Roshani, if you expect me to get on my knees to propose, that's never going to happen. You know me well. I am not that person. You are the most interesting, intelligent, beautiful soul I have ever met, and I know you think the same about me, except for the beautiful part. I am deeply, madly in love with you and can't wait to start our life together," Rudra says, looking into her eyes.

"Sit," replies a straight-faced Roshani, pointing towards the seat of her scooter, hiding her smile. Rudra doesn't comprehend the reaction and, like a good puppy, follows her order.

They reach, and Rudra gets off the scooter. While going towards his house, he utters hesitantly, "You didn't answer."

"Was there a question?" Roshani asks and heads home.

15

Déjà Vu

Rudra's phone screen illuminates.

Hey, do you have any plans for today?

No, I'm in bed.

Get ready, I need to go to Naini for some work. If you are free, come along.

OK, what time?

In another thirty minutes, by 9:30 a.m.

Done. I will be there.

Rudra has spent the night restlessly waiting to hear from her. Upon getting her text, he jumps out of bed and rushes into the bathroom, shouting, "Ma, I am leaving in half an hour, please get me something to eat."

"Breakfast is ready for an hour," his mother yells back.

Rudra gets ready, eats his breakfast hastily and darts out to wait for Roshani. As soon as he opens the main door, she is already there.

"Hi, good morning," says Rudra, and gets on the scooter.

"Good morning? You have never greeted me before," says Roshani cheekily. Rudra changes the topic and starts discussing something else.

They take the old Yamuna bridge from Gau Ghat and reach a small finance bank in Naini. Roshani asks him to sit and wait outside, and goes to the branch manager's office. She returns after some time.

"Done, what to do now?" she asks.

"You are asking me? I thought you had some plan," says Rudra.

"Chill. Didn't you see how beautiful the Sangam is? Let's go there," Roshani says.

"Come on. You brought me along to visit the banks of the Ganges? I have a better idea," he whines.

"Have you ever been to the Sangam, Rudra?"

"No, I have never been there, though I live in Allahabad," he replies very casually.

"Sometimes we should do such things too, you will feel good, trust me," she insists.

"But..." Rudra doesn't want to go to the Sangam. He expects to drop by a better place, a nice restaurant maybe, but he reluctantly agrees.

Roshani starts her scooter but doesn't turn for the old bridge. Rudra says, "You were supposed to take this turn," pointing towards the road.

"Let's use the new bridge. I love the wide, smooth roads, with a clear, beautiful view of Ma Ganga. You can also see the Kumbh area. Yes, the Magh Mela is over now, but we can go to the Panchmukhi Hanuman temple, Viman Mandapam, Ganga—"

Rudra cuts her short, "Is there any cemetery around? I don't want to end up there. Eyes on the road, please."

Roshani straightens her head and says, "Right."

It's a beautiful day in March with clouds floating by, and pleasant air blowing. Rudra looks below on his left, and the water level is so low that shining white sand is visible. There aren't many people below, just a few of them going towards the great confluence point of three rivers, the holy Ganga, mighty Yamuna and mysterious Saraswati. He can hear a medley of prayers being offered to the gods on loudspeakers. They leave the bridge and turn towards the Sangam. They reach a point beyond which personal vehicles are not allowed, so Roshani parks her scooter, and they start moving on foot.

"I know you are not much into mythology, but I will like to be your guide, whether you like it or not. So, do you know why this area is called the Sangam?" Roshani asks, elbowing Rudra.

"Why is this area called the Sangam, Roshani?" he asks to play along.

"So, there are many debates about the origin of the word Sangam. Some say it comes from the Tamil word *Sangu,* an instrument which was blown for the assembly of scholars. There were three such sangams organised in ancient Tamil history. Others believe its origin is from the Sanskrit word *Sangama,* which means confluence of two or more rivers. No matter where the word originated, it not only means confluence of rivers but of cultures, beliefs, and people too. Devotees from all over the country, even foreigners, come to experience this, to take a dip in the holiest of the rivers. You know, some people spend a whole month here in the bitter cold, called Kalpvas. Technically, it starts from the eleventh day of the Hindu month Pausha and ends on the twelfth day of Magh; this period of one month is called Kalp, which is equivalent to one day of Lord Brahma. One Kalpvas gives you punya worth a hundred years of worship. Now, that is mythology, but imagine the mental and spiritual growth in that month, one can achieve," says Roshani, looking immersed and throwing her arms in the air.

Rudra gazes at Roshani, awestruck by such words coming out of a modern girl, whom he has known from their childhood, but has never seen this side of her.

"This is Adi Shankar Viman Mandapam temple," says Roshani, pointing in front of them.

Rudra looks ahead at the four-story temple and says, "Doesn't it look like a South Indian temple?"

"Yes, it is a Shiva temple made in South Indian architectural style in memory of Adi Shankaracharya."

They both enter the temple and climb the stairs to the second floor, from where a vast area of the Sangam is visible. Rudra notices that the ground is unusually cold, and that relaxes him. They stand there, looking at various idols, appreciating the magnificent view of the Sangam, and observing people. Roshani grabs Rudra's hand and pulls him towards the sanctum sanctorum. They enter the inner chamber, and she leaves his hand to fold hers and closes her eyes. Rudra does the same.

The priest applies a tika on Rudra's forehead and hands some flower petals and holy water. He drinks the holy water and exits the inner chamber to the open area, leaving Roshani praying inside. He again looks at the river. This view, all the noise around and the cold ground calms Rudra's troubled head. He closes his eyes and feels at ease.

Rudra opens his eyes and finds Roshani smiling at him. She raises her eyebrows, asking, *Are you OK?* He nods with a smile on his calm face.

They go towards the stairs to explore the upper floors, but it is prohibited, so they leave.

Next, they head to the famous Hanuman temple. Roshani says, "Where are the clouds? There is so much sunlight. Do you need a cap?"

Rudra questions back, "How much more time are we going to spend here?"

"Aren't you enjoying?"

"Yes, I am, but if the next temple is last, why should I buy a cap?"

Roshani says, "Right. We will be here for another hour, maybe."

"In that case, I will get a cap."

They go to a makeshift shop and buy a cap for Rudra and a fancy hat for Roshani. They step into the Hanuman temple, and Roshani starts, "This is an interesting temple where Hanuman-ji is in a sleeping position. In mythology, there are many stories about this form. One of them mentions that when Hanuman finished learning from Lord Sun, he insisted his guru ask for his fee. In ancient times, pupils had to do whatever was asked as guru dakshina, which means fee."

"I have also watched shows on the Ramayana and Mahabharata, Roshani. I know what guru dakshina means," interrupts Rudra.

"OK, OK. Somehow, you come across as somebody who doesn't have any interest in mythology or history. Anyway, Lord Sun asked Hanuman to protect Shri Ram from any mishaps. Hanuman flew to Ayodhya. Lord Ram thought that if Hanuman accompanied him, he would kill all the rakshasas, wasting the purpose of Ram's incarnation on Earth. So, he sent Maya to make Hanuman fall asleep. This is the spot where Maya met

Hanuman. It was nighttime, and Hanuman didn't want to cross the holy river Ganga at night, deeming it disrespectful," says Roshani, folding her hands and bowing her head. Rudra follows. "As per another 'realistic,'" quoting by her fingers in the air, "story, a businessman was travelling in his boat in the Ganga with this statue of Lord Hanuman. When he reached here, the statue got heavier by itself, and ultimately, the boat sank. After many years, when some people discovered the remains of the boat and this idol, Akbar was the emperor of India at that time. He commissioned this temple for his Hindu citizens."

They stop at a shop to grab some snacks. The shopkeeper opens the cold drinks and hands them to Roshani and Rudra. "A quick question," asks Roshani, "It is said that the three rivers, Ganga, Yamuna and Saraswati meet here in the Sangam, but where is the Saraswati?"

Rudra says, "You tell."

The shopkeeper chimes in. "There used to be an underground river flowing through the fort, you can find the Saraswati Koop there. It dried up eventually due to mistreatment," he says, dejected.

Roshani pays him, and they leave the shop. She says, "He was very sad, wasn't he? Anyway, it is said that the Saraswati is invisible. Saraswati is the goddess of knowledge, and Prayag used to be a major centre of education. So, the concept of the Saraswati merging here comes from that."

"In fact, the Saraswati is mentioned in the Rigveda and the Mahabharata. Like the Ganga and Yamuna, the Saraswati also originated from the Himalaya, and its origin glacier is called Swarga Rohini. It's the same place where Yudhishthira found the stairs to Heaven. About 3000 years ago, due to a shift in tectonic plates, the direction of flow changed. The main river eventually dried up. Whatever is left exists in the far north but is no longer known as the Saraswati. Now, Allahabad is far from where the Saraswati has been mentioned in the Vedas. Also, what that shopkeeper shared is a widely known myth. After the change in flow, the Saraswati became an underground river. There are some places where it can be seen, like the Saraswati Koop. So, the Saraswati meets here in the Sangam, flowing underground," explains Rudra.

Roshani is impressed by his knowledge and says, "Wow, you know such things?"

"This is our history, this is who we are." Roshani nods while Rudra thinks, *Where did I learn this?*

They keep walking ahead. The Ganga is on the left, far away due to depleted water levels, and the Hanuman temple is on the right. Roshani walks on Rudra's left, holding the chips packet, and both focus on munching. She takes in the temple's aesthetics, and Rudra appreciates the Ganges.

She says while eating chips, "You know, Allahabad fort used to be closed to the general public, but from last year it has been open for all. It has boosted religious tourism. This fort has the Akshayavata in it, the immortal banyan tree. It was closed yesterday, though, due to some maintenance work." Rudra zones out of the conversation, as a few chips are left. He concentrates on getting as many as possible before Roshani starts doing the same.

"So, here we are. Take the packet, Rudra, I don't want it," Roshani says playfully, and Rudra finally looks to his right. He finds himself standing in front of an incredibly high stone wall. The wall has guarding posts like medieval military forts. A cool breeze is blowing. In the background, he can hear the flowing water, people chanting mantras, and bhajans playing on speakers. Rudra turns white and pale, like all his blood has become water.

"It is also a common belief that Lord Brahma…" Roshani looks around her and doesn't find Rudra beside her. She turns to see him standing shocked, looking at the fort's front wall. She approaches him and asks, "Rudra, what happened? Why aren't you responding, Rudra?"

Rudra walks briskly towards the fort entrance. To enter, you must climb a long, inclined surface with separate pathways for incoming and outgoing tourists. He ascends the stairs with Roshani at his tail. After a few steps, he finds a huge banyan tree to his left. There are two temples near that, the Akshayavata temple and the Patalpuri temple.

Rudra moves towards the Patalpuri temple, the temple of the underworld. He goes down the stairs at the temple entrance and finds a long tunnel at the bottom. The tunnel is extremely narrow, and its ceiling is a few inches above his head. He starts feeling claustrophobic. Ignoring his dread, he crosses the tunnel and at the end of it, is an irregularly-shaped temple with various idols carved inside its walls. He recognises some of the gods amidst them. Upon looking closely, he starts hallucinating and hears the sound of someone digging a hole behind him. He turns around to discover a cordoned-off area with its floor in a different colour than the rest of the temple.

He examines it and realises it has been recently plastered; the cement colour is visibly different. Rudra leaves the tunnel and climbs out of the temple into the open air. He falls to his knees, gasping.

Roshani comes running behind him and puts her hand on his shoulder, asking, "What happened, Rudra? You are scaring me."

"I am scaring you? Really? Who are you, Roshani?" Rudra barks, clenching his fists.

"What are you talking about, Rudra? What happened? Please tell me," Roshani asks, apprehensive of his condition, thinking he will get a seizure if not comforted.

Rudra looks at her and questions crossly, "Why did you bring me here?"

"Because Uncle asked me to," replies a teary-eyed Roshani.

"Which uncle, Roshani?"

"Your father, Santosh uncle."

Rudra asks, unnerved, "What? My father asked you to bring me here?"

"Why would I lie? What happened, Rudra?"

Rudra walks towards the exit and says, "Let's go home, it's time to get some answers."

They both come out of the fort and go towards the parking lot. They are about a hundred metres from their scooter when Roshani notices Santosh standing there and informs Rudra. Rudra strides up to him and asks, "You knew all along?"

Rudra's father turns to Roshani and says calmly, "Thank you, beta, you have been of great help. I am really sorry for putting you through all this."

Roshani is mystified. The last few minutes have been too intense, leaving her with a lot of questions, but she simply replies, "It's OK, Santosh uncle." She is confused by the sudden turn of events and doesn't even know how to look her best friend in the eyes.

Rudra is seething with rage. His father continues, "Roshani, you go home. Rudra will come with me," and then he turns to Rudra, "I think you should apologise to Roshani. I will explain everything."

Rudra is dazed at his father's behaviour. *How can he be so normal?* He doesn't say anything. Santosh repeats, "Apologise to Roshani, Rudra. Life is unpredictable. One should not hold unnecessary grudges against loved ones for long, who knows when it's your last time together."

Rudra's expressions change from anger to surprise, but after noticing his father's downcast face, he understands something big is about to happen. He turns to Roshani and says, "I am sorry for not trusting you, Roshani. I shouldn't have shouted at you."

Roshani is still baffled and says, "It's OK, Rudra," and leaves on her scooter.

Rudra faces his father, but before he can say anything, Santosh says, "Not here, Rudra. I don't want to talk about it in the car either. Let's go somewhere for a coffee and talk."

Rudra gets scared. Why? The answer is in his father's expression—plain, pale face, like he is about to meet his death.

16

Unwinding

Santosh stops the car at the India Coffee House. They both come out of the car, enter the cafe, and sit at the farthest table in the corner. Santosh goes to the toilet and returns, scanning the whole place with his eyes. He sits on the table, inspecting underneath with his hands. Seeing all this, Rudra queries, "What are you doing, Papa?"

"You don't know who you are fighting against."

"I am not fighting against anyone. I am a common man, minding my own business."

"You are not common, and yes, you are doing what you were born to do."

Rudra gets more puzzled and asks, "What is it all about, Papa? Please tell me."

"First of all, Rudra, I am not your father, nor is Nandini your mother. These are not even our real names." Santosh drops a big bomb on Rudra.

Rudra's mouth opens in disbelief. "What do you mean, you are not my father? Papa, I know you are not joking, you cannot plan such an elaborate prank."

"What is your first memory, Rudra?" Santosh asks.

"What kind of question is that, Papa? How can I remember my very first memory?"

"OK. Let me rephrase it. Do you remember anything about the time before we moved to Allahabad? Anything before you were eight years old, to be specific?"

"Yes, before that we lived in Varanasi. We moved here because of your transfer," Rudra answers hastily.

"I am a businessman, Rudra; we don't get transferred. This is something that an eight-year-old doesn't understand, and after some time, people don't even think about why they moved cities. That was a mistake. I could not even lie properly then," Santosh chuckles nervously and continues, "Do you remember anyone from your Varanasi days, any friend, your school?"

"I used to study in a convent school there?"

"Do you remember the name of your school?"

"Yes, it was Mahamana Convent School."

"Do you remember the building, your classroom, classmates, any friends from school?"

Rudra nods a yes and tries to remember any detail. He closes his eyes, jogs his memory, but fails to recall anything. He opens his eyes in disappointment.

Santosh clarifies, "That is because you were never in Varanasi. You were not even with us before the day we moved to Allahabad. You remember the things we told you multiple times. We were directed to raise you."

"By whom?"

"That's a difficult question. I am just a pawn in this game," Santosh sighs. "And it is not a person. It is a society of powerful people, in fact extremely powerful people, who run this country, economy, policies, industries from behind the curtains. This society is so mysterious that even the people involved don't know who they work for. People like me do what they are asked to do. In the power struggle, there is always good and evil. One side aims to control the power from being used, and the other side struggles to gain that power to use for their benefit. In our case, it is the same."

"So, which side are you on?"

"I told you, Rudra, I am so tiny an entity that I don't have the luxury of choosing sides. I was born on the wrong side, and it seems like I am on no one's side now. That's why I am with you here, telling you all this," Santosh says, frustrated and anguished. "So, what I know is that there is an ancient weapon, which is protected by a group of people. Nobody knows who these people are, but they have been protecting it for thousands of years. There is another society which has been trying to locate this weapon, and I belong to the latter one."

"What kind of weapon is it?"

"Frankly, I don't know. This weapon can be anything. Only the people at the top know."

"OK. Who are my parents?" Rudra asks, hopeful to know.

"I am sorry, Rudra. I don't have answers to most of your questions. As I told you, you were given to us when you were eight. We have never been told about your parents or family."

Rudra gets frustrated, and Santosh senses it, so he says, "Now, I will tell you whatever I know. We were entrusted to take care of you and keep you in sight since you were eight. Even when you were in school, park, garden, playing with your friends, cinema halls, or college, you were never alone; there was always somebody watching you. Do you remember that your college had a strict rule for all students to reside in the hostel, but only you were allowed to stay outside because of your health? What condition do you have? All the documents proving you have a weak heart are forged. You don't have any health issues; you are fit as a horse. It's fed into your head that you have a heart condition, so that your mother always lives with you. From the very first day, you are drugged. Most of the people you have ever been in contact with are either part of the society or people with a proper background check."

"Is Roshani also an agent?" Rudra asks with a heavy heart.

"No, but without you, her life would have been better. You both became friends in your childhood, and she was sent to a boarding school. As soon as she completed her schooling, it was ensured that she got admission in a college, far away from Allahabad. Now that you are not living in Allahabad, she has finally got time to spend with her family," Santosh answers, empathising with her. "Regarding the recent days, you disappeared on the morning of 27 January from the factory, no police complaint was filed, and you were not seen in any security cameras."

"But the FM informed me about it," Rudra says, bewildered.

"Everybody around you is a part of the society, Rudra. Do you think they would let you work somewhere they are not in control? I think the whole factory belongs to them and so does the factory manager," answers Santosh.

"This factory is not some family-owned business; it is a huge multinational company. How can somebody in India have control over a company like this?" Rudra cuts him.

"Logic fails when you are dealing with such powerful people. They may not own the company, but those who can make decisions, like not filing a police complaint or promoting you to a general shift job after the dog attack to ensure you are safe at night, are definitely part of that society," explains Santosh and continues, "So, during those 11-12 days, you were in search of that weapon..."

"What are you saying, Papa? I am a normal guy who works in a factory. Why would I go searching for an ancient weapon?" Rudra interrupts again, frustrated.

"You are not a normal guy," says Santosh, looking into Rudra's eyes. He emphasises, "You are special. You were born to do this. You have been trained to read ancient languages and understand ancient books. Even at the age of eight, you had the knowledge of all the Vedas, Upanishads, and Puranas." Rudra is taken aback, but it also explains how he quoted ancient literature during a lot of interactions.

"In those eleven days, you discovered some parts of the weapon and gathered leads on the other. Something happened, and they stopped the mission, but you hid the leads and parts somewhere. They have been searching for those, and that's the only reason you are still alive. The moment they find those things, you will be executed. I don't want that, so I sent that letter and asked you to stop taking the medicines," says a concerned Santosh with tears in his eyes.

"You sent the letter?" Rudra asks in utter surprise.

"Haan, even the hospital and doctor are not genuine. The medicines you take are prescribed to make you forget about those days, until they locate the weapon," answers Santosh. All of a sudden, his expression changes to fear. Before Rudra can ask anything, he says in haste, "Go to the toilet. There is a back door, open it and blend into the crowd. Don't look back and don't make the mistake of going home." He hits Rudra's foot multiple times under the table to move.

"But, Papa..." Rudra resists.

"They are here. You need to leave immediately. Remember, you might not be my biological son, but I loved you like one, always. Don't run, just stand up and go to the washroom normally, without looking at me," Santosh instructs, looking at Rudra, poker-faced.

Rudra takes a good look at Santosh's face. Santosh smiles a little, and then Rudra moves to the toilet, locates the back door and exits into a busy, narrow street. He disappears in the crowd, not knowing what happened to Santosh.

Rudra takes a left turn, following the wave of people, without knowing where it leads. He creates a maze of lefts and rights to avoid getting traced, but he is hysterical. The last sad smile on Santosh's face is haunting him. He feels every person on the street is looking for him. He enters a wider road and hops into an autorickshaw to escape 'them'.

"Bhaiya, move."

"Where to?"

"I will tell you; just keep moving in this direction. Ouch, what kind of seats are these? It's pricking like needles." Something pierces Rudra's back while shifting on the seat from one side to the other.

The driver responds, "Sir, these are old seats."

Rudra shoots back, "Then get it repaired..." He collapses on the seat, and everything blacks out.

17

The Story Unfolds

An autorickshaw with a sleeping passenger takes a sharp right at a traffic signal, which is about ten kilometres from the location where Rudra is last seen. It heads to the outskirts of Allahabad and crosses a bridge on the Yamuna. After driving for forty more minutes, the autorickshaw reaches an area with no human establishments and trees all around. It takes a left turn off the road and disappears in the jungle. After another fifteen-minute ride, the autorickshaw arrives at the ruins of some old structure. The driver comes out, wearing a hoodie and a mask which is covering the lower half of his face. He looks very well-built, with broad shoulders and good height. He lifts Rudra over his shoulders and takes him inside.

It gets dark, and the chirping of crickets and howling of jackals occasionally disturb the jungle's silence.

Rudra opens his eyes and finds himself lying on a shattered floor of an old building. There is a single source of light in the centre of the room. He adjusts his eyes. His head is spinning, but he tries to sit with his hands' support, sighing due to stiffness in his body. Once settled, he looks around again and shivers in horror as he notices something in the farthest corner of the room. With the dim light, he fails to identify what it is.

"How is your head, Rudra?" a voice comes from the same corner. Rudra is terrified, but after listening to a human voice and realising he is not in command, he starts a conversation.

"Who are you?" Rudra asks, masking his fear behind his steady voice.

"Relax, I am not an enemy," the voice answers softly.

"Friends do not kidnap." Rudra's voice is firm this time.

"I had no other option. You were about to be captured by them again. They would not have left you alive this time. I didn't have the luxury of time to explain."

"Do I know you? Why does your voice seem familiar? Who are you?" Rudra asks in incredulity.

The figure stands up and walks to the centre of the room. He becomes more and more visible with every step and stops near the light. Rudra struggles with his eyes, so the figure adjusts the light by rotating a knob. Rudra now clearly sees a large, masked figure. He unveils his face, and Rudra shouts in astonishment, "Kshitip? Aren't you Kshitip?"

"Yes, I am Kshitip, Rudra."

Kshitip gestures at Rudra to relax and offers him a burger and a glass of juice. Rudra unwraps the burger and finds it very crumbly and cold. Kshitip says, "I bought it when you were talking to Santosh."

Hearing Santosh's name, Rudra's eyes well up. He keeps the burger aside and asks Kshitip, "What happened to him? Is he alright?"

"I don't know, Rudra, but he is not your real father. Why are you getting emotional?" Kshitip says carelessly, eating his burger.

"He told me he is not my real father, but he did take care of me."

"He told you? How could he?" asks a surprised Kshitip.

"That's what he was telling me in the coffee house."

"What else did he tell you?" Kshitip asks in excitement.

Rudra notices the eagerness in his voice and replies, "Nothing much," and stares at the light.

"You don't trust me, right? You think I am also from their side," scoffs Kshitip, finishing his burger and wiping his fingers.

"For twenty years, the family I lived with was not my family. That woman, whom I considered my mother, is not my mother, and that man is not my father. I don't know who is right. I don't even know who I am," vents Rudra, looking into Kshitip's eyes. "And you expect me to trust you, whom I have known for merely a couple of months and who is my kidnapper?"

Kshitip comes closer to Rudra and says, "You are absolutely right, you should not trust anyone. I just hoped you would trust me after all that we did together in those days."

Rudra is stunned and asks immediately, "You were with me during those eleven days?"

"You don't remember anything at all?"

"No."

"Huh. They are known for such things, making people forget specific parts of their lives. Don't…"

"Who are they?" Rudra asks, cutting Kshitip in the middle, irritated of hearing about 'them' all the time.

"They are the Guruputras, powerful people from ancient India. They have control over almost everything today, except one thing which they have been searching for centuries," says Kshitip, "Once they were rulers of this country, but, as it happens in the struggle of power and throne, one great dynasty takes over another. They were defeated, and whoever remained alive had to go into exile to save their lives. They took an oath to take revenge and believed that one specific weapon could make that happen, the most powerful weapon ever made. After all these years, they have gained power again, but the search for that weapon has become their obsession. They still believe they can become rulers of the world using it. They can do anything to get their hands on that weapon. But, if they find that, only God can save humanity."

Rudra has been listening to Kshitip's words prudently and asks, "How do you know all this?"

Kshitip takes a deep breath and says, "There is another society, equally powerful, that has ensured that the weapon is always out of the Guruputras' reach. We belong to that society."

"We?"

"Yes, we. We were born in that society and spent our early days of childhood together. We were taught ancient history, languages, scriptures, fighting and survival skills, but you were kidnapped one day. Since then, we have been looking for you. Somehow, we got information about the Guruputras and their establishments, so I joined one of their factories. I gathered as much information as possible about their young manpower in factories to possibly locate you. Then I heard about a twenty-eight-year-old guy in the Goa factory who lived with his mother because of some illness.

"People made fun of you in our factory, but I sensed a cover-up. I shared the information with our people. As soon as they started following you, they realised something was wrong, and the security around you was so impenetrable that there was no other option but for me to transfer to the Goa factory. By the time I could gather relevant information about you without being noticed, you had disappeared again," reveals Kshitip.

"But you said you were with me in those days," Rudra asks, still suspicious.

"You don't trust me yet?" Kshitip calmly elaborates, "When you disappeared on the morning of 27 January, nobody paid attention as they thought you had gone to your hometown on leave, but I did a little investigation and realised that you didn't leave the factory that day, at least not from the main gate. Your last known location was the tower's second floor. There I found your mobile phone, which ascertained my theory that you were either kidnapped or sent somewhere else."

"But it still doesn't explain how you found me," Rudra says, eyeing him.

Kshitip replies, "I noticed something peculiar on the chocolate tower. The roof was clean, as if it had been swept recently, but the wall was extremely dirty. It seemed all the dirt from the floor had shifted to the wall. That is possible by only one thing, a lightweight helicopter."

"A helicopter? Are you nuts?" Rudra mocks Kshitip's theory.

"That is the roof of a hundred-acre factory. The structural area must be more than forty acres, and it is an industrial hub where there is always noise of machines, hooters and whatnot. Also, there are smaller, silent helicopters designed for fewer people that land in a smaller space," justifies Kshitip.

"Okay, if you say so," Rudra nods, unconvincingly.

Kshitip resumes his narration. "Moments after I went up to the roof, I was called and handed over my tickets to go back to my old factory. I boarded my flight, but when I reached Delhi, there was no cab to take me to the factory. I didn't call anyone and waited for some time. When nobody from the HR department or the driver called, I understood that they sent me back just as a precautionary measure. They booked my tickets to Delhi, but the rookies in HR didn't inform my factory that they were sending me back. That was a golden opportunity for me to track you."

Rudra stops him abruptly. "Now that you knew who I was, and I was 'abducted again,'" he says putting imaginary quotation marks in the air, "You could have disappeared rather than waiting for a moment like this. It is not like they would have tracked you, or that job was important."

"Haha, you are absolutely right." Kshitip laughs and then says, "No, that job was not important to me. I didn't even bother about being tracked because I know nobody would be able to do that if I went incognito. But it was important not to let them know that we were aware of you. If they suspected, they would have relocated you or changed the plan, and our whole effort would have gone futile. Also, I didn't even know that the work would be completed in one go."

Rudra doesn't express his acknowledgement, but it seems logical to him. He questions after a pause, "So, how did you track me?"

Kshitip says, "I will share the entire story with you, but first, I should go out and do a perimeter check." He leaves the room and steps out.

18

Vasant Panchami

Kshitip returns and takes a seat. He recounts what follows his arrival at Delhi.

He was having dinner in a restaurant that night, and on the TV, they were running news coverage of the ongoing Kumbh Mela in Allahabad.

Kumbh is the biggest congregation of faith and religion in India. Religion that forms the basis of this weapon and both societies. Kumbh is the ideal place to fit in the sea of people without being noticed.

Then, they had mentioned the Shahi Snan of Vasant Panchami on 29 February. That was when it struck Kshitip that Rudra might have been taken to this location to do something there.

Rudra asks, "What does it have to do with Vasant Panchami?"

"Oh, everyone in the society knows that somehow Goddess Saraswati is linked with all this," Kshitip answers, but Rudra looks unconvinced. Kshitip shrugs his shoulders and says, "You can call it a hunch, déjà vu."

They both sit in silence before Rudra says, "You said you found my mobile phone. Do you have it?"

"Oh yes, sorry I forgot to give you," replies Kshitip while unzipping his backpack. He finds Rudra's phone and hands it over. Rudra presses the power button, but the phone doesn't switch on, so he looks at Kshitip.

"I charged it just a few days back, I thought it would still have some battery left." He rummages through his bag again and takes out a power bank. "Here, use this. But I will suggest you switch it on here, get whatever information you can and then destroy it. There is no signal here, so nobody would be able to trace you. If you use it somewhere else, you know the consequences."

Rudra connects the power bank to his mobile and queries further, "Then?"

Kshitip takes a while to decode the abrupt question. Then, he shares how he had taken the next flight from Delhi to Lucknow and a train from there to Allahabad.

He had reached around 9 a.m. and had directly gone to the Kumbh Mela to look for Rudra. He kept searching for several hours, on the ground, inside tents, or in akhadas, but he could not find him. He checked every temple there, even the nearby hotels and lodges.

One just could not find someone in that area; it was so huge and crowded. The sun started setting, and so did his heart, thinking his hunch was wrong. He was standing near a temple when he overheard a group of people talking about their experience. They discussed visiting the Akshayavata and Saraswati Koop inside Akbar's fort on the banks of the Ganga. They were talking about the fort being open to the public. Kshitip knew he was at the right place.

By then, it was dark and the fort was closed, so he had to find a way to get inside. He checked the surroundings and found easy access. He climbed the north wall of the fort to enter. There was nobody, so he sat in a dark corner and waited for hours for something to happen or someone to show up, but nothing happened that night.

The sun came out, and visitors started pouring in. Kshitip walked out of the corner and left the fort. He was disheartened and decided to go for a dip in the holy Ganga. He still remembers how cold the water was.

After taking the dip, he sat on the shore for a moment. Beside him, a family was talking to a priest about the muhurta of a ritual they wanted to perform since it would be the most auspicious time to make the puja fruitful. Then it struck Kshitip that days in the Hindu calendar do not align with the Western one, so there would be a certain time of the day when Vasant Panchami would start, not precisely at midnight. He ran to a shop, bought a Panchanga, and discovered that Vasant Panchami would start at 10:45 a.m., so he again entered the fort and planned to spend the whole day there.

Kshitip spent most of his day near the Akshayavata and temples. Again, nothing happened the entire day. People left the fort, but he hid in the same corner. From there, he could see the temples clearly. Kshitip waited for more than six hours, but there was no activity at all.

Right after midnight and before the end of Vasant Panchami, two figures emerged from the other side of the fort. One of the guys was at least seven feet tall, built like a giant. Till today, Kshitip gets chills thinking about that guy, in the dark, quiet surroundings. They both were wearing face masks and moved to the Patalpuri temple. The other guy seemed a little edgy. He kept looking over his shoulder and walked hastily to keep up with the bigger guy. After they reached the temple, they discussed something, and the seven-foot guy stood outside guarding the entrance, and the edgy one went inside.

After a while, the bigger guy also entered the temple. Kshitip heard a few muffled gun shots "pop-pop" and then complete silence. He could not gather the courage to go and check inside, but he went a little closer, still in hiding. A few minutes passed, then he heard footsteps. It was that edgy guy; he was shaking and struggling to breathe. He stepped out and removed his mask. Kshitip recognised that guy.

"Me," Rudra blurts out, interrupting Kshitip.

"You remember?" Kshitip asks, amazed.

"Not everything, but I have visions sometimes of that night, and now that you are narrating it, I can recall a few things," says Rudra, "And the huge guy was called Thirty-six."

"Yes, yes, I know. You told me later," replies Kshitip and smiles. "I see, your memory is back."

"I can relate my visions to what you are saying. Surprisingly, my memory is much better now, but I am unable to put them in order. You continue, I will pitch in whenever I think it's necessary," Rudra answers.

"So, now you trust me?" Kshitip grins.

"100 per cent. Now, I do have some memories of what we went through in those days, together." Rudra smiles back.

"Good. It took me more effort to convince you this time. When we last met in the fort, it was easier," says Kshitip.

"Yeah. Those were different circumstances and..." Rudra stops abruptly.

"And?"

"I was scared," Rudra responds, looking at his mobile. He avoids sharing something. Kshitip notices that, but decides not to pry. Rudra changes the topic and asks, "What happened after that?"

"Ah, right. Then I came out of my hiding and you recognised me too. You asked me to help remove the bodies from the temple."

When Rudra had said "bodies," Kshitip thought Rudra was in shock since only one person was inside with him, Thirty-six. Kshitip was so scared while walking across that narrow corridor to the temple that he still can't describe it in words. Who knew it was nothing compared to what they would face in the coming days? He first saw the lifeless body of Thirty-six, lying on the floor, bleeding from his neck and head. Behind the pillar, there was another body in a white dhoti and kurta with blood everywhere.

"The body of Amatya Baahudhwaj. When Thirty-six entered the temple, he immediately shot Amatya twice. He first shot his left leg. He wanted to capture him alive, so he shot a second time at his other leg, but it hit him in the chest as he awkwardly fell due to the first shot. When Amatya was struggling, Thirty-six went and sat beside him, holding his head. Amatya swung his hand and hit Thirty-six's neck. He fell with a fatal knife wound. I could not believe what happened. I was fear-struck. Then Thirty-six spoke his last words to Amatya, 'Now, you can't stop the inevitable. The end is near,' with a devilish grin on his face and then died," recollects Rudra.

"But why did Thirty-six go close to Amatya when he was already dying?" Kshitip asks. He has always believed that Thirty-six killed Amatya, and Rudra killed Thirty-six. Rudra never shared this story earlier.

"Because Amatya said something to me, after the second shot. Thirty-six could not hear, so he went to interrogate," replies Rudra, and asks, "Didn't I tell you about these things at that time?"

"Last time, we didn't even have time to talk. We were just engrossed in solving the clues to find the pieces. By the way, what did he tell you?" Kshitip asks curiously.

"I don't remember. He said something like billions of lives are on stake, and gave the location of the first clue. He died while trying to tell me something. He kept on repeating, 'yellow brick.' I panicked and rushed out of the tunnel," shares Rudra.

"That time, I didn't explain much for you to trust me. I just said a few things, and you got persuaded easily," says Kshitip, quizzing Rudra further.

"That was all gut feeling. Thirty-six's last sentence with that grin on his face made me realise that the people I was working for were wrong. Whatever conversation I had with Amatya Baahudhwaj was also of the same nature, though I don't remember those right now. What happened afterwards?" Rudra asks.

"So, we took care of both bodies and cleaned the area. After that, you told me Amatya had asked you to visit the forty-fourth god in the temple."

They didn't know where to find it, as there were idols on all the walls of the temple. So, they decided to count from both directions. Kshitip started from the left, and Rudra managed the right side. There were many idols, sometimes with two or three gods in one frame. They completed counting and met again at the entrance opposite where they had started. They both had a tally of forty-three idols.

They thought they missed a particular idol due to its small size, and started again. They checked every carving carefully, looking for any god in the background or its symbolic presence in any of the frames, but again ended up with forty-three.

Rudra had mumbled, "What does aavirbhava mean?" Kshitip had explained that it's manifestation, someone's physical presence.

Before dying, Amatya had asked Rudra to look for the aavirbhava of the forty-fourth god, but Rudra didn't comprehend his Sanskrit properly.

They were both baffled by how a god could be physically there. Rudra guessed either the earth or the Akshayavata as the two possible options, but then dismissed the former as the temple was vast. Amatya had said that he would get answers when in front of it.

Kshitip had mentioned, "Look for yellow bricks."

Rudra had refused, "There are no bricks on the ground, Kshitip. Also, it would be foolish to hide a clue for something so mysterious and powerful, openly on the floor that can be disturbed for any maintenance work, anytime."

Rudra sneers, "Why are you getting into so much detail? Just tell me where we found it."

"I am trying to bring back your memory. If I tell you what happened in two lines, how will you remember? You may recall something critical," Kshitip replies calmly, and Rudra nods.

After eliminating the other option, they had shifted their focus to the Akshayavata and inspected every brick on the wall around the roots, but again, there was nothing. The walls were clean, and so were the bricks.

While again looking here and there, Kshitip saw something written on a small pillar. It read, "This ancient Saraswati Koop was covered by the Mughals along with Dev Aangan. The top of the well is painted red," with an arrow pointing downwards. Behind that, a small area was red with four pillars on all its sides, making it partially visible.

Kshitip remarks, "This was idiotic. I had entered the fort after hearing about the Saraswati Koop, and it never crossed my mind."

"A goddess, the aavirbhava," says Rudra, almost mesmerised.

"Those were your exact words when you saw that writing," Kshitip reminds him.

They had then gone outside the temple to find something to break the floor. Luckily, there was renovation going on in the fort premises, so they found the perfect tools, a sledgehammer and a mattock. Then, they got back in.

"The thing I hate about fairs is that they are loud. In the Kumbh Mela, the nights are also not quiet. There is always some religious thing going on, but that night, the amalgamation of sounds covered our clatter," says Kshitip.

"I have nightmares about the fort and digging in this temple. I keep seeing a person in there, now I know it's you," says Rudra, relieved.

"So, you never saw that person's face in your dreams?" Kshitip asks.

"No. I simply remember feeling a sense of relief after that," Rudra says. They both smile at each other. Kshitip resumes recounting those days for Rudra.

It hadn't taken them long to break that floor, and after a few hits, the first piece fell, making sounds as though hitting some obstruction, and finally, they heard a splash. They removed the pieces carefully and soon had an entry hole. The Saraswati was flowing approximately 30-40 feet below. The only way to find a yellow brick was to enter through that hole and search every brick manually.

Surprisingly, Rudra carried a bag underneath his overcoat, which had metal cord, harnesses and hard hats with a torch. They tied it on one of the pillars, and Rudra went down the well. Kshitip was peeping through that hole while Rudra cleaned the bricks. After a while, he finally found that brick. While he was removing it, Kshitip heard a noise outside the temple. There was no way to hide, so he rushed towards the tunnel entrance to find the origin of that sound, and Rudra remained silent, hanging in the well. A patrolling guard was on the stairs. Kshitip didn't know what to do if he entered the main temple. But he decided to hit the guard's head if he entered.

Kshitip was ready to hit him, but the guard turned back and left the tunnel, singing a religious song. Kshitip took a sigh of relief. After ensuring it was safe, he came and pulled Rudra out of the well. They noticed the brick was hollow, and there was a red cloth inside it. They put that red cloth with brick in Rudra's bag and thanked Goddess Saraswati for the gift. Kshitip also silently apologised for whatever destruction they had caused in the last couple of hours. Then, they left the fort.

Kshitip finishes narrating, and a silence blankets the room.

Kshitip and Rudra both have many questions for each other, but they are apprehensive about changing the topic. When Kshitip doesn't talk for some time, Rudra finally says, "Right. This weapon that we are talking about, the weapon which the Guruputras have been searching for thousands of years, Amatya Baahudhwaj sacrificed himself to keep it safe. Thirty-six was smiling, even when he was dying, at the thought of his people owning it. What is this weapon, and why is it that important?"

Kshitip takes a deep breath and says, "This weapon gives immense power to the owner. The person wielding this weapon will rule this world."

Rudra cuts him short, "I know all this; you said the same thing a few minutes back. Does it have a name?"

Kshitip pauses for a few seconds and says, "You know the name, Rudra. In fact, everyone does. It is the deadliest weapon in our history."

Rudra asks eagerly, "Tell me what it is, Kshitip."

"Gandeev."

"Gandeev? I have heard the name. That bow of Arjuna? From the Mahabharata?"

Kshitip nods affirmatively. After a few seconds of silence, Rudra bursts into laughter and says, between his chuckles, "Do you think I am an idiot? You started with history and transitioned to mythology. The Mahabharata is mythology, my friend. Somebody wrote a great book about gods and devils, people flying, weapons of mass destruction, people worshipping to get a child, and you took it seriously?"

Kshitip remains unmoved. He smiles at Rudra's denial and replies calmly, "I wish you were not kidnapped before the completion of our training, then you wouldn't be laughing at this. Nonetheless, it doesn't matter whether you believe it or not. You have already seen to what extent people have gone to hide this weapon or even the knowledge of it from mankind. You will believe in it someday."

Rudra stops laughing and says, "Kshitip, I understand that what they are searching for is extremely important and may cause mass destruction, but it is also necessary for us to be logical. People say the Mahabharata is our history, and took place thousands of years ago in our country, but do they have any proof?"

"In fact, they do. But then again, somebody who doesn't want to believe, won't. There aren't just circumstantial proofs but scientific ones too. Astronomers have proven that the position of various planets and the moon, which have been described in the Mahabharata on multiple occasions, can be traced back to approximately 3000 BCE. Various radioactive materials have been found in the area where the war is supposed to have taken place. Some of them are present only at places where the temperature crosses thousands of degrees, like atomic bomb blasts. Several cities' ruins mentioned in the Mahabharata have been found at the exact location. The..."

Rudra interrupts, "OK, Kshitip. That is not the point. It doesn't matter what I believe about the Mahabharata. What about my mobile? Is it charged now?" Rudra reaches out to his mobile. He pushes the power button, but it doesn't work. He turns his head towards Kshitip.

Kshitip says, "I bought it from a street vendor, man. I will give you another one." He takes out another power bank from his bag. Rudra stares at Kshitip, questioning this power bank's authenticity. Kshitip understands and says, embarrassed, "This will work, trust me. It is branded." Rudra connects the new power bank, and Kshitip goes outside again to check.

19

The Travel

Kshitip returns after checking and continues narrating their journey to Rudra, vividly recollecting those days.

It was early morning, but the streets were not deserted. They had taken an autorickshaw, and after finding an isolated area, Rudra had opened his bag. Kshitip took the red cloth and unwrapped it. There was an old parchment paper in it with Sanskrit inscriptions:

> **mahoksha harya rakshnartham dadruh pragyan shyena**

Rudra had said, "Mahoksha means bull, harya means snake, dadruh is tortoise, and shyena is eagle, I think."

"What does it even mean?" Kshitip had questioned, but Rudra had no idea either.

"I remember, you thought that the bull could be Kamdhenu," says Rudra, laughing incessantly. "Kamdhenu, a bull, hahaha.".

"You don't have any memory of the important things, but you didn't forget this? Yes, I said that, but it's not so funny that you laugh at it even after a month. It's a poor joke at its best. I didn't realise what I said in excitement. I forgot Kamdhenu was a cow, not a bull," complains Kshitip and joins Rudra, chuckling.

"What an idiotic thing to say."

"But because of this, we thought about mythology, and the most obvious answer was the Nandi bull."

Zeroing in on any place based only on Nandi was impossible because every Shiva temple had Nandi guarding the linga. It was the same with the serpent; it could be Sheshnaag. Whenever there is a Shiva linga, you would find Sheshnaag covering it. So, they focused on the tortoise as it seemed unique. The first thought was obviously of Vishnu's second incarnation, Kurma or Kachchhapa. Kshitip was astonished when Rudra said he was aware of a Kurma temple.

The temple was in Andhra Pradesh's Srikakulam district. As the tortoise seemed the most difficult hint, they assumed they had decoded it and left for Varanasi. From there, they took a flight to Visakhapatnam.

Kshitip comments, "How easy it is to now think we took a flight. Every step, every place, every person was so spooky, like somebody was following, or at any moment, something terrible would happen. I had not slept in two days and was tired, but I couldn't rest on the train, flight or even in Visakhapatnam. Whenever I closed my eyes, the faces of Amatya and Thirty-six would flash in front of me. I was dying to get a proper sleep."

They had reached Visakhapatnam around 3 p.m. and had immediately taken an auto to the bus stand to board a Srikakulam bus. They were not 100 per cent sure about the temple, but they knew they would find Sheshnaag and Nandi.

Their only challenge was the eagle, but they had no option but to visit and verify.

Though the journey was less than three hours long, the bus stopped at a hotel for evening snacks. They felt safer away from Allahabad. They came out of the bus, sat at a table and ordered something to eat. This restaurant had picture boards of places to visit in the city and state. Rudra and Kshitip read all of them. One of those boards caught their attention. That picture had a huge Sheshnaag made of rock and an enormous Nandi. The inscription on the board read:

> The Lepakshi temple is situated on a low rocky hill called Kurmasaila, which resembles the unique shape of a tortoise. The temple complex is renowned for the amazing Vijayanagara style of architecture with the magnificence of a hundred-pillared Natya Mandapa with intricately carved walls and exquisite sculptures, a miraculous hanging pillar, timeless paintings on ceilings, colossus sculptures of monolithic Nandi and Naga linga guarded by a humongous Sheshnaag, an unfinished Kalyana Mandapa, and above all, many mysteries and legends. Every stone here has a story to tell, and every pillar has an episode of an epic. The main deity of the temple is Lord Veerabhadra, the fiery form of Lord Shiva. The historic town of Lepakshi is related to an occurrence in the Indian epic of the Ramayana. According to Valmiki's Ramayana, when Ram, accompanied by Hanuman, met the dying Jatayu, they helped him attain moksha by

> uttering the words "Le Pakshi," which means "Rise, bird."

"And we were going in the opposite direction. We left that bus and boarded the one going back towards Visakhapatnam. If only we had a mobile phone, it would have been easier to Google and find that place," recalls Kshitip.

"We could have bought a SIM and phone in Andhra Pradesh, we had IDs, didn't we?" Rudra asks.

"None of us had an Aadhaar card. Anyway, it would have been easier to track us with a SIM in our name."

"But for tracking, people need a mobile number," retaliates Rudra.

"Are you sure?" Kshitip asks sarcastically. Rudra doesn't reply. "I have seen on *Crime Patrol* that the police take dump data of a certain area and get the details of all the users in the vicinity. We had limited money, Rudra. We were not in contact with anyone, and we were travelling a lot. Most importantly, we had used a real ID to book that flight, which was dangerous enough," explains Kshitip, and Rudra nods.

Lepakshi was approximately 900 km from Visakhapatnam. As booking a flight was not an option anymore, they had again taken a bus. After two sleepless nights, they finally slept like tired horses in that bus. They woke up when the bus stopped at a hotel for the second time. They didn't have the slightest clue about when it halted for the first break. That was the last time both slept without one of them guarding.

"Now, while telling the story, I realise what a blunder it was. Anything could have happened," remarks Kshitip.

They had reached Lepakshi in the second half of the day and had directly gone to the temple. It was a magnificent work of architecture, well-maintained and vast. After a sound sleep and a full stomach, it appeared even more glorious.

Kshitip had asked, "What are we looking for?"

"The parchment doesn't say anything," Rudra had replied, straight-faced.

"Oh, so any ideas on what to do?" Kshitip had questioned in bewilderment.

Rudra had already moved towards the entrance, so Kshitip followed. He recalled the picture board's lines, "and above all, many mysteries and legends. Every stone here has a story to tell and every pillar has an episode of an epic," and he knew they would spend days there.

They entered the Natya Mandapa, which had one hundred pillars with intricate carvings. Every single pillar was a subject of study in itself. There were paintings on the ceiling, some of which were not even visible due to the lack of sunlight, and gorgeous sculptures. After spending an hour in the temple, they were more confused than before.

Rudra had asked, "Where is Nandi? Did you see it anywhere?"

"No."

They went outside and learnt that Nandi was about 200 metres away from the temple. It was a huge monolithic structure with ornate designs on it. They decided to start with Nandi. Just thoroughly checking that one rock sculpture cost them more than thirty minutes. It was already 4 p.m., and they didn't have time. They decided to head back inside.

In the temple, they had seen a monstrous footprint, and Kshitip had said jokingly, "Is it Thirty-six's footprint?" and Rudra had given him a side-eye.

"But seriously, it's a mystery why that footprint always has water in it, without any known source of water," ponders Kshitip.

"We were not solving that, Kshitip, please be on track," says Rudra, in irritation.

"Yeah, right. We went inside and started with the serpent. Sheshnaag had seven hoods, but nothing was out of place or mysterious. So, we inspected the inscriptions on all the pillars. There were hundreds of them with elaborate carvings," Kshitip recalls.

They had been extremely frustrated because they could only solve a problem if they understood it first. They were not aware of the mythology of that part of the country. Though it was a Shiva temple, everything was very different.

The closing time was approaching fast, so they decided to hide inside the temple to continue their search. Then, they saw something remarkable. An elderly man and his wife were sitting at the base of one of the pillars, passing a piece of cloth under it with closed eyes, praying to the Almighty and wishing for something. One end of the fabric came out from the other end. They held it briefly and then removed the cloth from the other side. It was the famous hanging pillar of the Lepakshi temple. It was enormous with a sufficient gap between the pillar and the ground. It was a marvelous piece of architecture and engineering.

They watched all this in awe, with their mouths wide open. In their hearts, they knew they had found what they were looking for. Before they could reach that pillar, an announcement was made on the loudspeakers that the temple would close in five minutes. People started leaving the temple premises. Rudra and Kshitip went in the opposite direction towards the unfinished Kalyana Mandapa and hid behind the bushes. They planned on coming out after five minutes, but once devotees left, other formalities like cleaning and checking started, which lasted until 8 p.m.

It was completely dark when they heard the gates being locked. They waited a few more minutes to ensure nobody was around and then stepped out of the bushes. Only a few lights were on to ensure the temple did not remain dark. They once again needed Rudra's hard hat with a torch to see the carvings on the pillar. He wore that hat, switched on the light, and they started inspecting every figurine.

Unlike other pillars, the hanging pillar had no gods carved on it but had various frames, with its top distinctly designed like a boat. They needed to see the complete pillar from the ceiling to the base.

The only thing they had was Rudra's climbing kit. He climbed the pillar without support, like farmers climb a coconut tree, with the bag on his back. Once he reached the top, Rudra fixed the wire between the pillar's arch and ceiling and hung it. He fixed the harnesses and shifted to the wire to inspect the pillar minutely.

"What does an empty frame indicate? If it had any god's figure on it, we could easily link it with a story. These empty frames are beyond my understanding," Rudra had whined, a minute into the inspection.

They found this pillar the most uninteresting in the temple; there were no words, no fancy carvings, and nothing linked to the Ramayana or the Mahabharata. When Rudra started inspecting the pillar, he took several minutes to check every single centimetre, but by the time he was about to finish, it was swift. After one side was done, they tied the rope on the other side of the pillar and inspected all four sides in the same fashion. They couldn't find the slightest hint towards what they were looking for. Once Rudra finished his part, Kshitip also tried. Even after closely reviewing every inch, they failed to find anything. It was past midnight, and both of them were despondent.

Kshitip was sitting on the floor, contemplating whether they were at the wrong site, while Rudra stood nearby, looking towards the sky. It was not a full moon night; the moon was half lit, but the small town of Lepakshi softly glowed under it.

They were so dejected that they hadn't talked for over half an hour when Rudra suddenly started walking towards the temple entrance again. Kshitip thought Rudra needed more time alone, so he didn't stop or follow him. He waited for 15-20 minutes before he saw Rudra returning energetically.

"Do you have a measuring scale?" Rudra had asked.

"No."

Rudra searched nearby, came back with a thin thread in his hand, and measured the sides of the empty frames carved on the pillar. He measured its length and width and superimposed the measurement on the rope.

Kshitip had observed incredulously and couldn't understand anything. "What are you doing, Rudra?" Rudra had not answered.

Rudra sat down, evaluated the pillar's base, again superimposed the thread length of the smaller side on the bigger one, and cried, "I was right," in ecstasy.

Kshitip had again asked, "Rudra, what have you found?"

"Allahabad fort was constructed around the 1580s. Just imagine you hid something so important inside the Patalpuri temple, and the king of your country starts constructing walls around it, what would you do?"

"Recover it and hide it somewhere else."

"Exactly," Rudra had exclaimed, returning to what he was doing.

"So?"

Rudra had eyed Kshitip as if he was an idiot. "So, they hid it, and this is where it is."

Kshitip was still clueless. Rudra grabbed his shoulders with both hands and explained, "As I told you, the Allahabad fort was constructed in the 1580s. Knowing that our people would lose access to this weapon, they relocated it. Around the same time, this temple was being constructed, so they removed the weapon from the Saraswati Koop, left a clue there and hid it here.

"Now, why they did that, I can't say. But in religion, symbolism cannot be overlooked. They could have left that clue as a symbol of the weapon itself. The other possibility is that they don't communicate with each other to keep their identities hidden, which seems far-fetched. So, I assume the clue was kept symbolically. The construction of this temple was also completed around the 1580s. There are multiple empty frames on this pillar of various sizes and dimensions, but for all the frames, the ratio between length and width is the same as the ratio of its base. Whatever is hidden here, it's under the pillar."

"How do you know?"

"When we entered the temple, there was a board at the entrance with all the details of who built it and when. I just went outside to see that board again, and the moment I realised it was constructed almost simultaneously, it struck me. There is a reason for the gap between the ground and the pillar base. I confirmed this by measuring the dimensions of the empty frames. These frames indicate that whatever is hidden is under this pillar itself. Empty frames obviously mean something is missing," Rudra had answered with a scent of victory in his voice.

Kshitip was ecstatic too, but it was already close to 2 a.m. and removing the stones beneath the hanging pillar was not an apt job for two exhausted men. He reasoned with Rudra that the temple would reopen at 6 a.m., so the management committee would reach by 4 a.m. They could not remove the stones and put them back in just two hours.

"What is the need to fix it? We left the Patalpuri temple without fixing the floor."

"People from both societies know that something is going to happen. I am not bothered about the common mass; they will not understand. If this becomes news, the Guruputras will know where we are. It will put the whole mission in jeopardy," Kshitip had justified.

Rudra had dropped his shoulders and sat there in despair. He had said, "You are right, we can't put this whole thing in danger. The lives of billions of people are in our hands, but we have to be quick. We have to get it done by tomorrow night, no matter what."

"Don't you think it is too easy? Finding a weapon like this, I mean. Do you doubt that the weapon is under this pillar?"

"Let's get some sleep. We will find out tomorrow. We have only a couple of hours, let's take turns. First, you sleep, and after an hour, I will wake you up when I sleep."

They got a namesake sleep, sufficient for straightening their backs.

"I hope you are not taking advantage of my memory loss. Was it really you who said those logical words about only two hours remaining, and if we left it as it is, people would know about our mission?" Rudra jokes.

"That was my role: to make sane and logical decisions. The way you were transfixed on the result, you would have done anything to get the weapon," responds Kshitip. "Many times, you insulted me, shouted at me, left me alone, but I understood that you were under pressure and..."

"OK, OK. It was meant to be a joke. I know I'm a passionate man. I lose my temper over little things, but I don't mean any harm," Rudra says, getting emotional.

"I know."

"We have been sitting in these ruins for hours. Are you sure it is safe?" Rudra asks, pointing at the damaged walls and broken floor, to change the uncomfortable topic.

"Yes, yes. It is safe. It is a jungle and there is no human establishment on either side for several kilometres," Kshitip assures Rudra.

"Thank god, the battery is charging now," says Rudra, checking his mobile phone. "Let it get charged at least 25-30 per cent. So, what happened next, what was our plan?"

"When the temple opened and devotees started pouring in, we blended into the crowd and stepped out for breakfast. We found a small stall nearby. We couldn't even book a hotel and didn't even care about those little things. We had to go to such extremes. So, we sat there and finalised our strategy."

They had discussed at length a way to remove and fix the stones. Kshitip proposed gently scraping off the binding agent from the joints of the stones. Once sufficient, they could use a crowbar to detach the stone from the ground and then lift it. Rudra thought removing the binding agent to that depth with a scraper would not be possible since they didn't even know the depth of the individual stones.

"After the failed attempt to find the clues on the pillar, I was sitting on the edge of the floor at night and realised the stones were not very deep. It would be approximately two inches. I think, while constructing the temple, after levelling the ground, the engineers used the first layer of stones to prepare the base for the temple construction. Later, to raise the level of the Natya Mandapa, they put another layer of lean stones. I hope you noticed that the gaps filled with binding agent between the adjoining stones are sufficient to use a steel scraper and reach the bottom," Kshitip had opined.

Rudra lauded Kshitip's observation and suggested that, rather than lifting the stones by hand, they could buy some pulleys and vacuum cups. He already had wires to arrange the pulley system. With the resources they had, they could not afford mini cranes. They decided to pull the wire themselves, but a pulley system would ensure they didn't get tired.

"Why do we need pulleys, and why do you keep saying stones, not stone? It's a matter of one stone, we can lift it ourselves," Kshitip had asked.

"The gap between the pillar and the floor is less than an inch. Do you think you will be able to remove that stone without first removing the neighbouring ones?" Rudra had replied, shaking his head.

Kshitip had to change the topic to avoid further humiliation. "So, who is going to buy these things? I don't think we will find them in this town, and Anantapur is more than a hundred kilometres from here."

"Bangalore is also at a similar distance. Now that we have the whole day to plan, you go to Bangalore and buy steel scrapers, vacuum cups, crowbars and try to come back by 4 p.m. I will buy some cement and other stuff."

Kshitip had reached Bangalore, found a shop, bought all the required stuff, and got back by 3 p.m. By that time, Rudra had also arranged everything.

They again went into the bushes and waited for everyone to leave while sleeping in turns.

Around 8 p.m., when the temple was locked, they came out of the bushes and moved to the wall where Rudra had kept the cement and tools. They brought it to the Natya Mandapa and started arranging the pulley system. They began with the smallest rock, east of the pillar's base. After setting the pulleys up, they scraped the binding agent off. After creating a gap on two sides of that stone, they worked on the remaining two.

They could not guess if it was because of age or the type of binding agent, but it was not too difficult to scrape it off. Once they succeeded in creating a sufficient gap between the stones, they used crowbars to detach them from the ground.

Kshitip held the rock with the crowbar, and Rudra pulled the wire to activate the lifting. The rock was elevated from the ground, and they were overjoyed as they expected it to be more demanding. After removing the first rock, they drew out all four neighbouring ones and were finally left with the most important base. As the gap between this base and the pillar was less than one inch, they decided not to use the pulleys to lift it.

They planned to detach it using a crowbar and then slide it. The moment of truth was so close. Their hearts were racing like F1 cars when they moved that rock. But they were scared stiff when they looked at the area underneath. It had nothing except the same stone as the other four. In fact, the stone underneath the first layer was bigger than the upper ones, five of which they had just removed and wasted two to three hours.

It was devastating. After all the planning and all the sweat, they drew a blank. Kshitip fell on the floor and wanted to wail. Rudra stood there, looking at the moon.

Within a few minutes, Rudra had queried, "Kshitip, what is built first while constructing a building, be it a temple, house or bungalow?"

"Have you gone mad? What are you asking?" Kshitip had screamed in frustration.

"First, we prepare the floor, and then the rest is built—walls, pillars, carvings, windows, ceiling and all. So, when Akbar started the construction of the fort in Allahabad, the flooring work must have been completed here. There is no possibility of anything being underground. Whatever is here is in the base of this pillar."

Rudra slid his hand under the pillar through the space created after removing the stones and examined the bottom surface. Kshitip could read in Rudra's eyes that he found something there, but they had no idea how to see the carving there. There was no space for them to put their heads inside, and they were not carrying mobiles.

Rudra glanced at his palm. There were some indentations on it which resembled some Hindi letters. He screamed in excitement and rushed out of the temple by jumping a wall, with Kshitip following him. After crossing some time, they were on the road outside the temple.

Kshitip had no idea what was going on in Rudra's head. He had asked, "We left everything there. What if somebody comes and finds them?" There was no response from Rudra.

After crossing the restaurant where they had their breakfast, there was a T-junction. They took the right and arrived at a stationery shop. Rudra regretted not carrying the crowbars and told a puzzled Kshitip to break the lock. They found some stones nearby and broke the lock of the shop's shutter. Luckily, it was a small market, not a residential area, so nobody could hear them. Rudra entered the shop, grabbed some white chart papers, some paint and glue, and asked Kshitip for 2000 rupees. Kshitip gave him the money, and Rudra kept it on the counter with a handwritten letter. They rolled down the shutter, hung the lock in such a way that it didn't look broken and walked back to the temple.

While going back, Rudra had spoken about his theory, "Do you know how showing the first two fingers became a sign of victory?"

Kshitip had not answered as he knew Rudra was showing off his knowledge, so Rudra had continued, "The legend is that the V sign comes from a gesture made by longbowmen fighting during the Hundred Years' War. This origin legend states that English archers who were captured by the French had their index and middle fingers cut off so that they could no longer operate their longbows. The V sign was used by uncaptured and victorious archers in a display of defiance against the French. Today, when people use the V sign for victory, they don't know about this legend. Similarly, in this temple, when people pass that cloth under that pillar, they don't know what they are doing. They think it would bring good luck. It must have some origin story, right? Somebody might have seen some wealthy person passing a cloth and misunderstood it as a good luck thing. But, was that person just passing the cloth or printing the inscription on it?"

Kshitip could not fully understand what Rudra was trying to say, but what Rudra did after that made Kshitip a big admirer of him. Rudra stretched one of the chart papers, poured some colour and a little glue on it and smudged it uniformly. He held two corners and asked Kshitip to hold the remaining two. They put it under the pillar, keeping the coloured side up towards the base and stuck it to the bottom. Rudra pressed the paper firmly, and a few minutes later, they removed it gently. The paper had printed instructions on it, but in some places, it was torn. They put another piece of white paper without any colour on the bottom, pressed it for a couple of minutes, and removed it. It had clear prints which read:

krishna nirmita, vasuki pratiyudh chaturdasham uparishtat pradidhi sarvebhyo, chakshu sarosh

"But what are these shapes on the paper everywhere? Why didn't they simply write rather than putting effort into beautification?" Kshitip had commented.

They were elated after they found what they were looking for. They put the papers aside and scraped the floor to fix it. Kshitip made the cement mixture, and once Rudra finished levelling the base, they spread a thin layer of white cement before putting all the stones exactly as they were. They filled the gaps with white cement and debris, cleaned the five stones and scattered dust on them. They repeated this multiple times to make it look exactly as it was earlier. They removed their setup and left the temple around 2 a.m. without anyone noticing. In that small village, even dogs were sleeping carelessly.

They reached the bus stand. It was a small building with a few benches inside. Right beside the bus stand, there was a hotel. The hotel was closed, but they knocked at the door. A poor guy came rubbing his eyes, "E Sodarudu?" He understood their confusion and repeated in English, "What brother?"

They had gestured that they were hungry, and he had said, "Closed, closed," but upon seeing their desperation, he became considerate. That guy opened the hotel door and asked them to sit. He went to the kitchen, prepared food and came back with two plates. The food was delicious.

He sat there the whole time while they were eating like dogs. They offered him money, but he refused to take it and simply smiled back. Kshitip and Rudra left appreciating the gesture and the town's culture.

Since it was a small town, at 4 a.m., only one bus was available, which was going to Visakhapatnam. They could not spend any more time in that town as the temple would open soon. The bus had very few passengers, so they took the last seat, and Kshitip unfolded the paper:

krishna nirmita, vasuki pratiyudh chaturdasham uparishtat pradidhi sarvebhyo, chakshu sarosh

In Chaturdasham, the gap between the alphabets was abnormal and reading it that way was going to cost them a lot of time later.

Kshitip had translated the hint:

"Krishna constructed it, fought with Vasuki, the fourteenth,

He is watching everyone from above, with anger in his eyes."

"Are you aware of any temples built by Krishna?" Rudra had asked.

"I can't remember any temple built by the gods. Why would a god build a temple? Oh yes, there is the Rameswaram temple, but Ram built that."

"Hmm, I have also never heard about any temple built by Krishna."

"Does Dwarika qualify?" Kshitip had asked hesitantly.

"Dwarika was a city, not a temple. I don't know about any temples in the city of Dwarika. But if it's there, then the fight with Vasuki makes sense, since it was in water. But now that the city is submerged, somebody watching over everyone doesn't make sense."

"What about the Yamuna and Gokul itself, where he fought with Vasuki? He was in Mathura, where there are numerous temples. I am pretty sure one of them would be linked to Vasuki."

"Makes sense, but in Mathura, he was treated as a god because he had killed the tyrant king Kansa, so I doubt any temple was built by him there. I could be wrong; I am not a temple expert. There is another side to this, though, because Gokul was the place where he grew up like a normal kid. Keeping all the power aside, he might have built some temple, but all the big temples in Mathura are of Krishna only," Rudra had said.

"Could it be the Govardhan hill? I mean, that explains the 'He is watching everyone from above' point."

"Is there any temple on the Govardhan hill?"

"Yes, I have been to Mathura. There is a temple on the Govardhan hill called the Giriraj temple. I remember this hill is often considered a physical form of Shri Krishna."

They had contemplated in silence for some time, and then Rudra had reasoned, "To me, it seems like a diversion. Though it's very convincing, it doesn't seem right. The temple is of Krishna, so obviously it should have been built by someone else. Krishna being Govardhan is interesting, but what about the angry eyes part?"

"Has there been any other famous king named Krishna? Why should we consider Shri Krishna only?"

"The Kailash temple."

"What?"

"The Lepakshi temple has been built like a fort, and the Patalpuri temple is inside a fort, so the Giriraj temple doesn't fit. Both temples have some element of mystery, and the most mysterious temple in the whole world is the Kailash temple, built by Krishna of the Rashtrakuta dynasty. How can I miss this? I have watched so many documentaries on this temple," Rudra had spoken with confidence.

Rashtrakutas were ruling that part of the country before the tenth century. The two temples they had visited so far were built in the sixteenth century, and all this started after the Allahabad fort construction began in the 1570s or 1580s. So, Kshitip challenged how anything could be present in a temple so old, when the clue leading to it was carved almost 500 years later.

"We are an awesome team. You know about dynasties and medieval history. I am interested in mysteries and have a genius brain," Rudra had said, chuckling. "Now, the thing about the Kailash temple is that it was built over a long period of time. Allegedly, it was built in eighteen years, but that is humanly not possible. Some parts of it were constructed even after hundreds of years. There are proofs also in the varied construction styles of different sections."

"But that still doesn't explain anything. What about Vasuki and fourteenth?"

"The Kailash temple has numerous carvings of incidents from the Ramayana and the Mahabharata. I am 100 per cent sure we will find a carving of Vasuki's incident somewhere, and the fourteenth of something will be where the next piece is. Trust me on this," Rudra had said, folding the paper and putting it in his bag. He had leaned on the chair to sleep, but Kshitip was not convinced and had a bad feeling about it.

There were no direct buses or trains from Visakhapatnam to Aurangabad. They should not have travelled to Visakhapatnam in the first place, but they didn't think about getting off the bus as they badly wanted some sleep. They thought, as Visakhapatnam was a big city, they would get buses to Aurangabad from there.

After changing multiple buses, they reached Aurangabad in the early hours of 3 February. They slept on the bus stand until morning and then took another bus to Ellora. They arrived at Ellora and skipped all other caves to go directly to cave number sixteen.

"Sir, guide, sir? Only 1000 rupees for the whole day, sir. It is a man-made marvel, and there are amazing things to know, sir," an excited man had come rushing to them.

"I know everything about this place. We don't need a guide," Rudra had dismissed the guide, who left, cursing Rudra under his breath.

Rudra had always dreamt of coming to this place. The moment they entered the temple, their jaws dropped to the floor, witnessing the grandeur and magnificence of that amazing building. Just at the entrance, there was this intricately carved majestic pillar, at least 80-100 feet in height. The whole temple was black in colour. It was a basalt mountain, carved from the top down to create this architectural wonder. People believed that the entire temple was constructed within eighteen years.

"So, eighteen years is a long time?" Kshitip had made a mistake by questioning it.

"Yes, it is, but if you think logically, you will understand what it means. The amount of rock removed from this site for the temple's construction was close to 400,000 metric tons. If you consider that thousands of people worked here for straight twelve hours without any breaks for twelve months a year and for eighteen years, it's a lot. Assuming there were no holidays, rain, or natural obstructions, the rocks were excavated at a rate of five metric tons, or 5,000 kg per hour." Rudra had been throwing his arms in the air to explain its scale.

"So?"

Rudra had shot back sharply, "So, it is not even possible today. Even our advanced technology cannot remove that much basalt rock per hour. And this is considering no carvings on walls, pillars, such intricate designs like elephants, lions, and designs on the ceilings, paintings and idols. There are so many mysteries like this, but one of the biggest ones is, where did they dispose of the removed rock, that 400,000 metric tons of rock? The pile of that rock would have created a crag of its own. And, please don't think a king can put his entire kingdom to construct this temple. Also, consider the space available here. Anyway, look for anything related to Krishna's fight with Vasuki."

"How do you know about all this?" Kshitip had asked while searching for Vasuki's depiction in any possible form.

"I have always been interested in mysteries. I like reading about conspiracy theories, alternate theories, and realistic fictions. So, I came to know about this temple and ultimately ended up watching more than fifty hours' worth of documentaries. I realised that they all somehow indicate that it was built by a more advanced civilisation, not humans. At that time, the tools that humans had were chisels and hammers, and this could not be done with those," Rudra had clarified, still admiring the stupendous architecture.

Surrounding the temple, there were various caves. Man-made caves with paintings on the ceilings and huge idols of various gods. They almost forgot about their mission after witnessing that marvel. Several times, Kshitip tried to make Rudra search for the Vasuki carving, but he simply wanted to admire the temple. After a few attempts, Kshitip also joined Rudra in exploring the place, and before they could know, it was 2 p.m.

They had their lunch and realised that even in daytime, various paintings were not visible inside the caves and temples, so at night they won't be able to see anything at all, even with a torch.

They hurried their search for a snake in any of the paintings or carvings and found plenty of them, but none that they could say was of Vasuki. They were getting frustrated, and Kshitip saw the guide nearby, so he went and asked him about Vasuki.

"Go ask your friend, sir. He knows everything about this temple," the guide had scoffed and moved ahead with a group of tourists.

"You shouldn't go to people and ask about these clues. Anyway, the second line of it doesn't make sense," Rudra had said.

"That's why we are looking for Vasuki. It is a temple of Lord Shiva, who is always angry and has thousands of idols, carvings and paintings."

"Shiva is not always angry. His Taandav or Natraj form is the only angry form, or when his third eye is open."

"OK. I see a Natraj on that pillar, another on the one beside it, and there is also an idol of Natraj carved on the wall behind," Kshitip had replied, frustrated.

"I understand, Kshitip. We have to look for Natraj, who is looking at everyone. A carving on the temple walls cannot be considered 'watching everyone' because its face is in a certain direction. What was the second line exactly? 'He is watching everyone from above, with anger in his eyes.'"

They had entered the main hall of the temple while talking. Rudra pointed his finger towards the ceiling and lifted his head while repeating, "...from above, with anger in his eyes," and stopped there. Kshitip realised after a few seconds that Rudra had stopped. He looked back, and Rudra was standing in the middle of the hall, still staring at the ceiling with his index finger pointing up and trying to have a good look at something by tilting his head in all directions.

Kshitip looked up, too, and saw a huge Natraj carving on the ceiling of the temple. The natural light in the hall was poor. It was challenging to see the whole carving, and he knew that by tilting his head, Rudra was trying to see Natraj's eyes.

Then, Rudra scanned the hall with his eyes and walked briskly to the same guide. He almost snatched the torch from his hands. The guide shouted in Marathi, so Rudra apologised while walking back to Kshitip and focused the light on Natraj's face. His eyes were wide open, painted red.

Rudra took 500 rupees from Kshitip and gave the torch and the note to the guide.

He was surprised to earn 500 rupees in just a minute and looked at Rudra like he was a lunatic.

Rudra had exclaimed, "Uparishtat pradidhi sarvebhyo, chakshu sarosh," pointing his finger towards the ceiling.

"There is no depiction of Vasuki in this temple or even in the nearby caves," the guide had yelled and walked away.

"At least we have the answer to one of the questions."

"The important thing is, now we know we are at the right place," Kshitip had sighed.

"It was the right place from the beginning. Krishna built this, which was decoded yesterday itself."

"I still had doubts. Now I know we are at the right place. We need to strategise. There is no Vasuki here, so what should we look for? Let's have a cup of tea and think about it."

"Yes. Let's go."

"By the way, if you must give someone a tip next time, give 100 rupees, not 500. I don't have much cash left," Kshitip had taunted.

They sat at the tea shop and started thinking. Rudra was quiet for the first few minutes, and Kshitip was having tea.

Finally, Rudra had asked, "So, what are the important things about the story of Vasuki?"

"Water, river, the Yamuna..."

Rudra had questioned the shopkeeper before Kshitip could finish his sentence, "Bhaiya, is there any idol or carving of the Yamuna in the temple?"

"Yes, the two deities at the entrance are Ma Ganga and Ma Yamuna. The left one is Ma Yamuna," the shopkeeper had answered while cutting onions.

"Let's go." Kshitip had to leave his tea and follow Rudra.

They went to the entrance, where there were two statues greeting them. They focused on the left one, but at first glance, it was clear they would not find anything. It lacked that element of mystery. Yet, they spent close to half an hour examining the rock on which Ma Yamuna was carved. It was a small rock, nothing enigmatic, and after thirty minutes, Rudra also lost interest in it.

They again started roaming around the temple, searching for any hint. Time was running out, and finally, the temple closing announcements were made, and people began leaving. Knowing that they won't be able to find anything in such a short time, they also left.

"I am tired. Let's book a room at a nearby hotel," Rudra had suggested.

"But we cannot. We have already made the mistake of flying by air. We cannot disclose our identity."

"I know you have forged identity proofs, Kshitip, and many debit cards, which you destroy after every use. You can book a room on your forged ID card," Rudra had said, straight-faced. Kshitip was impressed, but the problem was that these days, hotels ask for the IDs of all the guests.

Rudra says, still sitting on that autorickshaw seat in the ruin, "You know, Kshitip, I have started recalling the name on your forged ID, too. I am recovering fast, and I am not feeling weak anymore."

"Do you know what is helping?"

"That injection," Rudra smiles.

"I thought you won't be able to decode that," Kshitip smiles back, but suddenly his expressions change.

Rudra tries to open his mouth, but Kshitip puts his finger on Rudra's mouth to direct him not to speak. Kshitip closes his eyes to focus on hearing something and almost jumps to his feet. "Stand up, we must leave now."

Rudra is startled and asks, "What happened?"

Kshitip packs everything in his bag as fast as humanly possible. "I think somebody is watching us. If you focus, you can hear a mechanical humming, like a drone. Let's leave! We don't have time."

Both of them come out of the room and move towards the main door, but between the door and them is a vast, open hall. They can't remain hidden anymore. They see some beams of light outside the exit door. Can *these be lights mounted on automatic guns?* Kshitip holds Rudra's hand and pulls him back. They run towards the backside of the building and hear a loud thud on the main door.

'They' have entered.

Kshitip takes Rudra to a huge staircase.

"Are you mad? They have drones, we won't be able to escape from the upper floors," screams Rudra.

"Stand still, don't move," instructs Kshitip, calmly, while touching the nearby wall at various places like he is pressing a keyboard. Suddenly, the floor slides open, and both fall into a tunnel. Then, the floor gets back to its original position. Kshitip opens his bag, takes out a torch, switches it on and moves slowly. He looks back and questions irately, "Where is the seat you were carrying?"

"When the floor opened, it fell off. I think it is in the mansion now," answers Rudra, and realises that by the location of that seat, the secret door can be found now.

"Then, run!" cries Kshitip and asks angrily, "Why the hell were you carrying the seat, by the way?"

"Master, we have located them. Twenty-seven is at the scene himself, and soon we will get the good news," an old man addresses an incredibly tall figure.

The voice of the old man is filled with pride and joy, but his head is bowed down. The figure, wearing a black gown, stands with his back towards the old man. They are in the centre of a grand hall, which is decorated with incredible artefacts.

He says, "Never underestimate them, Vahanus. Tell me when Twenty-seven confirms."

"They will not see tomorrow's sun, master," replies Vahanus in excitement.

"How many times do I need to tell you? They have to be alive, not dead," the figure turns towards Vahanus in anger. Even in that dimly lit room, the redness is visible on his forehead.

Vahanus falls to his knees. "I know, master, I know. I just said those words without any such intentions. Twenty-seven knows what he is doing."

"That's why Twenty-seven is there, not you. They are involuntarily working for us," the figure again turns his back towards Vahanus, indicating that the conversation is over.

Right next to the figure, on a huge wooden table, a massive bow is lying with its strings detached. Yes, strings; it doesn't have a single string like usual bows, but has thousands of delicate strings, glittering in that dim light.

"They don't even know what they are searching for," the figure mumbles.

20

The Power of Them

Rudra and Kshitip see the end of the tunnel after walking for half an hour, and they push it open like a door. They come out of the trunk of a tree and close the door behind them. Rudra stands there and puts his hand on his back, stretching to straighten up after walking hunched in the cramped tunnel.

Kshitip hisses in anger, "We can't take rest. After finding the seat at the bottom of the staircase, they may have understood."

"I don't understand your logic. That seat will get caught, but what about the auto you captured me in?" Rudra shot back.

"I disposed of that autorickshaw while you were unconscious. Even their forefathers won't be able to find it," Kshitip answers in annoyance. "Let's not waste our time, Rudra. Please move."

"But where are we going?"

"That, we need to figure out while walking," Kshitip replies, and they continue in the direction the tunnel leads them. That mansion is still visible in the moonlight at some distance, behind them.

"We didn't book any room, and like tonight, we were roaming around in the nearby jungle. We didn't go back to Aurangabad," Kshitip restarts the story. "Now that you remember everything, tell me what happened next, and I will correct you."

"No, no. Let it be the way it is. You are a good storyteller," Rudra says hesitantly.

"I have been narrating it to bring back your memory, not to entertain you. You start now," Kshitip says firmly.

Taking a few minutes to gather his thoughts, Rudra starts, "I don't remember how long we were in the jungle and how we came out, but soon we reached a local bazaar. There were many small shops and people were selling souvenirs, designed like the Kailash temple, Ellora caves and other carvings. We had our dinner in the same market, sitting on a bench, in the open. I hope I am correct till now?"

"Yes, yes. Everything is correct," assures Kshitip.

Rudra feels confident and resumes, "After having dinner, we started roaming around again. And, I think it was close to the bus stop, near a park. Right?"

Kshitip nods.

They had seen children playing with a toy in which a string attached four lions to a square-shaped box in the centre. All the lions were looking in four directions, opposite to the box. Whenever kids turned the key, the lions pulled the box in their direction and at the end, the box opened with a ball in the centre. It was a replica of the Kailash temple's top view.

They had observed the children for a moment, and then Kshitip had said, "No, it can't be." He had rushed to an old shopkeeper there and had asked, "What is that toy about? I mean, the ball coming out of that box, what is it?"

The shopkeeper had replied, "It is a folklore that the ball for which Lord Krishna fought with Vasuki is in that box. Just a story."

"What?" Rudra had queried.

Kshitip had explained hastily, "Lord Krishna fought with Vasuki for a ball, Rudra. And I think the last word of the first sentence is not 'chaturdasham' but 'chaturdisham'. It doesn't mean fourteenth of something but four directions."

"Oh my god. It was right in front of our eyes the whole time. Let's go back!"

"But how?" Kshitip ran here and there, like a maniac, looking for a ride.

"The way we came. Nobody should know that two people are going towards the temple at night, when it is closed. It will raise suspicion."

They had stridden towards the temple. Knowing that they won't get entry through the main gate at this time and that there would be tight security, they headed for the adjacent cliff on which the Kailash temple was built. Using Rudra's climbing kit, they landed in the temple. Both knew where those lions were, so they went directly to the location and tried to find a way to remove that ball. They failed to get any clues.

"Should we break it?"

"How can you even think about it? It's a national monument," Kshitip had said. They contemplated for a few more minutes, and then Rudra realised that Natraj, with an angry eye, was mentioned in the clue. He must be the key to get the ball. They went to the hall where Natraj was carved in the ceiling and decided that Kshitip would climb up to Natraj. Rudra would wait next to the lions.

They had arranged a setup for Kshitip to climb close to Natraj, and Rudra went to the lions. Kshitip put on his harnesses and climbed up. It was not a difficult ascent, but the difficult thing was not knowing what to do. Kshitip examined the carving meticulously. When he could not find anything out of place, he went back to Natraj's eyes and started examining them more closely.

Those eyes were painted red. He noticed some dust around the irises of both eyes. Kshitip pressed both irises, and to his surprise, it went deep into the ceiling. He could hear a loud thud on the ceiling that echoed outside. After a few seconds, when the noise stopped, he heard something breaking.

Rudra had screamed, "OH MY GOD."

At once, Kshitip pulled his fingers out, the irises regained their position, and he climbed down. He ran towards Rudra with the harnesses still on his body and saw him standing with the ball in his hand. The ball was glowing. Rudra was in a trance, spellbound by the series of events. Kshitip tapped him, and Rudra dropped the ball on the floor. It stopped glowing.

Kshitip had walked closer, and Rudra had warned, "Watch out. The teeth are on the ground." Kshitip noticed four stone teeth, one from each statue, lying on the floor. Rudra picked them up. They were heavy and had a weird kind of material in them, like metal.

Kshitip picked up the ball, but it didn't glow. "Did you press something on the ball? Why was it glowing in your hand?"

"The box cracked open, and when I picked it up, it started glowing. I didn't do anything."

Kshitip gave the ball back to Rudra, and it started glowing again. So, he guessed that maybe it glowed only in Rudra's hands since they first came in contact with it.

"You didn't theorise. You were so damn jealous," Rudra says sarcastically.

"Come on, grow up. We are not kids. I was not jealous because it was glowing in your hands," Kshitip refutes.

"Hahaha. You were, anyway. Maybe because I was worthy of holding that ball."

"Why do you think you are worthy? It was just because you were the first one to hold it," Kshitip says the same thing again, getting irritated. They continue walking while Rudra narrates their journey.

They had noticed something written on the ball:

> **satyawadi nripa tyaj kutumbam, garvit madhya taramati rohidas**
> **pancham stambha samaveshita, shakti sakshat**

They put those teeth in the bag, along with the ball and turned towards one of the lions. They were shocked to see his mouth had all its teeth intact, like nothing had happened. Rudra suggested that it was to ensure people didn't suspect any foul play. Then, they moved to the hall, removed the setup, and left for the cliff.

Kshitip reached the top when Rudra had not yet started climbing, still looking at the temple and admiring it. Rudra didn't want to leave that place. So, for the last time, he stood there, mesmerised by the art, architecture, vision of the artists, and scale of that brilliance. He wanted that perfect picture in his mind, etched for eternity.

"We will go again, my friend," says Kshitip, cheering him up.

"I don't know, I have a fear deep in my heart that our lives are not going to be the same after all this," Rudra says, avoiding Kshitip's eyes, to hide his tears.

After a few moments, Rudra says, "So, when we reached the top of the cliff, we decided to go to the bus stand, where we had seen that replica of the Kailash temple, to take a bus to our next destination."

While walking, they had started their discussion about the next stop. Kshitip's guess was Ayodhya.

"Shri Ramchandra is considered the best king, most just, and the saviour of his people, but when it comes to satyawadi, the first name that comes to my mind is King Harishchandra," Rudra had countered.

"Do you know which kingdom Harishchandra was king of?" Kshitip had asked, but Rudra was clueless, so Kshitip had continued, "Ayodhya. He was an ancestor of Shri Ramchandra. When I said Ayodhya, I also thought of Harishchandra, not Lord Ram. When it comes to mythology, I also have some knowledge."

They took a bus to Aurangabad. The distance between Aurangabad and Ayodhya was close to 1500 km, so rather than taking buses, they decided to hop into the general compartment of a train to save time. They got lucky as there was a special train from Aurangabad to Varanasi, which was on the platform ready for departure. They jumped into the train when it left the platform.

While on the train, they requested a ticket collector to assign them a berth in an air-conditioned compartment. After ensuring the benefit of both parties, they got adjacent berths, which were vacant. They had comfortable berths to sleep on and enough time to analyse the hint.

The next morning, when the train had reached Nagpur, Kshitip had asked, "Do you have any other suggestions about our destination?"

"Oh, so you also have doubts?"

"I could not stop thinking. Both times, I mean for the Lepakshi and Kailash temple, the first lines were about the location. Here, the first line talks about King Harishchandra leaving his family. He had abdicated the throne and left Ayodhya with his family. So, I think we are going to the wrong place."

"And, I think we are going to the right place. He sold off his wife and son in Varanasi," Rudra had opined.

Kshitip had been elated as he shared the same line of thought. "And the most important thing is, on the previous occasions, the temples have been of Lord Shiva. Varanasi is considered the city of Lord Shiva. There is an ancient temple too, the Kashi Vishwanath temple," Kshitip had concluded.

"Yes, there is also the Nageshwarnath temple in Ayodhya. It was built by Kush."

When Kush, son of Lord Ram, was young, he used to take a bath in the river Saryu. While swimming, he lost his arm's amulet. When he came out and realised that his amulet was gone, he was scared. He thought it was a bad omen, and he would be punished for that. He started searching, but he could not find it. After some time, a nagkanya came out of the river and gave him his amulet. She had taken it as a remembrance, as she had a huge crush on the prince. Kush could not do anything about her crush, but he built a temple of Lord Shiva in her memory at the same spot on the banks of the river Saryu.

"In ancient times, people used to build temples to commemorate love," Kshitip sighs.

"I know, it could only be a story, but just think about the person who created it. He has compared love with worship and the gods. Such stories build character and make people believe in true and eternal love," says Rudra, looking the other way.

"So, any progress with Roshani?" Kshitip asks, and Rudra stares at him in surprise. "After recalling this love story, I know you are thinking about her. Last time when we were running around, you shared a little about her."

"No, nothing special. It is the same as it was," says Rudra without any emotion in his voice, and again starts thinking about her.

21

Never Underestimate Them

It's 30 January. A deep blue Mercedes G-Class stops at the entrance of a huge villa. A tall and fit man, wearing an Armani suit, shades and expensive red shoes, comes out of the car. The guard opens the door and the man walks through the hall and enters a room. There are two people sitting inside already.

The man in the Armani suit asks, "No sign of them yet?"

"No, sir. They should have been here by now," answers one of the guys, shaking in fear.

"What have you people done till now?"

"Sir, we went to Kumbh and combed the whole area," the other man replies.

"It is impossible to comb an area like that. We had also disabled the CCTVs, so nothing could be obtained from that," he mumbles to himself.

"Sir, we checked the CCTVs of the Allahabad bus stand too, but we could not find anything."

"Nobody will go to the bus stand. There are bus stops near the Kumbh area, and anybody can board from there. I am sure you won't find any CCTVs in that place. Get the details of travellers going out of Allahabad, Lucknow and Varanasi airports. I want the list on my desk in an hour," he orders calmly, and the two guys leave the room immediately.

Within an hour, the list is on his table.

"So?" he asks.

"Rudra has travelled alone to Visakhapatnam from the Varanasi airport, sir, but no news of Thirty-six," one of them answers.

"Book tickets for Visakhapatnam on the next available flight. We are leaving."

The flight lands in Visakhapatnam in the early hours of 31 January. They search in the hotels, restaurants, and temples, but can't find anything. The entire day passes, looking for leads.

It has been three days since their arrival in Visakhapatnam, but they have not been able to find any clues.

On the night of 2 February, the gentleman sips tea in his hotel room and picks up a local newspaper. While glancing through the news stories, he finds an interesting headline: *The Gentleman Burglar*.

The news reads:

> An interesting crime happened in the temple town of Lepakshi. A gentleman thief broke into a stationery shop to steal some colours and left money with a note. The money was more than enough for the colours and the lock. The note read, "Sorry, had no other option."

The man picks up his phone and dials a number, "We are leaving for Lepakshi in two minutes. Get ready. Settle the bill."

They reach Lepakshi around noon. By then, the management committee of the temple has already received orders to close the temple for the general public and vacate it.

The expensive car stops at the gate of the temple. The doors open for the car to enter. The man and those two people go inside and start looking for anything suspicious. The hawk-like eyes of the man notice a faint blue patch on the floor near the hanging pillar within the first hour of inspection. He puts his fingers underneath the pillar and rubs off some colour. He gestures to one of the guys to remove the floor and asks the other to bring some colours and papers.

The next day, early morning, the car stands in the parking area of the Ellora caves.

"Any leads?"

A new guy, standing in front of that man, says, "Nothing is broken or stolen, but a local guide shared a weird story. Yesterday, some guy gave him 500 rupees for using his torch for a minute."

"Did you ask him where this happened?" the man asks.

"Yes, he was in the entrance hall, and he looked up at the ceiling," the new guy answers. "We checked the CCTVs of the temple and nearby railway stations, but we could not find anything."

"But there are CCTV cameras in the temple?" asks one of the guys with the gentleman. "That's surprising. I talked to the management here. They said that they were facing some technical issues yesterday. Particularly with cameras in the Kailash temple."

"Of course," mumbles the gentleman. "Circulate the picture of Rudra at bus and railway stations. Somebody must have seen him boarding a bus or train. Check the list of passengers of the nearest airports too, but I think he will avoid travelling by air. He must have realised his mistake by now."

He starts moving towards cave number sixteen, the Kailash temple.

Early morning of the 6th, one of the guys comes to his hotel room and says, "Sir, we were circulating his picture at the railway station and one of the ticket checkers started behaving suspiciously, so we…" The man glares at him, ordering with his eyes to cut it short. "They left for Varanasi. We checked; the train reached Varanasi just half an hour ago."

"They?"

"Yes, sir, there is somebody with him. The TT could not see the other guy as Rudra was dealing with him."

"Book flight tickets to Varanasi and make sure my car gets there by the time we reach," he orders while typing on his cell phone, and the guy leaves.

22

Back to Square One

Rudra and Kshitip had reached Varanasi on 6 February. It was dawn, but they directly went to the Kashi Vishwanath temple. To their surprise, the temple was open and aarti was in progress. They roamed around but could not find any idol of King Harishchandra, or even any mention of him there.

This temple was relatively new in comparison to the other ones they had visited in the last few days. So, they bought a booklet from a stall to learn about the temple's history.

They read that this temple was demolished and rebuilt several times in recent history. The original Vishwanath temple was destroyed by the army of Qutb-ud-Din Aibak when he defeated the king of that area. The temple was rebuilt by a Gujarati merchant afterwards, when Iltutmish was ruling the country, just twenty years after the demolition.

It was destroyed again during the fifteenth century. Raja Man Singh built the temple during the rule of Mughal emperor Akbar. Raja Todar Mal further rebuilt it with Akbar's funding at its original site in the sixteenth century. In the seventeenth century,

Aurangzeb tore it down and built the Gyanvapi Mosque in its place. The remains of the erstwhile temple could be seen in some parts of the mosque. So, to check the mosque, they visited that too. But again, there was nothing related to King Harishchandra anywhere.

While leaving the mosque, they saw a group of four or five people going towards the Kashi Vishwanath temple. From there onwards, the game of hide and seek started.

"I should not have screamed at that time. It was all my fault," says Rudra, recalling that incident. "But if you had given me a sign before grabbing my hand and pulling me back, I wouldn't have screamed."

They heard Rudra scream and turned. Though Kshitip had pulled him from the main street to a narrow lane, they spotted the duo before Rudra could be out of their sight, and started following them. The streets of Varanasi were a maze. Rudra and Kshitip kept changing the streets, running here and there, but could not escape them. Those people had scattered and were on 4-5 streets behind Rudra and Kshitip. Though none of them had seen their faces till that point, the sound of their boots was becoming louder and louder, and that's when the duo decided to separate.

While running, Rudra came out in the open, and there was a railway line around 30-40 metres from the end of the street. There was a train running on the tracks. He gathered all his strength and courage to sprint as fast as he could and managed to jump into the last compartment of the train, just before the bridge. The people standing at the door pulled him in. By the time he turned to see the group chasing him, they had given up. Rudra leapt out of the train at the next station, Vyaspur. It was a small station. But he had no idea where Kshitip went.

"I went to Delhi and from there, I took a train to my hometown," Kshitip recalls.

"You have a family?" Rudra asks, surprised. "You said you were raised in some secret place with other children."

"Like you, we all have a decoy family so that people do not suspect. How can I join a company if I don't have a family? Every company does a background check," Kshitip answers while walking briskly.

"My bad. This time, you seem like a completely different person, like a lone wolf," Rudra winks at Kshitip. "But didn't they suspect you when you returned to the factory? You were gone for those days, too."

"Before leaving Delhi, I had handed over my mobile phone to my so-called brother, from my fake family. He went back to our hometown and was roaming around with my mobile in his pocket. Before giving the phone, I had sent a message to my manager about my mother's health: 'My family admitted her to a hospital.' So, I was fully covered on that front. Most importantly, they had no solid information about the other guy with you. It was only that guide and TT, who didn't even see me. They were not credible sources for anyone," explains Kshitip. "But they were still keeping an eye on me, 24/7, when I returned to the factory."

"Why did you go back? I mean, you could have disappeared," Rudra thinks out loud.

"You asked me this question earlier in the evening. Had I disappeared, they would have known that your cover was compromised. And since nobody had seen me, all I had to do was behave normally for a few days to avoid suspicion, which is what I did," Kshitip clarifies. "Now, the important question. Where is the bag? Where did you hide it?"

"When I left that train at Vyaspur, I don't know why, the only place I could think of going to was a small town in Ballia. Ballia is the easternmost district of Uttar Pradesh, about 120 km from Varanasi, after which Bihar starts."

"You might have read the name somewhere on any banner or millstone."

"It was something like a memory. Like I had been there, in my childhood. I don't know what triggered me, but in that moment of fleeing from those people, that's the first place that came to my mind. After switching multiple means of transport, I finally reached Maniyar, a small town in Ballia. I was very paranoid. Every person looked like a mercenary, and somehow, I could feel that the gap was closing, and I could be caught any minute. So, I hid the bag in a temple and hours after that, I was caught," says Rudra. He abruptly stops walking and falls on the ground, shivering.

Kshitip drops his bag and immediately bends down to hold Rudra's head with both hands, trying to calm him down. "Rudra, Rudra. Everything is okay. Everything is okay. We have come very far from those people; nobody is following us. Shhh, shhh." Rudra keeps trembling. It gradually stops, and he sits still on the ground.

"What was that, Rudra?" Kshitip asks firmly.

"Please don't talk about it, Kshitip. I get panic attacks."

"No, Rudra, we need to talk about this. This must not repeat. What if it happens when we are being chased?"

"It's not that simple, Kshitip. I faced a near-death experience. I thought those dogs would kill me," says Rudra and again panics.

Kshitip holds Rudra's head and shouts, "So what?"

"Those were huge dogs, and they were barking like, like, like…" Rudra stutters and puts his palms on his ears.

Kshitip forcefully removes Rudra's hands, yelling, "Like?"

"Kshitip, stop, don't do this," Rudra begs.

Kshitip continues, "Like?"

"Their…their…growling sound…ah…was so loud, like, like, like a lightning. Fo-fo-four people were holding the leash of those do-do-dogs and were chasing me. After a point, they unleashed those dogs. In fear, I stepped into a mu-mu-muddy field. I could not see the mud because of the tall grasses. I could not run, and one of the dogs attacked me from behind, and I fell on my face. After that, I woke up in the hospital in Allahabad." Rudra stops shaking by the time he shares the entire episode.

"Those were just dogs. You cannot keep fearing dogs for your whole life. Stand up and start walking. We lost our precious time because of your drama," Kshitip says bluntly, picking up his bag and moving. Rudra stands up and follows him.

After a while, Rudra says, "So, I was found in that field in Ballia, not Allahabad. Now we know where to go. But why aren't there any vehicles on the road?"

The old man opens the door of his master's dimly lit room. Before he can say anything, his master says, "They ran away?"

"Yes, master. They used a tunnel," replies the old man, trembling in fear.

"Hmm. Aren't our people already aware of the tunnel in that mansion?"

"There are more than one, master," the old man pleads. "We need to do something, master. How will we catch them?"

The master waves his hand, and the old man immediately leaves the room.

Rudra and Kshitip have been walking for quite some time along the road, and finally, they see a small shop. They are hungry, so they go to buy something to eat when they hear news on the radio:

"Janta Curfew has been imposed in the country. On 22 March from 7 a.m. to 9 p.m., you are advised to stay inside your home. Kindly do not panic; there is no need to stock anything. All transport services will be suspended. Essential services will operate without any disruption. Tough times are ahead; this is to prepare the people of India for the upcoming difficult days."

Rudra and Kshitip look at each other.

Rudra says, "How are we going to travel? How powerful are they? Who are we fighting against? It is all over."

"It is not over. It is a new challenge. They will do everything in their capacity to slow us down, to stop us, but we must not. We must finish what we started. We cannot let them win. Let's buy whatever we can. We still have one day before the curfew starts. Let's not waste even a single minute," prompts Kshitip. He buys biscuits, chips, water bottles, whatever the shop has, and soon they hit the road to finish what they have started.

23

Let the Game Begin

It is about midnight; everyone is inside their homes. A milk tanker runs on the deserted roads in the city of Ballia. Usually, they move at a slower speed, but as the roads are completely empty, even the milk tanker is running at 100 kmph.

"Stop, stop, stop. There is a police barricade ahead," warns the co-driver.

"They are everywhere these days. Rather than stopping, it will be better to take a turn. Otherwise, they will become suspicious," answers the driver without flinching. He takes the left. "We are in Ballia now. Our agreement is up to here. Let's find a quiet road and unload."

The co-driver locates a dark and secluded spot and signals the driver to stop. The driver parks the tanker, and the co-driver climbs onto the top to open the lid. Before opening, he taps three times near the lid in a rhythm and then climbs down. After a while, a head pops out, then hands, torso and finally a man's entire body. He looks to his left and right before getting off. One more man comes out, followed by another, followed by another and ultimately forty people emerge from that opening. Two of them look familiar and disappear into the dark after coming out of the tanker.

"My head is still spinning. Walk away from me, I may vomit anytime," says Rudra, unable to walk in a straight line.

"My condition is no better than yours. Man, we should have booked the whole tanker. It was horrible that everyone was rolling on each other," whines Kshitip, twitching his lips.

"At least there were people in this case to prevent banging our heads on the ends; had there been no people, we wouldn't have survived this torture," replies Rudra. "It took us two days to travel 250 km. How will we find the rest of the pieces?"

"The way we found a way here, we will find everywhere. I need water. I am very thirsty," says Kshitip, walking briskly. Rudra controls his shaking legs and tries catching up.

After walking about 500 metres, Rudra hears the sound of water. "Somebody left a tap open, it seems," he says and turns to his right, in the dark. They spot a sweet shop with a faulty tap. Rudra walks towards the tap and drinks water.

Kshitip stands behind him in the dark and suddenly exclaims, "Wow, I didn't expect to see such an expensive car here." He is spellbound by a Mercedes SUV running in the same direction as theirs.

Rudra immediately stands up and looks at the car, "I think I have seen the same car in Goa."

Kshitip looks at him, surprised, and says, "So, they know that we are here?"

"It is not that difficult to guess. I am again on the run. They know I was in Ballia last time before they caught me. I was expecting them here, anyway," Rudra replies, looking in the same direction.

"I was also expecting this. But they don't know the bag's location, so they can't guess where we will be. Let's walk away from the road, keeping an eye on the car," suggests Kshitip and Rudra nods.

Rudra and Kshitip walk for approximately three to four hours to reach the Maniar bus stop. They are extremely exhausted and sleep deprived, but cautious too. The temple of Navka Baba is visible from the bus stand. They enter the wheat fields, hiding from any possible threat.

"You know, every year during Navaratri, a festival of ghosts is organised here. People from all over the country visit this place. Lots of incomprehensible things take place here, like people talking in the voice of some dead relative, show of baffling strength, even levitation," says Rudra while approaching the main structure of the temple.

"It's 3 a.m., Rudra. Don't you think it's not the right time to mention all this?"

They arrive in front of the main temple. There are lots of carved stones scattered everywhere, some in the shape of Shiva linga, others look like small temples. Some have been kept with the support of a tree, and some are lying on the ground.

"I think we are alone. I will go inside and retrieve that bag; you stay back to guard. I still don't remember where exactly I kept that bag, so it will take time. If I don't return in thirty minutes, come and check carefully," instructs Rudra, walking towards the temple.

Kshitip hides behind a tree and keeps an eye on the temple entrance as well as one of the roads. There are four roads from different directions with structures on all sides, so it is not possible to find a place to watch over the entire area.

The main temple is comparatively smaller, but the various structures scattered across the vast field make it look like a graveyard. It has dormitories, shops and smaller temples in the same complex. Rudra crosses the dormitory complex to reach the main temple with a huge black linga. It is not a usual Shiva linga; it's in the shape of the English letter C. He looks around, but there is nothing else. Rudra gets confused about what to do now. He comes out of that temple and goes into the adjacent one. Rudra finds that the second temple also has a Shiva linga and some other small idols.

Where did I hide it? Rudra ponders and stands there, puzzled. Kshitip observes Rudra from a distance, but doesn't understand what he is doing. Suddenly, Rudra moves to his right, and Kshitip stands to follow him. At the same time, he hears some sound coming from the pond behind him. He stops and contemplates for a moment, and decides to follow the noise.

Rudra sees a tiny temple on the base of a huge tree and has a flashback of hiding the bag on its roof. He remembers the name "Aughad Baba temple" written on it.

He climbs up on the foundation and opens the door. The temple is so small that he puts his hand inside to inspect the ceiling. There he finds his bag, firmly attached to the ceiling with heavy-duty tapes. He cuts the tape with the help of some miniature utensils kept in the temple and finally takes out his bag, checks it, closes the gate and turns around to get off the foundation.

As soon as he turns, he finds a man in a white angavastram standing behind him.

"Everything is in place?" he asks, calmly. Rudra shudders in fear, unable to see the man's face in the dark, but he seems old, of average height, bald, with a round stomach. "Is everything in place, Rudra?"

"How do you know my name?" Rudra retorts, hiding his fear.

"I know everything about you. It was I who had suggested to name you Rudra," he answers with infectious calmness.

"What is your name?"

"Vishnugupta," he replies. Rudra stands there, confused. He expects a confrontation any moment, but it progresses as a quiet and normal conversation.

Vishnugupta repeats, "Is everything in place?"

Rudra answers, "Yes," surprised. *Why did I answer?*

"You replied because you recognised my voice and you know who I am."

"How did you know what I was thinking?"

"We don't have much time here, ask the right questions," the man says firmly.

"Who are you?" asks Rudra, but the man doesn't speak and keeps staring. Rudra thinks for a while and questions again, "What are we searching? Who are the people who are following us? What did Amatya Baahudhwaj mean when he said that the fate of the world is in my hands? Who am I, and what the hell is going on?" With every question, his pitch increases due to frustration, and he almost ends up screaming the last part.

"The answer to who you are is something that you will get at the right time. The only thing I can say is that you are special. You are born to do some exceptional things," he sighs. "I know you don't believe in mythology, so it is tough to explain what is happening. Just assume the Mahabharata was real. Would you?"

"Umm, OK."

"The Mahabharata was the greatest war that mankind has ever witnessed. All kinds of weapons were used. The weapons could do anything, from crippling a person to killing 10,000 people, in different ways. By the time the war ended, there was not even a single family without a martyr. There were so many disgruntled hearts at the end; people who wanted revenge. The fire in most of the hearts died down eventually. But a group of people has not forgotten yet and has been looking for the right opportunity to strike. Their fight is not between families; it's against humanity. They want to kill every living soul. They have been planning such catastrophes for centuries. Catastrophes like World War I and World War II are their plots to end the world. Spanish flu, the black plague of Europe, various rebellions in different countries, invasions, famines, and the invention of religion are all planned by them. The highest donor of the Large Hadron Collider is still unknown. But..."

"The LHC is a science project, not some kind of mass destruction weapon," Rudra interrupts him, trying to see his face in the dark.

"Yes, it is, for people like you. When that project started, many people had different agendas. There are some reasons why it is not functioning now. Anyway, these people tried many times and succeeded in starting these catastrophes. Still, they could never achieve their goal because people like us work tirelessly to prevent such things from happening. Those people have seen the weapons which were used in ancient times. They know that if they get hold of those weapons, nobody in this world can stop the destruction of humanity.

"But the problem for them is that the location of these weapons has always been a mystery. When the war ended, these weapons were hidden in locations that only a handful of people knew. But everything changed about two years back when Gandeev was unearthed and taken by them, the Guruputras, in Sinauli. And, when you find one link of a chain, sooner or later, you start finding the adjacent links. That is what happened, which we didn't notice."

"They are the Guruputras. Who are you people?" Rudra asks.

"You can call us 'the Protectors,' protectors of those weapons. So, the pieces of these weapons, after being dismantled, were given to different people. These were influential and powerful people, even famous kings, who took an oath to keep the pieces safe, even at the expense of their lives. These were passed on from one generation to the next. After the father, the first kin became its protector. But with time, the kingdoms started shrinking, foreign attacks became frequent, and these protectors got weaker. During all this time, the Guruputras were looking for these weapons.

"When the protectors became vulnerable, the Guruputras intensified their search, but even at that boisterous time, we managed to remain hidden and keep our weapons safe despite many protectors losing their lives," Vishnugupta sighs sadly. "The weapon in question here is the most calamitous of all. It remained unused during the war, and afterwards it was possessed by certain people before it subsequently came to King Harshvardhan. King Harshvardhan was a noble and just king who respected history. He was known for being a Shaivite. By his time, attacks by foreign invaders had increased, and he himself fought the Huns of central Asia. He knew that one day his dynasty would not be able to protect the weapon any longer, so he made it a part of religion.

"He was known for organising a ceremony in Prayag called 'Daana,' in which he gave away all his wealth to the poor. At the same time, Prayag was considered a holy place by devout Hindus because they believed that drops of Amrit fell there when asuras and devas were fighting for the pitcher during Samudra Manthan. Harshvardhan mingled both. The weapon is of Shakti origin. Out of all the forms of Shakti, Saraswati is known as the most peaceful form, so he kept the weapon in that well near the Ganga and called it Saraswati Koop. From there, the concept of Sangam and Kumbh Mela started.

"People started worshipping that well. Harshvardhan shared this secret with only one person, the next protector. The weapon remained there for hundreds of years until the sixteenth century, when Akbar started constructing a fort around that well. The then-protector of this weapon removed it from there, dismantled it, hid the pieces in different locations and left the clue to the first piece there."

Rudra interrupts again, "What is the point of leaving a clue?"

Vishnugupta answers, "It is difficult to understand a human mind. Even we were not aware of this. Maybe he left that clue as a symbolic presence of the weapon. By the time we came to know about it, Gandeev had already been taken from the Sinauli site, and they knew about the Sangam. We sent Baahudhwaj to retrieve the clue, but it was too late."

"OK. You answered my question. But why? I mean, why are you explaining all this to me?"

"So that you know, what your success or failure can lead to. The stakes are too high to be complacent. All this is much bigger than you. People have been protecting it for thousands of years, and many have sacrificed their lives, but you are meant to complete the task. From now on, be more vigilant. Until now, I have been making sure that you don't get captured on any CCTVs and that you travel carefully. The pieces cannot be destroyed in isolation; the weapon needs to be assembled before that. Only a worthy person can wield this weapon. And there is only one such man in this world, today," he stops for a few seconds and extends his hand towards Rudra to give something.

Rudra hesitates at first and then stretches his hand to take whatever Vishnugupta is giving. Rudra notices the skin of his hand is pale yellow.

Vishnugupta instructs, "Go to the other side of the pond, you will find Kshitip there. Use this to go to the places where you need to, and when everything is over, go to…" Rudra cannot hear the name of the place as a mild thud sound disrupts them. Before he can understand, the man who calls himself Vishnugupta falls on his knees. He says calmly, even when he is hit by a bullet and dying, "Run! Don't worry, they will not be able to catch me." Then Rudra hears the approaching boots.

Rudra looks at the man for the last time. Vishnugupta is in light now, all of a sudden, his pale-yellow skin starts glowing and smoke comes out of his skin. Before Rudra can see further, a bullet passes close to his ear, and he runs for his life. He reaches the other side of the pond, and behind a mound, he finds a black metallic structure which resembles a ball. One of its sides opens like a door, and Kshitip pulls him in, closing the door and pressing some buttons on the panel. With a whirring sound, Rudra feels like his weight has increased. He turns his head to see Kshitip sitting in the opposite direction. There is a small window in front of him. He peeks out; they are not on the ground anymore. The ball's flying, soon the speed increases, and Rudra falls asleep.

24

Harishchandra

Rudra opens his eyes and finds that he is still inside that flying ball. He turns back to find Kshitip sleeping and shouts in panic, "Wake up, Kshitip. How can you sleep while flying a... whatever it is?"

Kshitip gets up, startled and yells, "It is on autopilot, Rudra. It doesn't need somebody to operate all the time."

"But autopilot doesn't mean the human pilot can fall asleep," Rudra retorts.

"This technology is much advanced than ours. You only need to put the destination, height and speed at which you want it to fly, and some effort during landing. That's it," says Kshitip, admiring the craft.

"How do you know about landing?" Rudra gets suspicious.

"When we reach the age of sixteen, we are trained to operate this, Rudra," replies Kshitip, emphasising the word 'trained'. Kshitip reads Rudra's uninterest on his face, so he instead asks, "What happened there, Rudra?"

"I don't know. I am still trying to understand. A priest-like guy appeared from nowhere who knew everything about me and told me what we were doing and the history behind it. Then some people came and killed him. While dying, his body was glowing, not like a bulb, but that shimmering glow, you know. Whether it was my tired mind's illusion or reality, I don't know," says Rudra in bewilderment and with the same expression, Kshitip hears every single word.

"They killed him in front of you?" Kshitip asks.

Rudra nods and says, "For the first time I have seen somebody dying that way. That moment is etched in my memory. His face, his expression while dying, his open mouth, the way he fell have been imprinted in my memory."

Kshitip rubs Rudra's shoulder. "I can understand. What did he tell you about the history anyway?"

"That the Mahabharata was real…"

"Didn't I tell you that?" Kshitip interrupts.

"But the way, when he shared all this, it seemed real. My mind didn't question anything, I felt he had seen those things himself," recollects Rudra, awestruck. Kshitip shakes his head in affirmation. Rudra continues, "He said the same things you told me last time about both societies and…" Rudra stops putting his hand in his pocket. He is about to show Kshitip both things that man has given him, but diverts the conversation, "Where are we going?"

Kshitip notices his behaviour but doesn't stress on it. "You forgot Harishchandra?"

"Oh, right. Harishchandra. I know where to go now," says Rudra with determination.

"We knew last time, too," Kshitip comments sarcastically.

"There is a difference between last time and this time. Now we know what we are doing and why. We know that some person has hidden it to protect it, so we have to think like him." Rudra clarifies.

"And you thought like him in a fraction of a second and figured out the place?" Kshitip taunts.

"No, I watched on TV," Rudra says, looking away from Kshitip.

"What?"

"Now I realised why I have been thinking about Harishchandra. During all those days in Goa, Harishchandra was in my head after the incident, so I watched some documentaries and came across an intriguing place in Maharashtra. What was the clue?"

"Satyawadi nripa tyaj kutumbam, garvit madhya taramati rohidas

pancham stambha samaveshita, shakti sakshat"

"In the Ahmednagar district of Maharashtra, there is an ancient fort, Harishchandragad. It is situated between two cliffs, and what are their names?" Rudra asks Kshitip how singers point their microphones at the audience during live concerts.

"Taramati and Rohidas?" Kshitip guesses.

"Ta-da!" Rudra throws his hands in the air in excitement. "So, you know the destination now. Key it in and let's sleep for some time."

"Sleep? Fifteen minutes back, you were scared to death of this idea."

"Now I trust," he murmurs with a smile on his face, but sadness soon replaces it. Kshitip looks outside, and a deadly silence covers the cabin.

25

Journey Continues

It is about 09:30 a.m. Kshitip lands the flying ball about two kilometres from the temple in a jungle, and they cover it with tree branches. They walk towards the temple. It's a stiff climb, and the wind howls like a dragon. The roar of the wind and its speed are so fast that they struggle to keep moving in a straight line. For the first 500 metres, they plod slowly, but eventually the roaring wind calms its pace.

They reach the cliff, and Rudra turns to realise that Kshitip is not walking beside him. Kshitip is standing at the edge, looking towards the other cliff. Rudra panics and runs to him.

"Kshitip, what are you doing?" shouts Rudra, stretching his right arm towards Kshitip.

"Don't be dramatic, Rudra. I am not doing anything. Just see how beautiful this place is. The air, the weather, and the view are so pure. Isn't it amazing? A great place to spend a life like ours. Useless lives, no family, no friends, no home," Kshitip replies dryly, still looking towards the horizon.

Rudra walks a few steps towards Kshitip to see his face and notices teardrops on his cheeks. Kshitip wipes his face hastily. Rudra puts his arms around Kshitip's shoulders and says, "I will marry Roshani after all this. She has a beautiful friend, and I will ask Roshani to introduce her to you. After all this is over, you will have a life, a family, a home, and everything else. Don't worry."

"Hahaha, if you are joking, you are a very strong man. But if you are serious and really think that you are going to have a normal life when all this is over," Kshitip says, making imaginary inverted commas with his fingers on 'when all this is over.' "Then you are very naive. Just a few days back, you were picturing the Kailash temple in your head for the last time. You don't even have the slightest idea what is going on and what your life will be like. Chances of survival of both of us or even one of us are extremely low, and you are thinking about having a double date together," Kshitip laughs sarcastically and sits down.

Rudra also sits down with a storm of emotions bubbling in his heart. They both sit there without any dialogue for some time. Kshitip stares blankly into oblivion, free of thoughts. But expressions on Rudra's face can tear away any heart. After a long gap, Kshitip says, "So, is she gorgeous?"

Rudra remains silent, stands up and starts walking towards the temple. "Let's go."

Kshitip follows Rudra's lead, rubs off the dirt from his clothes and starts walking. They walk for quite some time without speaking a single word. Once they climb the last peak, they get the first glimpse of the back side of the Harishchandreshwar temple. They climb down the cliff and walk towards the temple's main entrance.

It is an ancient temple constructed of black stone. Its entrance, stairs, walls, doors, idols—everything is so antique and stunning that you forget everything and immerse yourself in its grandeur. But the duo doesn't. They come out of the temple, and Kshitip turns to his left, but Rudra grabs his hand and signals to follow him.

Finally, Rudra says, "Do you know anything about this temple?"

"No."

"On the left side of the temple where you were going, there is a pond, named Saptatirtha Pushkarni, which used to have idols of Vishnu on its bank. Those have been shifted to the Kedareshwar cave, where we are headed."

After walking for a few minutes on the rough pathway, they reach the Kedareshwar cave. There are trees, and behind them is a dark cave. It's a natural cave like a huge hall, filled with water, approximately 3-4 feet deep. There is a Shiva linga in the middle of the water, covered with a structure with four pillars on the sides, but three of these four pillars are either completely collapsed or severely damaged. Surprisingly, the ceiling of this structure is still in place, and it is attached to the roof of the cave. Kshitip gapes in disbelief.

"The four pillars represent four yugas—Satya yuga, Treta yuga, Dwapara yuga and Kali yuga. As we know, we are currently living in the fourth and last yuga; the pillars representing the other three yugas have collapsed. It is said that the rear right-side pillar represents Satya yuga; that's why it's completely destroyed. Similarly, the one on the front right represents Treta yuga and is more than half destroyed. The third one on the rear left side represents Dwapara yuga, which is nearly 50 per cent damaged. The final one on the front left side is Kali yuga pillar, which is undamaged. The belief is that whenever this pillar collapses, the world will end," elaborates Rudra.

"Amazing. The people who made this were geniuses," Kshitip says, admiring the masterpiece in front of his eyes.

"The cave is natural, but if you look closely, the walls have been chiselled to make it a proper room. There are designs on the wall," Rudra says, inspecting the cave.

"But why the Harishchandreshwar fort? How is it linked to King Harishchandra?"

"It is said that the merchant who bought the wife and son of King Harishchandra was from this area, and Harishchandra worshipped this Shiva linga for years," says Rudra and turns back abruptly. "Breakfast?"

"Breakfast? We didn't come here for food, Rudra. We need to find the piece and the next clue," Kshitip gets irritated.

"Despite the lockdown, there are so many people around. It's daytime and the number of people is increasing. So, let's eat, take proper rest and strategise. We are going to have a pretty long night again," Rudra answers while already walking towards the main fort, where he has seen some food stalls and camping sites.

They reach the area and enter a small hut where an old lady is serving some local cuisine with tea. They order two plates, and it's so delicious that they order two more. They book a tent for sleeping. Finally, after the ordeal of three nights, they lie down on a proper mattress and fall asleep immediately.

26

One More Busy Night

Kshitip wakes up and finds that Rudra is not on his bed. He jumps off his bed and comes out of the tent without forgetting the bag. He is searching for Rudra when somebody puts a hand on his shoulders. Kshitip turns; it's the attendant of the camping site.

"Sir, are you leaving? You have not paid yet," says the attendant, looking at the bag on Kshitip's back.

"No, no, I am looking for my partner," Kshitip replies, still scanning the area with his eyes.

"I saw him going inside Amma's hut. I think he likes her tea." He points at the same hut where they have eaten their breakfast. "Sir, I am not saying you are that kind of person, but since you people are carrying only one bag, which is already on your back, please don't run away without paying us. It's not a hotel; we don't earn much."

"No, no. How much do I need to pay you?" asks Kshitip, putting his hand in his trousers' back pocket. He takes out a 2000-rupee note and puts it in the attendant's palm.

"It would not be more than 500 rupees, sir, but I will check with Saheb."

The sun is setting. Kshitip glances at his wristwatch; it is 6:30 p.m. He goes to that hut and finds Rudra sipping tea with fritters.

"Oh. I woke up, so I thought of having a good cup of tea. Sit, have some."

Kshitip sits and gestures towards the old lady for another cup of tea and fritters. He starts eating from Rudra's plate and asks, "So, what is the plan?"

"Let's finish tea first. We will discuss outside."

After a while, they both come out of the hut, and Rudra stares at the sky where the clouds are still orange after the sunset. Kshitip looks at Rudra and thinks of finally consoling him, because since morning, Rudra has not talked much.

Kshitip stands beside Rudra and says, "Rudra, sometimes life takes strange turns. Few things are not in our hands. And who knows, we will get to spend a normal life after all this is over. I can understand that all your plans have shattered. But not everybody gets to do such things." A surprised Rudra looks at Kshitip with an expression that is part smile, part 'oh what a good man… but such an idiot too'.

"Do you remember the two lines, Kshitip?" Rudra asks. "Clue about this place?"

"Oh, yes, yes."

"What do you think it is about?"

"I have been wondering about the same, and now I understand why you are not speaking. Is it possible that it is not the right temple, or the riddle is talking about some other structure here in the same complex?"

"I have been awake for a couple of hours. I explored the whole complex. There is nothing like this, and it is quite clear that it is the only structure," says Rudra with unease in his voice.

"Satyawadi nripa tyaj kutumbam, garvit madhya taramati rohidas

pancham stambha samaveshita, shakti sakshat

But which one is the fifth pillar? There are only four pillars in the temple, and out of those four, three are already damaged."

"I have been thinking about this. I think it's safe to go to the cave now that people have left. Let's go."

They both move towards the Kedareshwar cave. After crossing the fort and rough terrain, they reach the cave, which is completely dark now. Kshitip's explorer's hat is going to come in handy again. Rudra wears the hat, takes off his trousers and steps into the water; Kshitip follows. He switches on the light and says, "There are only four pillars, as you can see. I am scared of my own theory, but have been wondering about the fifth pillar. Is it?"

"The Shiva linga?" says Kshitip, and Rudra turns to him immediately. Kshitip's face is white.

"Yes. But why are you so scared?"

"The riddle says that the piece is inside the fifth pillar. Whichever of these two is the fifth pillar needs to be broken to get the piece. If the Kali yuga pillar is the fifth pillar, as per the folklore, Earth will be destroyed if this pillar is damaged. And, if the Shiva linga is the fifth pillar, I can't even dare to think about damaging a Shiva linga," explains Kshitip, folding his hands.

"I know and I understand your point. Though I don't believe in gods the way you do, even the thought of breaking the Shiva linga is scary."

They both spend some time standing in that chilled water without talking to each other. Though they are in waist-deep cold water, they are perspiring, especially Kshitip.

"Let's sit outside and think it through," says Kshitip. He steps out of the cave, puts on his trousers and sits on a rock below a tree, with his back towards the cave, and his right foot shaking, completely out of control. Rudra also walks out and notices Kshitip's panic. He puts his hand on Kshitip's foot, but it keeps trembling. Kshitip stands up and says, "It is not the right location, Rudra. I mean the location is right, but it's not the right temple. It must be that pond or the main temple, let's go there and explore. Nobody in our society will ever think of hinting at demolishing a Shiva linga. The story associated with the Kali yuga pillar is itself scary enough."

"I have already explored the whole complex, Kshitip," Rudra assures softly.

"Please let's explore again. You might have missed something. Isn't it possible? Tell me," Kshitip talks like a madman. Rudra agrees, and they walk towards the main temple, which doesn't have pillars at all; it has walls.

They go to the Saptatirtha Pushkarni pond. Kshitip exclaims, "Didn't I tell you that you were wrong?"

"What happened?"

Kshitip replies victoriously, "Look, there are pillars on one side of the pond. The pillars in the cave are not the only pillars in here. Oh my god!" Kshitip's mouth opens in disbelief.

"What happened now?"

"Do you see that structure in the background?" Kshitip points at a hut-like structure. Their backs face the temple. The side of the pond just next to them has all the pillars. Kshitip points to the terrain behind the side with pillars. As the area surrounding the pond is elevated, it seems that the hut is above the pond. Kshitip completes his sentence, "Isn't that hut constructed just above the fifth pillar from the right?"

Rudra focuses on this observation. He has switched off the torch on the hat to avoid anyone's attention, so he tries to focus with almost zero natural light. "It looks like that, but don't you think, with the change in our point of observation, that will also change?"

"I understand your point, but let's draw a line, extending the line of this wall," Kshitip says, pointing towards the wall on the right, "And then a parallel line from Pillar-5. If the line from Pillar-5 meets the structure on top, it will indicate that it is the pillar that we are looking for."

Rudra hesitantly agrees to Kshitip's proposal, just to calm him down. Deep down, he knows that the fifth pillar is in the cave, not here. Now, they must find something to start drawing parallel lines.

"Let's find a long rope and, if possible, a measuring tape," instructs Kshitip.

"Where can we find a rope and measuring tape? Also, this cannot be done in the dark; we will have to use light. Won't people get suspicious?"

"It's a trekking destination, ropes and measuring tapes will be easily available. Enthusiasts do all kinds of stuff here. I don't think measuring something will catch anyone's attention. And I know who can help us with all this," says Kshitip, and walks towards the main complex.

As they approach the centre of the complex, all of a sudden, a fire erupts, illuminating the place, and people start screaming.

"I told you not to put petrol. Why don't you people listen to me?" a guy shouts, and then somebody switches on a battery-powered music system and all of them start singing in unison. It is a group of young college students who have just arrived and started a bonfire. Being a site for adventure enthusiasts is of great help, sometimes. They are dancing, shouting, singing, and exploring. Kshitip finally finds the attendant of the camping service, to whom he had given 2000 rupees earlier, and asks for a rope and measuring tape. He gives him the best possible ropes and a ten-metre-long measuring tape, maybe thinking that Kshitip will not take the rest of the money.

They both go back to the pond and realise that the area has enough light due to the bonfire. They start their work, extending the line of the wall. They measure the distance between the wall and the fifth pillar and draw a parallel rope keeping the same gap between the lines as the fifth pillar and the wall. Metres before that structure, they both realise that this rope is nowhere near it, and they stop extending the rope any further.

They both sit silently. Then, Rudra says, "Let's go."

Kshitip stands up reluctantly with slumped shoulders, desolate and beaten. He doesn't even want to go to the cave, but his body starts moving in that direction.

"Oh, Lord Shiva, forgive me for the sin I am going to commit. This is the only way to save this world from this catastrophe. My belief should not come in the way of saving the whole mankind," prays Rudra with folded hands and enters the cave.

They both stand looking directly at the Shiva linga. Kshitip asks, "Where should we begin?"

"Let's start with the Shiva linga."

Kshitip closes his eyes in grief. "Do we really need to break it?"

"Let's push it first, breaking it is the last option."

Kshitip replies quietly, "This Shiva linga is approximately five feet high, made of stone and has a base. I don't think it will move by the force of only two people."

"Do you want to break it then?" Rudra replies in frustration.

"You are right. Let's get in," says Kshitip, and they both start removing their trousers.

The water is icy cold now, and the Shiva linga is about 20-25 feet from the entrance. They somehow reach the Shiva linga and decide to push it from the right side. They use their whole muscular power to tilt or displace the Shiva linga, but fail even to shake it. They try again, from different sides, but nothing happens—zero, zilch, nothing at all. Their bodies are drained, and due to the cold water, they are shivering badly.

Kshitip says, "I need to get out of this water," and he starts going back.

Rudra remains in the water and says with bowed head, "Now we don't have any other option but to break it."

Kshitip turns back, but Rudra turns towards the left side to avoid Kshitip's gaze. Rudra is wearing the hat with a torch. The moment he turns his head to the left, the light hits the corner of the entrance, where the wall meets the ceiling.

Kshitip says angrily, "It's not just about how I feel, Rudra. I understand the world is in danger, and I am fighting with my belief to do what is right, but don't you dare provoke me."

"Shhh..."

Kshitip gets angrier, but then he realises that Rudra is not listening to him but rather focusing on something else. He jumps back in and looks at the spot along with Rudra. There is an indentation just above the entrance where the wall meets the ceiling of the cave. It has a specific shape; it's definitely not an indentation caused by breaking off a stone. It has clear, smooth edges and resembles a cylinder or an oval.

"Shiva linga. Find a Shiva linga of that size," says Rudra, almost mesmerised. "It is a classic example of: you see what you want to see. With this clue in my unconscious mind, I watched all those documentaries and videos, and when we came here, I blindly believed that it was about those four pillars and linga. These five pillars were in front of our eyes the whole time," says Rudra, pointing towards the entrance. It has five pillars, supporting the ceiling of the cave. "We entered and exited through them multiple times, but we were blind. You see, there are five pillars, and these don't look the same age as the cave and Shiva linga."

They start searching for the Shiva linga. It doesn't take them more than two minutes to spot a Shiva linga of that size on the right wall. It is sitting in a square slot in the wall. Rudra climbs on the shoulders of Kshitip, respectfully removes the Shiva linga from there, and puts it in the slot.

As soon as he puts that Shiva linga in the slot, a piece from the ceiling falls into the water. Rudra jumps off Kshitip's shoulder, and they both get into the pond. Kshitip finds it and starts crying, "Thank you. Thank you. Thank you." Rudra hugs him tightly. They both come out of the temple and bow their heads to Lord Shiva.

Kshitip says, "Next time, before hugging me, please ensure your trousers are on," and they leave the temple complex.

Before leaving that amazing place, Kshitip sits for some time at the same spot where he cried while coming, and they leave with one more piece in their bag.

The attendant waits for those two strangers so that he can return the remaining money to them, but they don't return, at least for the next few months.

27

What's Next?

"So, what is the next clue?" Kshitip asks after sitting in their aircraft and closing the doors. Rudra is already unzipping the bag; he takes out the piece. It looks like a thin brick, approximately two inches thick, six inches long and three inches wide. Rudra inspects it closely and hands it over to Kshitip. On one side, there is a glass-like material in the centre, and on the other side, something written in Sanskrit is clearly visible.

"This glass would have broken, had the floor not had waist-deep water," says Rudra while inspecting the brick.

Kshitip smiles and replies, "People were saying that water seeps from the walls the whole year, and nobody knows the source. The water level is always maintained inside the temple. Just wondering, if all this is done to ensure that when this brick falls, it doesn't hit a hard rock floor."

"Wow! That would be an amazing engineering achievement. How cool is this theory?"

Kshitip focuses on the Sanskrit inscription:

brahmandam santulan vrat surya sangati
drignimilat, shardha, aatmanam tyajatu devnaam

"I have no clue," says Kshitip.

"But I know. Set Jaipur as the destination. I don't remember the name of the place exactly, but the temple is in Jaipur," says Rudra ecstatically. "I have lived in an industrial area in Jaipur for a couple of years and visited this place too. There is a temple in a beautiful rural area in Jaipur, approximately forty kilometres from the city. Its midst hills and greenery. It is said that the Shiva linga in this temple is not placed by someone, but it is a self-manifested one. Somebody discovered the linga and constructed a temple around it. This Shiva linga is in a body of water. It is very narrow; I don't remember correctly, but I think the diameter of that water body would not be more than 30-40 cm. The interesting thing is that it tilts towards the sun's direction twice a year when the sun changes its position. It happens twice a year, which is called the solstices or, in Hindi, ayana. Uttarayana and Dakshinayana."

"I know what solstices are."

"So, it is said that this Shiva linga balances the effects of change in the position of the sun, on Earth," concludes Rudra.

Kshitip starts the craft, sets Jaipur as destination and turns to Rudra, "Just wondering, Rudra, you were with the other society when you started working, right?"

"Yes."

"I mean, you visited this temple when you were with them. How did they allow you? Were they aware that you were visiting that temple? Were they preparing you for this escapade?"

"Or, they might not have been aware of any pieces being in this temple. They would not have been very high-ranking people in the society, I assume," says Rudra, shrugging his shoulders. Kshitip just nods and turns towards the control panel of the craft. Rudra lifts his head and starts wondering if what Kshitip is indicating holds ground.

It is very early in the morning when they reach Jaipur. They leave their craft in a secluded train parking area and go to the Jaipur railway station to see if they find any clues about the name of the place. Generally, railway stations have pictures and names of the tourist attractions. Nobody is nearby—no officials, no passengers, no trains, no announcements, it's like a ghost town. They go to platform number one, and there are some pictures of such places. One hoarding is about the Maleshwar Mahadev temple in Samod.

"That's the place," Rudra identifies the temple immediately. "That is the first waterfall I have ever visited in my life." He hesitatingly adds, "as much as I remember."

They go back to their craft and leave for Samod. By the time they reach, it's about 4 a.m. They park their craft in an area where there are dense bushes on the hill and come out. From the edge of that hill, the Samod temple is visible, nestled in high hills with a waterfall in the vicinity.

Rudra moves towards the edge of the cliff to climb down, but Kshitip hesitates and says, "Rudra, I will not enter any temples any more like a thief or by breaking in. Now, because of the lockdown, there will be very few people, or they may not even come at all. Let's enter like devotees this time rather than thieves." Rudra wants to go inside right away without wasting any time, but he agrees, as Kshitip has gone through emotional distress of late.

"So, what do you suggest we do?"

"It's a village, people wake up early here. Let's find a shop and grab something to eat. I know it's 4 a.m., but still."

They climb down the hill, which takes about half an hour and from there they head towards the nearby market, but every shop is closed. When you don't think about something, you don't need it, but when you start searching for it, you feel its necessity. Now they are both hungry; earlier, they were not.

They reach a sweet shop on one corner of the market; shutters are down, and there is no sign of any human being. This is their last hope, so they turn back to go to the temple.

"Are you hungry, kids?" a frail female voice asks. They both turn and find an old lady coming into the streetlight, with a supporting stick.

"Yes, ma'am," replies Kshitip.

"Come with me," she says, waving them to follow her. Her small hut is not very far; it doesn't even have a door. They enter, and she fires her clay chulha and prepares tea and onion kachoris in no time. "I sell these for survival, but because of lockdown, nobody is coming here now. I fired my chulha after two days today… I didn't say this to make you sad. Please forgive me," she says while frying the kachoris.

They both sit patiently listening to her and waiting for the kachoris. As soon as she serves them, they start eating like animals. Before she can complete frying the next lot, their plate gets empty. The tea is already cold by the time they are done eating, but they cannot ask her to heat it up. They sip their cups of tea and stand up to pay her, but she waves at them to remain seated.

"Have a hot one too. Cold tea is not of any use," she offers and pours some hot tea into their cups. Their eyes well up, and they finally taste how amazing that tea is.

They stand up to leave and the lady comes out of hut with them and says, looking at the road, "I also have two sons; they are stuck because of lockdown. They used to call me on telephone of this shop," she points at a shop. "But this shop is also closed due to the lockdown, and I have not heard their voices since. I hope they are not hungry. Every mother wants the well-being of her kids. How can I take money from you? This is my house, not my shop. Now, go," she says, not even looking at them. Rudra and Kshitip are speechless, their eyes teary, and their hearts full of emotions.

Kshitip comes closer to the old lady and touches her feet. She blesses, "May you live long, son." Rudra follows suit. "May the victory be yours."

They wipe their eyes and head to the temple. After walking for approximately 500 metres, they enter the complex of the temple. As they get closer, they notice that the aarti is already in progress. As a pleasant surprise, only the priest is present there. They wait outside the temple and are surprised by how amazingly the people of Jaipur and that village are following COVID protocols. The head priest turns after finishing the aarti and is taken aback to see two tourists. He finishes all rituals, puts on his mask and comes to them, "I have never said this to anyone, but you are not supposed to be here."

"We know, Pandit-ji. If we say we started this journey before the lockdown was imposed, would you believe us?" Kshitip asks. Pandit-ji looks at them suspiciously and then smiles.

"Pandit-ji, we have come from very far. Obviously, the prime objective is to visit the temple, but he also wants to see the waterfall before sunrise and wants me to click some pictures of him. I have injured my leg and won't be able to walk on the stones, so if you can just ask somebody from your staff to accompany him, we will be really grateful," Rudra politely requests.

Pandit-ji looks at his foot and then at Kshitip's face and says, "Come, I will take your pictures. These days, nobody is in the temple but me."

Kshitip gives Rudra a hateful stare like he is saying, *It's disgusting, taking advantage of a man of God.* Rudra also shakes his head in agreement, *I know, but what choices do we have?*

Pandit-ji and Kshitip return after almost 20-25 minutes. Rudra is sleeping on the floor near the steps. Pandit-ji smiles and goes inside the temple. Kshitip shakes Rudra to wake him up. He opens his eyes and winks at Kshitip, showing 'mission accomplished'.

Pandit-ji comes out with a flower and some sweets, gives them to Kshitip and says, "I hope you found what you came for."

Kshitip looks at him suspiciously, and Pandit-ji says, "I mean, your pictures."

"Oh, yes, yes," he laughs nervously. Pandit-ji goes inside to do his daily chores, and when he comes out after some time, there is nobody in the hall.

28

What Do We Do When…

"What did you find? Where was it?" Kshitip asks in excitement while climbing the mountain. They are still fifteen minutes away from reaching the top.

"It was simple. The verse was to have faith and leave oneself to the will of God."

"Oh, right. So, it was in the water body, around the Shiva linga? Tell me in detail," Kshitip says, getting irritated.

"Yes, it was in the water. I put my hand in the water, up to my shoulder. My fingers felt an unevenness in the well, and there it was," says Rudra. "I will show you in the craft. It is a rod-like thing with something written on it. I couldn't read it."

"OK," says Kshitip. He takes a pause and then asks, "Rudra, we never talked about that night in Ballia; what did that priest tell you?"

Rudra doesn't expect this discussion while climbing a mountain with a heavy bag on his back, but he knows Kshitip is his partner, and he cannot keep him in the dark. Rudra sits down to catch his breath and says, "He said that after the Mahabharata war, some deadly weapons remained unused, so kings and warriors who remained alive kept those weapons with them. But, with time, their families became weaker, and they had to hide these weapons in secret locations."

"But the things we have collected don't look like weapons to me," interrupts Kshitip.

"These are not weapons; all these are pieces of a single weapon. He said that the weapon is so deadly that it can wipe out all forms of life, if used."

"And do you believe that?"

"Does it matter?"

"No, it doesn't, but what if the responsibility of taking a decision whether to use or destroy it comes on our shoulders," Kshitip wonders.

"We are pawns, Kshitip. This decision can never be ours, but even if such a situation comes, using that weapon is not an option at all. That's not rocket science, even if it doesn't cause annihilation, it may cause significant destruction," Rudra says with determination and Kshitip nods.

"And, what about the story being true?"

"What story?"

"The Mahabharata."

"I think we have seen enough not to completely doubt the story. Glowing dead body, an aircraft of the size of a cubicle which is an amazing example of advanced technology, people sacrificing themselves for a cause, such elaborate planning and technology to hide the pieces of this weapon. I mean who can have ever thought that a piece of rock, when fitted in an indentation, can release a piece of brick and get absorbed completely without leaving any trace or what about the glowing ball in the Kailash temple? I mean, all this has been done hundreds of years ago, that is mindboggling. You know that priest told me that King Harshvardhan had this weapon at one point in time, and the Saraswati Koop in the Allahabad fort once had this weapon hidden in it. And because of this weapon only, that well is called Saraswati, and that is the third river of Triveni Sangam," Rudra says all this in one breath in excitement, and his expression changes suddenly to disappointment.

He says, looking away from Kshitip, "But that is the problem. He said the weapon belongs to Shakti. Shakti means Goddess, right? And, as Saraswati is the most peaceful form of Shakti, this weapon was kept in a well named Saraswati. I mean, it is okay until you start talking about gods, goddesses, reincarnation, immortals, Shiva's third eye, destruction of the world by dance, blah blah blah," by the time he ends his sentence, he has completely lost interest.

"Hmm. I understand. It's logical what you say. But what if…" says Kshitip.

An impatient Rudra interrupts, "You start with 'What if,' the man in the Ballia temple started with 'Just assume.' That is exactly my problem; everything starts with these only."

"Okay, let's talk logically. When did people see electrons, protons or neutrons for the first time?"

Rudra scoffs, "Come on. Is this your logic?"

"Yes. Before Galileo, people believed the sun revolved around Earth. The initial models of atoms assumed that it was like a watermelon. We discovered telephones, automobiles, air travel, computers, and space travel recently. There are thousands of examples which you already know, and I am just talking about the last 100-150 years. Before that, people thought that there was a giant which ate the sun at the end of the day, every day. It has been just over a century since we invented air travel, but our folklores are flooded with vimanas and flying people. We were not aware of any form of life other than life on Earth, but now there are scientists who believe that we are not alone in this universe, my friend. Just because we have not seen something doesn't mean that it doesn't exist.

"Now, when it comes to reincarnation, Amrit, Dev Lok, Patal Lok and sages cursing people and converting them into something, I am also not a big fan. But we should understand that these stories are passed on orally from one generation to another, and people spice them a bit, incorporating their imaginations. I also don't think Lord Vishnu is sleeping on the lap of a five-headed serpent floating in an ocean of milk, but is there somebody looking after us from above? Definitely. Did he come to earth taking the forms of Ram, Krishna, and others? Maybe not. Somebody coined the term reincarnation, and people loved it. It became a great concept, and people copied it. Who knows? Or maybe it is something beyond our understanding. There are examples of babies born in one country who know some foreign language without any training or exposure to that language. They remember the names of people and their previous families. Their memories of previous lives are so vivid that they even remember how they died in that life."

"I am not aware of any such cases," says Rudra, shrugging his shoulders.

"Doesn't mean that it is not true, isn't it?" smiles Kshitip.

"You made your point, Kshitip. There are so many unsolved mysteries in the world, and most of those are beyond our understanding, but again, what does it mean that a weapon is from Shakti origin?"

"Hmm, does it really matter? I mean the origin. But, as per mythology, Shakti is the primordial cosmic energy and represents the dynamic forces that are thought to move through the universe. This energy is considered creative, sustaining, as well as destructive, and is sometimes referred to as an auspicious source of energy. She is also called Anadi, which means she has no beginning or end; she is timeless. She is the creator, birth giver, nurturer and destroyer. Now, thinking logically, it is not possible to have an endless life," Kshitip answers, takes a pause and adds hesitantly, "OK, a useless correlation now but I watched a movie long back: *The Man From Earth,* which shows a man leaving his job, friends, family, house to relocate to some other place for no reason and during his farewell, when his friends interrogate, he shares the reason that he doesn't age. And it was not the first time that he was leaving his loved ones, but he had done so multiple times in past. He was not even a homo sapiens but a Cro-Magnon, and due to some disorder, he just doesn't age."

"Interesting concept. But are you saying our gods are sick?" Rudra chuckles.

"Hahaha. I knew you would say this. I just shared a view, who knows what they are? We have spent sufficient time arguing here. Let's go," says Kshitip, and they start climbing again.

29

007

"Who is he?" asks the first guy.

"He is a secret agent, like James Bond," answers the second.

"Who does he work for?"

"Who knows? We have been with him for these many days, but we don't even know his name."

"But I like his car. What would be its price?"

"It is so costly that you will have to sell your house with everything in it, 9-10 times to buy this car... Shhhh, he is coming," answers the second one, straightening his back in attention.

"So, where are they?" asks a tall guy with an impressive build.

"Most probably, they are in Jaipur, sir," the first one answers, admiring his boss's incredibly costly suit.

"OK. Keep an eye on them," says the guy and goes inside his room.

30

The Old Clock

"I have set Delhi as the destination, we have about forty-five minutes to decode and finalise the next stop," says Kshitip while pressing some buttons and turning back to Rudra.

"OK. So, here it is," Rudra says with that shining rod of deep metallic yellow colour in hand. It is approximately two feet long.

Kshitip notices that something is written on it in Sanskrit:

azri antya prahara, dwitiya dand vighati peyuh
dhamma patan, rajya patan

"One more riddle to solve. It is the smallest one, though, and seems like it is talking about a particular time, but where?" Kshitip thinks out loud.

"Yes, the word 'prahara' shows that it is talking about time."

"It's not just about the word 'prahara', the whole sentence quite clearly mentions a specific time of day," answers Kshitip as if there is nothing to decode.

"I didn't understand," says Rudra, expecting some clarity.

Kshitip looks at Rudra's face and realises that he is genuinely asking for an explanation. "Dand and ghati are measures of time in ancient Hindu civilisation. In the Hindu calendar, there are eight praharas. If you convert it to the modern-day time system, every prahara is of three hours. Each prahara has seven and a half dand, and each dand has sixty vighati. It means one dand is equivalent to twenty-four minutes, and every vighati is equal to twenty-four seconds. Now, don't ask me where I learnt all this. You know the answer already."

Rudra is mesmerised and says with a smile, "I know, I know. I have also read all this, but applying it so quickly in today's world is incredible. Before I could even think, you calculated, that's amazing."

"I did it swiftly because I am using it right now. Didn't you notice?" Kshitip says while turning back and waving towards the control panel of the craft, the way magicians wave their hands. "Ta-da."

Rudra turns towards the control panel, and his eyes widen in disbelief. The entire panel is in Sanskrit. Even the messages appearing on the display are in Sanskrit. He swears, "Un-f*****g-believable."

Kshitip angrily hits Rudra on his head and shouts, "Come on."

"Sorry, Papa," laughs Rudra while rubbing his head. "What about the place?"

"Peyuh means the sun, right?" asks Kshitip, thinking about it.

"Yes, absolutely. But what does azri mean?"

"Is it the edge of a sword?"

"Could be. We are after ancient things; a sword makes sense. Otherwise, azri means corner too, like the corner of a room," says Rudra.

"Sun sword, sword sun, surya talvar, talvar surya, surya dhaar, dhaar surya," Kshitip babbles, and Rudra closes his eyes to deliberate. After a few seconds of silence, Kshitip asks, "Corner in Sanskrit and Hindi is kona, right?"

"Yes," says Rudra, pensive in his thoughts.

"Could it mean kod or kon, which means angle?"

"Could be," says Rudra, getting irritated now.

"Then I know our destination," says Kshitip gleefully, punching the air.

"What? Where?"

"All the places we have visited are temple towns, right? So, I started thinking in that direction. Azri means angle or kon. One of the synonyms of the sun is ark," explains Kshitip. He looks at Rudra, expecting him to decode the riddle now.

Rudra is clueless at first, but after five seconds, he says, "Konark?"

"Exactly, my friend." Kshitip is really ecstatic, but Rudra remains silent. Kshitip's excitement also dies down after seeing Rudra's reaction.

"But, isn't it a Sun temple?"

"Yes, it is a Sun temple," answers Kshitip.

"All the temples that we have been to are Shiva temples," says Rudra, gloomily.

"I know. But do you know the meaning of the last line 'dhamma patan, rajya patan'?" Kshitip asks. His smile starts coming back.

"No," Rudra answers plainly, knowing that Kshitip will flaunt his knowledge now.

"OK, so let me set the destination first. Don't worry, I know it's right," Kshitip goes to the control panel and runs his fingers on it.

Then, he starts the story after taking a deep breath, "So, this temple was built in the twelfth or thirteenth century by King

Narasingha Deva. When the temple's completion took longer than the estimated time because the architect couldn't put the headstone, he threatened the architect and workers to complete the temple before the next morning. Still, they had no idea how to do that. The son of the architect suggested a way, and he started the work. In some time, he successfully put the last piece in place, but the workers started opposing this and said that if the king came to know that a twelve-year-old kid did something that thousands of adults could not do, he would be furious and kill us.

"After hearing all this, the boy jumped to his death from the top of the temple to save his father and thousands of workers. The name of the boy was Dharmapada, lovingly called Dhamma. When the king learnt that the temple was completed this way, he banned worshipping in that temple and very soon, the whole dynasty fell."

"It must be the same temple then," Rudra agrees.

"And it's not only a Sun temple, but it also has idols of all major gods along with an ancient Shiva linga," says Kshitip. After hearing this, Rudra's eyes lit up.

31

Om Suryay Namah

It is close to 11 a.m.; Rudra and Kshitip are in the Konark town of Odisha. From where they have hidden their craft, the top of the Sun temple is clearly visible. They walk for about half an hour to reach the temple.

It is magnificent in size and grandeur, but unfortunately, it is in ruins despite being a world heritage site. Without wasting any time, they start searching for something that changes with time. The temple has been constructed in the shape of a chariot. In mythology, the sun moves in the sky in his chariot, which is pulled by seven horses. The temple has twenty-four wheels and seven horses. The wheels of the chariots resemble a clock.

Kshitip says, pointing at a wheel, "Oh, so this is that temple. There are many temples in India that have been constructed in the shape of chariots. I knew that in one of these temples, the wheels function like sundials."

Rudra says in excitement, "It must be what we are looking for, which changes with time. Do you know how it functions?"

"No, I don't. Let's ask someone."

"But, in lockdown, who will we find?"

"In temples, there is always somebody. Let's search," says Kshitip.

They look nearby to find someone. They walk for about fifty metres and see a sage sitting under a tree. They ask him about the functioning of the sundial, and he agrees to demonstrate the same. They return to the wheel, and the sage puts his finger in the centre of the wheel. Its shadow falls on the perimeter, and the sage predicts the time according to the place where the shadow falls. To their surprise, the time is accurate.

They both ask the sage to teach them how he does that.

The sage explains, "Do you see these eight thicker spokes, passing through the centre of the wheel? They cut the wheel into eight sectors. Each sector represents a prahara, which means three hours. Then there are these thinner spokes bisecting each sector into two. Now, all these smaller sectors are equal to one hour and thirty minutes. If you look at the perimeter, there are exactly thirty beads in a smaller sector, so each bead equals three minutes. Depending upon where the shadow falls, you too can calculate the time. The beads are big enough to differentiate between these three minutes easily. Bhole Shambhu." He turns and leaves.

"The knowledge our ancestors had is beyond our understanding. Every temple we go to, my respect for them increases immensely. I mean, how could anyone carve something with so much precision on a stone, which is reliable and relevant even after all these years," says Rudra, admiring the magnificent engineering of the temple. "What time do we need to check this sundial?"

"Antya prahara means last prahara, which will be 3 p.m. to 6 p.m. So, the exact time as per the riddle must be 3:25 p.m., twenty-fifth to forty-eighth second," replies Kshitip, calculating time in his head.

"Impressive. So, we have some time. Let's go and have some food," says Rudra and they both head to the nearest market.

They return around 3 p.m. to the temple and wait for the riddle's time. As soon as their wristwatch hits 3:25 p.m., Rudra puts his finger in the centre of the wheel, and its shadow falls on one of the beads on the perimeter. Kshitip marks that bead. Rudra removes his hand, and they push that bead with excitement. The moment of truth is here, but nothing happens. Kshitip presses it again to no avail. He presses every point from the centre of the wheel to that bead in vain.

The time has passed. They both sit down, facepalming, near the sundial, their heads between their knees.

"Are you sure that you read the riddle correctly?" Rudra asks.

Kshitip gets irritated, "Do you still have doubts? I explained to you everything, and you were convinced. This is it. This is the temple."

"Did we read the correct time?" Rudra asks again, this time replacing 'you' with 'we'.

"Yes, obviously. Antya means last. For a sundial, the last prahara would be the last one with the sun in the sky, that would be evening, 3 p.m. to 6 p.m.," says Kshitip, calmer than earlier.

"Then where did we make a mistake?" Rudra stands up and starts looking around. "You told me when we came here that there were two sundials. Why two?" Kshitip doesn't respond, not knowing the answer. Rudra continues, "If Antya means last, antya prahara should be 3 a.m. to 6 a.m., right? As per ancient Indian culture, the day starts at sunrise."

"And from where will you get light to cast the shadow? It is a sundial, Rudra, not a torch dial," Kshitip retorts strongly.

"I thought you would say, a moon dial," Rudra says while looking at the sky.

"There is nothing as a moon dial," Kshitip replies sharply, but thinks, *May be.*

Kshitip stands up, almost jumping, and runs to the other sundial, then the next wheel, followed by another. Rudra runs behind him.

"There are twenty-four wheels in this temple. Why exactly twenty-four? And one of the wheels works like a sundial. Why only one? All the wheels are the same, the only difference is the design inside the dial and on the perimeter," Kshitip puts his finger on his lips, crouches and starts examining the design on the dial and exclaims, "You are a genius, Rudra! A damn genius! Look closely at the design on these wheels, their dial and perimeter."

"Yes, the designs on all the wheels are different," notices Rudra, analysing the design.

"No. They are not. Till now, I have come across a few sets of wheels on which the design is the same. Though not all the wheels are in pristine condition, you can see the design on them," says Kshitip, taking a deep breath. "And I have a theory, just let me complete all twenty-four wheels first." He moves on to the next one. Rudra follows Kshitip in a relaxed manner, knowing that the situation is under control now and waits for Kshitip's theory.

Kshitip checks the last wheel, turns to Rudra, and says joyfully, "As I presumed, these twenty-four wheels are in pairs. I mean the same type of design is present on exactly two wheels, so there are twelve sets of wheels. What does that mean?"

"Twelve months of the year?" Rudra guesses.

"Exactly. And the other wheel of the set is for night, a moon dial!" Kshitip has his Eureka moment.

"Amazing! But how do you know which one is for which month and which one of the pairs is for night?"

"If you look closely, the design on these wheels is linked to different times of the year. Like in this one, people have been shown sleeping under a thick blanket, which means it is for wintertime. The other one has leaves blossoming for the spring season. Similarly, you can see rain, summer, autumn and the activities for night; see this one." Kshitip takes him to different wheels and shows the designs.

"Oh. Khajuraho is not the only temple with such designs," says Rudra, tilting his head to have a proper look at the design.

"This is the first wheel you are paying attention to," says Kshitip, playfully.

"It is the most interesting one, anyway," Rudra chuckles, but soon his smile disappears. "I hope it is purnima today."

Kshitip's expressions also change. "I don't remember seeing the moon last night. I think it is amavasya," he says in disappointment.

"Are you sure?" Rudra asks, and Kshitip nods. They both sit down quietly.

After a few moments, Kshitip says, "The time calculation on a moon dial won't be easy, by the way. The trajectory of the moon's motion is not always the same. The moon dial will be accurate only on the full moon night. If it is amavasya today, we will have to wait for fifteen days. Anyway, we don't even know how to calculate time on a moon dial," says Kshitip, in despair.

"But why didn't they teach you about calculating time on a moon dial?" Rudra comments in frustration. "Do you need a cup of tea?"

Kshitip nods.

They find a small shop about a kilometre from the temple. The owner is running it secretly. There is no other option for that poor guy but to run his business illegally to meet his requirements.

They sit down there and order tea. Their tea comes in five minutes; they don't talk for those five minutes.

Rudra holds the cup in his hand and just before taking the first sip, he says spontaneously, "I don't think that it is about the moon dial. In my opinion, they would have trained you on this if it was so critical. Watching time on a sundial is, anyway, something that even local guides know, so it's not a secret."

"So, do you want to say, the mechanism of releasing the piece is not in the sundial?" Kshitip says, sipping his tea.

"Oh no, no, from where did it even come to your mind? I don't think there is any engineering failure. You yourself said that there are clocks for every month, it can be possible that the clock we used was not for March but for some other month."

Kshitip stands up, takes out his wallet, hands twenty rupees to the shopkeeper in a rush and starts walking towards the temple.

"I have not even taken two sips of my tea," says Rudra, but Kshitip doesn't turn. Rudra leaves his cup and follows Kshitip.

"March is difficult to identify as it is the end of spring and the beginning of summer, but I think this one should be of March," says Kshitip, pointing at one of the sundials. "And it is a sundial as pictures suggest."

"I also think so because the other one is clearly of spring, and the rest two are of summer. This one is clearly of a transition month from spring to summer." Rudra adds, stating their biggest scare, "I hope it is not about a moon dial, else we will have to wait for fifteen days."

They don't talk, because they know what it means to be in the same place for fifteen days in such a scenario, when the world's future is at stake, and mercenaries are following them.

At nightfall, they go to the tea stall, have a cup of tea, bread and butter. Once the tea seller closes his shop, they lie down on the wooden benches, but sleep is far from their minds. They know it's a do-or-die situation. Sometime in the night, they fall asleep and wake up when the tea seller arrives. They have breakfast with tea and leave for the temple, where they spend their time looking for any other possibility.

It is 3:25 p.m. Rudra puts his hand in the centre of the wheel, which they know is for this time of the year, based on its design, and the shadow falls on a particular bead on the perimeter. With a pounding heart, Kshitip presses the bead, and one of the major spokes comes out. Rudra and Kshitip look at each other with a sigh of relief and overjoyed. A shiny metallic flat rod of about one foot falls out of it. They put it in the bag and place the spoke back to its position. It fits perfectly without any sign of its detachment.

They clean the area and leave that magnificent architectural and creative marvel.

32

The Help

"What next?" Kshitip asks, but Rudra doesn't reply and keeps staring at the piece in his hand. "Is everything okay?"

"Are you sure what we are looking for is Gandeev? We have not discussed this of late, but I remember you once mentioning that we are searching for Gandeev. This piece or the previous one, which is a foot-long straight rod—they don't seem like pieces of a bow."

"Gandeev was my guess. To be very frank, I don't know what we are searching for."

"These pieces look more like pieces of an arrow or spear. Anyway, what use will only Gandeev be of? It's a bow, and a bow is of no use without an arrow," says Rudra, and looks at Kshitip, who is eager to see the inscriptions on the piece more than listening to Rudra's logic.

He hands over the piece to Kshitip. The inscription reads:

sarp garbh, sarp raaj, sarp jaati nasht
aadi sarp dharyatu, dhara bharah

"Now that's a mouthful. It's almost a tongue twister," says Kshitip, mumbling the verse repeatedly. "The last line is about Sheshnaag, obviously, but the problem is that there are so many Sheshnaag idols in various temples. You remember there was a huge Sheshnaag sculpture in the Lepakshi temple?"

"Hmm. Sarp garbh reminds me of a narrow tunnel in the path of the Vaishno Devi temple," says Rudra, looking at the piece. "I have heard from the travellers that they have to pass through a very narrow tunnel which feels like passing through a..."

"A mother's womb. It is not called a snake's womb," Kshitip interrupts Rudra.

"Oh, that's bad correlation then," Rudra says, embarrassed.

"But, I think, the direction is right. I mean, sarp garbh means a tunnel, but there are so many tunnels, so it will be difficult to crack the riddle with this word. Let's start with sarp raaj," suggests Kshitip.

"I know so many serpent kings from mythology, starting from Sheshnaag to Vasuki to Kalliya to Karkotaka to Takshak. This is again very vague."

"But as the last line indicates towards Sheshnaag, can it be that this one also means the same?" Kshitip contemplates.

"Then what is the point of putting both the words and sentences to point at one deity only?" Rudra questions back. "What do you know about attempts at the annihilation of snakes?"

"Nothing."

"I also don't have any idea. I know about Parashuram attempting to kill all Kshatriyas and a few such cases, but nothing about the annihilation of snakes," says Rudra, worried about the future of this mission.

"If only we had a smartphone or a laptop, we could have got some information from the internet," says Kshitip in frustration.

They both sit clueless in the aircraft, not knowing where to go or even what to think.

"Is there any tunnel which is related to a snake?"

"We are near an ancient temple. There are many saints and sages around. Let's go talk to them, they will have the answer," Kshitip suggests so plainly that it seems like an obvious solution. He opens the door of the craft and signals Rudra to come out too. Rudra joins him hesitatingly.

"What?" Kshitip asks.

"Isn't it risky to go and ask people about clues?" Rudra shares his concern.

"Leave that to me. It's just a story for others."

The sun is still in the evening sky, and a cool breeze is flowing. It is a nice time of the day to sit outside your house on the lawn or your porch and have a hot cup of tea, looking at the horizon. But these two people are sleepless, hungry, tired, scared, frustrated, and have no idea what they are doing.

They don't talk throughout their walk to the temple. Once they are there, they start looking for the same sage who has taught them how to tell time on the sundial. After a struggle of 15-20 minutes, they find him meditating in one corner of the garden, so they wait. The godly man opens his eyes and gets surprised after seeing them again.

"Baba, we were discussing the end of the world. How does it happen?" Kshitip asks.

The sage keeps looking at him with a knowing smile on his face, as if indicating to him to come to the point, but eventually replies playfully, "Haven't you all seen on television that the world ends when Lord Shiva opens his third eye?"

Kshitip doesn't notice the tone of his reply because he is more focused on the sage finishing his sentence, so he can ask his second question. He is ready for a bit of humiliation, too.

Kshitip opens his mouth to ask his question, but Rudra notices that Baba is not taking them seriously, so he asks instead, "But, what do you think, Baba? We have come all the way to this temple to experience the presence of the divine, the faith in the divine. You taught us about the sundial yesterday. We have come to you only because you know more than others. Please tell us."

The sage looks at Rudra with the same smile and asks, "What do you want to know?"

"What causes the end of this world?"

Kshitip hisses at Rudra, whispering, "Really? Is this the time to discuss this with a sage? We are late already."

"All yugas have a certain age. When that ends, the world ends," the sage says. Rudra keeps looking at him like he will continue and explain further, but he doesn't.

"And how does it end, Baba?" Rudra asks again.

"Shiva ends the world with his Pashupatastra."

Rudra understands by now that there is no point in going in circles, as the sage already knows that this is not their actual question, so he asks, "Baba, as per mythology, has there been any such incident in the past when somebody attempted to annihilate the snakes from Earth?"

Baba's eyes light up, and he says, "Snakes are the most misunderstood creatures. They have always helped mankind and attacked only when instigated. Do you know, when Duryodhana and Shakuni poisoned Bheema and threw him in the Ganga, it was a snake that saved his life? And because of that snake, he got the power of a hundred elephants. King Vasuki gave him this power. There are many such examples where humans betrayed each other, but snakes saved them. Nagas or serpents are not only worshipped by Hindus, but in many other faiths, they are considered demigods or gods. But when a naga takes an oath of something, humans or even gods cannot stop it."

He pauses to take a deep breath and then continues, "But the challenging time for them started when Arjuna decided to burn down the Khandav forest. The chief of the nagas in that forest was Takshak. Takshak belonged to the Ikshvaku clan, so he was a descendant of Lord Ram. Aswasena, the mighty son of Takshak, was there when Arjuna killed Takshak's wife. To avenge the slaughter of his mother, Aswasena attacked Arjuna during the Kurukshetra war while he was battling with Karna.

"Years later, when the grandson of Arjuna, Parikshit, made fun of a sage, the son of the sage cursed Parikshit to die of a snakebite. In some stories, it is mentioned that, to ensure there are no snakes left on Earth, Parikshit commanded his son, Janamejaya, to kill all the snakes. In other stories, it is said that once Takshak killed Parikshit, Janamejaya did this to take revenge for his father's death."

"Did what, Baba?" Rudra asks.

"Janamejaya conducted a special yajna to kill all the snakes, and as the snakes were banished to the underworld, this yajna was done there itself," says the learnt sage. Rudra and Kshitip look at each other in confusion.

"That place is in the land of the gods, Uttarakhand. A temple called Patal Bhuvaneshwar is in Pithoragarh district. That temple is in a tunnel, and it is said that all gods and goddesses live there," completes the sage. The duo looks at each other with a sense of relief, thanking God that it's not the real underworld.

"So, how deep would that tunnel be, Baba?"

"I have been to that temple; the tunnel is about a hundred feet deep and very narrow." He sighs and asks, "Why do you people want to go to Patal Bhuvaneshwar?"

"After completing our education, this is the first time we are free due to lockdown, so we have decided to visit as many interesting places as possible," Rudra answers with a plain face.

"Isn't the lockdown for preventing travel?" the sage asks, smiling.

"Yes, Baba, it is. But we don't have anything in our hands," answers Rudra with an unspeakable pain in his voice that he doesn't expect the sage to understand.

"Everything is in your hands, and you are saying you are helpless. Hahahaha," the sage laughs while standing up. Then he walks away. Rudra and Kshitip look at each other, shrug their shoulders and walk to their craft.

"You listened to his words very carefully as if you believed all that about Arjuna burning a forest and a snake killing a king to fulfil a curse," Kshitip takes a dig at Rudra.

"You don't need to question my beliefs after every mythological story, Kshitip," answers Rudra, annoyed with Kshitip poking him. "As I said earlier, my belief doesn't matter. As far as the accuracy of the story is concerned, the real story could be the same except serpents being slithering reptiles, but of a different race in that time. They killed the king, so his son avenged his father's death. Whatever the reality may be, we know our next destination now. Have you read the *Meluha* series by Amish Tripathi?"

Kshitip shakes his head and gives him a look: *Really?*

"OK, I know that's not a book written by some sage. I am not referring to that series for any fact, just an interesting concept. In that book, the nagas are considered as humans born with disability."

"OK, OK, I got it. It is obviously interesting, but let's focus on the work at hand," Kshitip cuts him short.

They both stop talking and keep moving towards their aircraft.

33

Land of the Gods

"Wow, what a peaceful and beautiful place, man? How lucky are these people that they live in such a serene place," says Kshitip, looking down the craft.

They have reached Pithoragarh. It is just before midnight, the sky is clear, but there is that mild layer of fog on the ground, the kind that you can even smell—the smell of pinkish winter.

"I think that is the temple," says Rudra, pointing his finger towards a structure on the ground. "Don't fly too low, people will notice the craft."

"It is midnight. In such places, people sleep by 8 p.m."

"I know, but there are people chasing us. So, be careful," says Rudra.

Kshitip nods, and after some manoeuvres, he lands the craft in the jungle about one kilometre from the temple. They both come out, hide the craft under branches and leave for the temple.

They take about half an hour to get there. When they reach, the whole temple is wrapped in darkness, and there is an iron shutter.

"The tunnel is inside the temple, we will have to break open the lock," says Rudra, looking for something to break the lock.

"No, no, no, no, I will not let you break the lock. Anyway, climbing down the tunnel at night would be extremely difficult. We do not know anything about this temple. What if we need some clarity, but because of the broken lock, people get suspicious, and we do not get the required information tomorrow? It is midnight already, and considering the opening time of temples, I think people will start coming in the next 3-4 hours," Kshitip counters.

Rudra stands there for a minute, but agrees with Kshitip's point, "Let us find a safe place to sleep."

"I don't think there is any safe place to sleep here. This temple is for snakes, right? Let's go back to the craft and spend our night there."

It is about 5 a.m. when they return to the temple and find a pandit there. While walking, Kshitip picks up a clay pot and a red cloth from the ground. He ties the cloth around the mouth of the pot while Rudra looks at him in surprise, guessing what he is doing. Kshitip holds the clay pot respectfully with both hands and approaches the priest. The priest is astonished to see two visitors.

"Namaste, Pandit-ji," Rudra greets the holy priest with folded hands, and Kshitip lifts the pot closer to his chest and greets. The priest is startled by the pot in Kshitip's hands.

"This temple is not for scattering ashes, son."

Kshitip breaks down, "I know, Pandit-ji. My father wanted to visit this temple, but he left this world with this one last wish in his heart. I just want to fulfil his last wish if you allow us."

"But how could you people come here without any transport?"

"We walked all the way from Allahabad," answers Kshitip with tears in his eyes.

"Allahabad?" the priest asks in astonishment.

"It is about the last wish of my father," says Kshitip, looking at the pot, "Please, Pandit-ji." Kshitip starts crying. His tears seem real.

"OK, OK, son. Don't cry. I will open the gates and take you to the temple," the priest says naively, taking them towards the temple to unlock the gate. Rudra looks at Kshitip and shakes his head. Kshitip shrugs off his shoulder, gesturing, *I am also not proud of it.*

The priest takes them inside. They notice a small opening in the ground, sarp garbh. The tunnel has a lighting system, and chains are fixed on both sides to facilitate the descent and ascent of the visitors.

"Where will you keep your father now?" asks Rudra, smiling at Kshitip.

"You don't have to hold the chains necessarily, Rudra. There are stones to support your feet. I will not leave my dad here." He winks, and they start climbing down the tunnel. Kshitip holds the clay pot in his left hand and walks carefully while Rudra descends at a faster speed. The tunnel has many narrow points where Kshitip struggles a lot with that pot in hand, but he somehow manages to reach the bottom.

Though the tunnel is wide enough, almost like a room, its height is very low. Kshitip walks forward, bending his knees and back. Rudra is already waiting with Pandit-ji in that cave, admiring the magnificence and mystery of that place. Kshitip looks in the direction where Rudra is looking and puts his hand on Rudra's shoulder.

Rudra says instinctively, "Yes, I know."

There is a massive structure of stone with a hood of a snake with several heads. "This is Sheshnaag, supporting Earth on his head. As you can see, it has seven heads and venom glands, teeth, everything," says the priest, pointing at the structure after noticing their interest. *Aadi sarp dharyatu, dhara bharah.* They don't have any doubts in their head about the place anymore. Now, they must look for the next piece.

They move forward to find a hole in the ground resembling a betel leaf. "It is the same hawan kund where the ritual of burning all the snakes was performed."

Kshitip sits down on the floor and inspects that hole. The hole is hardly 1-2 feet deep and has nothing inside except some fresh ritual offerings. He lifts his head, looks at Rudra, and shakes his head, indicating, *Nothing.* The priest looks at them suspiciously but chooses to ignore them, as he cannot fathom the implications of not finding something in a hole in the ground he visits daily.

They next stop at a small stone edifice, which is wet as drops of water fall from a peculiar-looking thing on the ceiling. "When Lord Shiva cut the head of Lord Ganesh, while all the gods and goddesses were looking for a worthy replacer of his head, it was kept under this Sahasradal kamal or Brahm kamal. It is in the form of a lotus and nectar kept dripping from it on Ganesh's body, which kept his body alive. You can see the food pipe, respiratory system pipes and other things you would find in a headless body."

Rudra smiles as he doesn't believe in all this and rudely asks, "But Pandit-ji, wasn't the head fixed on Ganesh's torso? If yes, the head should be present somewhere in the temple, not the torso."

Anyone else like Kshitip will respond angrily to such a disrespectful question, but the priest smiles and says, "You are talking logically, people generally listen and believe. One should ask questions. Come." He walks ahead. Rudra looks at him, surprised, as he doesn't answer his question. Rudra taunts Kshitip, who is smiling, "Typical."

After walking for just a few steps, the priest stops and points at a set of structures. "You see, that one is Kedarnath, Badrinath, Amarnath and the rest of the gods and goddesses." Rudra is not paying attention anymore and is looking in all directions to find a clue to the next piece.

"But, Baba, the shapes of Kedarnath and Badrinath nodules look exactly similar to real Kedarnath and Badrinath lingams and the mountain," notices Kshitip, and Rudra turns back after hearing this.

"Exactly. Now look behind the Badrinath formation. Do you see that small cave behind? It's of the same shape as the real Badrinath cave. Where you are standing is a natural cave. It must have taken thousands of years to take its shape. Now, if you say that people tempered things, it's not possible. It is stone, not wood. Every single millimetre of stone is made over hundreds of years. What you see here is a blueprint of the future. The blueprint of what was going to happen, they planned it here. This place is called the second home of Lord Shiva and all the gods and goddesses."

Pandit-ji looks at Rudra, who is having goose bumps. He continues, "You entered through the mouth of Sheshnaag. Currently, where you are standing, you can see spinal column type designs, but I didn't tell you that earlier because it would seem dramatic. Asking questions is good; a lot of things in our religion have become business. You are a man of science and logic, I understand, but these stalagmites and stalactites have been formed over thousands of years. Why did the process stop after taking the exact shapes of Badrinath and Kedarnath?

"I am a man of faith; I like to believe that Brahma planned everything here. Some say that the lotus is the seat of Lord Brahma and that place, the seat of Lord Shiva," he points in two directions. "But, if you don't want to believe in Shiva, Brahma or any other god, somebody must have intervened, right? There won't be so many coincidences at one place, logically."

Rudra stands in amazement after listening to such words from the mouth of someone he considered a blind, faithful devotee. "You are right, Pandit-ji. I do not believe in gods as we paint them or worship them, but I do believe that all the things which are happening or have happened suggest that everything doesn't behave the way we think they do. There must be a higher power—God, nature, or somebody."

"Hmm. The world is imperfect, humans are imperfect, nature is imperfect, so how can we expect our ancestors, history or religion to be perfect? There are different versions of the same story since a lot must have deteriorated by the time we started writing. Anyway, let's move ahead," opines the priest and starts walking.

Kshitip comes closer to Rudra and teases, "He schooled you quite nicely."

"But it was amazing," he replies, mesmerised by the priest's words.

"So, did you find anything interesting or worth exploring for our piece?"

"Anything interesting? Man, everything is mysterious and interesting here. I am unable to understand from where we should start," answers Rudra, and Kshitip agrees.

"So here is Devi Bhuvaneshwari, the goddess of the underworld," says the priest, pointing at a structure which looks a lot like a human body. "See, she has eyes, mouth, head, limbs, a bow on her shoulders and a halberd in her feet, which is also where she keeps all her weapons." The priest keeps speaking, but Rudra and Kshitip look at each other and nod.

Rudra whispers, "Who is going to divert his attention now?"

"I have an idea."

After that, the priest takes them to a place where many Brahm kamals and lots of small beads are on the ground. The priest says, pointing at those beads, "These are thirty-three crore gods and goddesses, drinking nectar. That's it, we cannot go beyond this point."

"Thanks a lot, Pandit-ji, for accepting our request and showing the temple to us." They both fold their hands and touch his feet. The priest turns and starts going back to the exit.

Rudra looks at Kshitip and frowns: *Go back.* They start ascending, and midway, Kshitip says, "Pandit-ji, I forgot my father, I mean, his ashes below. I need to go back and bring him."

"Oh, OK. Please go," he says with a remarkable calmness.

Kshitip climbs down and goes directly to the idol of goddess Bhuvaneshwari and starts inspecting the halberd, but doesn't find any opening. Though by touching the halberd, he understands that it has enough space inside to accommodate something. He looks at the idol again, and something comes to his head.

He jumps and touches the stone, which is supposed to be the strings of the bow on the goddess's right shoulder. The halberd opens with a sound of hiss. He puts his hand inside, and the moment he removes a leather pouch, it closes automatically. Kshitip puts that pouch in that clay pot and rushes to the exit.

Kshitip comes out of the tunnel and then the temple door and sees Rudra standing in the middle of the open area. Kshitip smiles and jerks his head, saying, "Mission accomplished," but Rudra doesn't react. *Why is he so serious?*

Kshitip keeps walking towards Rudra. He notices Rudra's backpack is not on his back. *What the hell!*

Kshitip watches Rudra closing his eyes as if something is going to happen that he doesn't want to see, and suddenly feels a piercing pain in his head and falls. With his fall, the pot also lands on the ground with a muffled sound and breaks into pieces. He tries to turn with that unbearable pain and sees a man lifting the piece and pointing a gun at him.

He passes out with the echo of Rudra's scream, "I need him, I need him, don't, don't!"

34

The Man in the Armani Suit

A barely conscious Kshitip feels hot and sweaty. His tired mind struggles to gain consciousness. Everything around him is shaking violently. He wants to shout and ask to stop this, as it is adding to his dizziness. He feels a sudden rush of nausea and turns to his right and throws up without even opening his eyes.

After vomiting, he feels better and recoils to his original position, on his back.

He opens his eyes, and everything is blurry. It takes a few seconds before his mind and eyes start to focus. There is light in the room—not too bright, not too dim—sufficient light. The walls are black, and as far as his confused mind can understand, they are not made of bricks or concrete; they look more like metal.

The whole room is shaking, like it is a train compartment. *Train compartment? It explains the light, metal walls and shaking.* He instantly bends his back and sits with his legs still stretched. There is a man in an impeccable suit and sunglasses, sitting next to him, on a separate seat, not reacting to anything at all.

"Kshitip, are you okay?" a voice asks. The voice has the warmth of care.

Kshitip turns to his right and feels relieved after finding Rudra sitting on a berth. "Yes, yes, Rudra. My head is bursting. What happened?"

Rudra looks at the man in the suit and then back at Kshitip. "You were hit on your head in Patal Bhuvaneshwar, and you were unconscious," Rudra talks quite freely in the presence of that man, which makes Kshitip a little uncomfortable. He rolls his eyes towards the man and asks Rudra in signs about the piece, pointing at his pocket. Rudra fails to understand, so Kshitip again gives him a different clue.

Before Rudra can speak, the man in the suit says, "It is safe. In fact, it is in Rudra's pocket." Kshitip is startled by the man's sudden response, but he is more surprised that the piece is with Rudra and thinks, *Why is the piece with Rudra and not him?*

"How is your head, Kshitip? Is it still hurting?" the man asks without any emotion. He is sitting upright with both his palms on his thighs.

Kshitip doesn't know how to respond and more importantly, why to respond, but he nods, showing, *I am OK.*

Kshitip is still in the same posture as before, and there is utter silence in the cabin with occasional thuds from outside. He realises it is not a train compartment but a truck with thick walls because no sound from outside can be heard except some muffled noise whenever the tires hit something. Kshitip wants to sit properly, so he slides his leg, but stops after seeing his vomit. He drags himself towards the door of the truck and puts his feet on the floor.

They all sit in silence. Kshitip and Rudra keep looking at each other. Finally, the man says, "So, Kshitip, now that you are feeling better, let's find out about the next location."

Kshitip looks at Rudra, who is also stunned. Rudra holds the piece in his right palm tightly.

"Who are you, and why are you after the pieces?" Kshitip asks.

The man doesn't speak for a few seconds and then says, "Let's find out about the next destination. We don't have time. Rudra, show us the piece."

"We will not decode the riddle unless you tell us what is going on!" screams Kshitip. The man smiles. *He has emotions.*

He replies, "You are not required to decode the riddles. Any of us who have little knowledge of ancient temples and Sanskrit can do it. You are alive just because Rudra pleaded for your life."

Kshitip remembers Rudra's words before he passed out in Patal Bhuvaneshwar. He thinks, *If they can solve the riddles themselves, we are not required. They are, anyway, going to kill me, but why is Rudra important? He is so important that because of his request, I am alive. Why is Rudra so special? Or is he one of them? No, no, it can't be. All the people believed him; Amatya couldn't be wrong. They have never been.*

Kshitip asks the man while staring at Rudra, "And, why is he so special?"

"Rudra, give me the piece," the man demands.

"Answer him. We have plenty of time on our hands," Rudra shoots back firmly.

"But he doesn't matter," the man replies, in a dangerously calm voice.

"He matters more than you think," says Rudra. Kshitip is confused and thinks, *Why is that man listening to Rudra?*

The man takes a deep breath and says, "It all started when they unearthed the chariot of Karna in Sinauli."

Kshitip's mouth opens in disbelief, and he asks, "How did you know that was Karna's chariot?"

The man calmly stares at Kshitip and then at Rudra. He doesn't like being interrupted. He takes a deep breath and replies, "The design of the chariots in the Mahabharata era was the same for royalties. People used to customise it with specific things like flags, leather or cotton to differentiate it from others. In the case of Karna, it was the wheels. His wheels were designed like the sun. The centre was like the sun, and the rest was designed like rays spreading outwards. He was, after all, the son of Lord Sun."

"I am sorry to interrupt again, but..." Kshitip says with hesitation. The man looks at him and stops talking. Kshitip resumes after realising that the man is waiting for him, "As far as I know, Karna came to know about his real parents just hours before the battle of Kurukshetra."

"So?"

Kshitip is perplexed but answers to put his point across, "If he came to know about his father, Lord Suryadev, just hours before the battle, how could he get his chariot's wheels designed like the sun from the beginning?"

"Oh. Karna was an ardent Lord Sun worshipper. Now that you know all this about Karna, don't you know that he was born with the earrings and armoured breastplate, like his father? These had the symbol of Lord Sun on them, and because of that, he worshipped Lord Sun from a very young age," the man answers.

Kshitip nods, avoiding the man's gaze.

The man continues, "The moment our master saw that chariot, he knew it was Karna's. I immediately left for Sinauli to have it in our possession." Kshitip listens to every word carefully. The word 'master' makes him curious, but a sudden thought hits his mind, *But the chariot is still there in possession of ASI.*

"May I ask a question, please?" Kshitip interrupts again. "But, sir, the chariot is still in ASI's possession."

"Yes, so?"

"But you went to seize it."

"Why would I seize a useless chariot? And how? I mean, where would I put a damn chariot?" answers the man in confusion.

"But, sir, you yourself said so," Kshitip says, scared of the man. The man keeps staring at him.

"He went there not to have that chariot in his possession but for something else which was in that grave," Rudra's voice booms in the silence of that cabinet.

"Oh, yes. When Arjuna killed Karna that day, he decided to bury his Gandeev along with Karna's chariot," the man replies. Kshitip's eyes widen after hearing that Gandeev is already in their possession. The man continues, "But we found something unexpected: a stone tablet. That tablet had some inscriptions. The language was not Sanskrit or any other spoken language, but hieroglyphics." He looks at Kshitip, who seems confused, so the man explains, "It means the tablet didn't have letters or words on it, but it had pictures inscribed."

"I know what a hieroglyph means, sir. Actually, it is said that hieroglyphs were invented in Egypt."

"You know what they said about the chariots in India? That Europeans brought the knowledge of chariot-making with them, and we learnt from them. The chariot excavated in Sinauli is much older than the first invasion by Europeans in India. These are not my emotions; the chariot was carbon dated, and it was found that it was constructed at least 500 to 1000 years before the attack of Alexander."

"Yes, I have also watched *Secrets of Sinauli*," says Kshitip without thinking.

"What is that?" asks the man innocently.

"What?" exclaims Kshitip. "Never mind."

The man shakes his head and says, "So, by this I meant to say that we have not been historians' favourite child. As they say, history is written by powerful people. When the world started writing down history, India was under the control of invaders. Others wrote our history, not us."

He sighs deeply and resumes the story, "So, I found that hieroglyph, and it took us three years to translate that. The day we translated it, we knew we were going to bring back the respect and pride of Bharatvarsh, which was taken from us." The man's chest swells with pride.

"What are you talking about? If you found that weapon, there would be no Earth, let alone Bharatvarsh. The weapon will destroy the world," Kshitip almost shouts.

The man doesn't react and says calmly, "You don't have the remotest idea of what is happening."

"No, Twenty-seven, *you* don't have the remotest idea. *You* are being lied to. *Your* master is using *you* in this. *You* are not ready to listen to anyone. *Your* stubbornness is going to destroy humanity," Rudra shouts, and his voice echoes in that small container for a while.

When it gets quiet, the man says, "You are supposed to be calm, and that is why I am following your requests; otherwise…" he minces his words and doesn't finish his sentence.

Rudra keeps staring at him, and Kshitip gets confused now.

The container stops, and the door opens with a hiss. The man stands up and walks to the door without looking at either of them. He opens the door and steps out of the vehicle.

The man informs his team, "Let's go towards Delhi. I will come with you."

"But what about them?"

"They are not going anywhere," says the man, locking the door.

Kshitip looks at Rudra with many questions and doubts in his eyes. He shoots the first question, "Why was he listening to you? Who is he?"

"Just keep in mind, they can obviously watch and listen to us, so don't do anything stupid," Rudra alerts Kshitip, and Kshitip scans the whole compartment with his eyes but fails to find anything in that light except some holes in the walls. He looks at Rudra, and Rudra says, "He is just a member of the Guruputras, extremely devoted to his master and will never listen to anything logical but only his master's orders. He is very skilful and knows everything about temples."

"Then why did they send you on a mission, not him?"

Rudra remains silent for some time and then says, "For wielding a mighty weapon, you need a mighty bow. They already have Gandeev." Rudra looks towards the door, avoiding Kshitip's piercing gaze, who is trying to understand where Rudra is leading with all this. Rudra continues, "You just don't need a special bow; you need a suitable man who can wield a bow like Gandeev."

"And you are that suitable man?" Kshitip asks spontaneously, almost mocking him.

"That's what they told me. That is why they kidnapped me in childhood to wield Gandeev one day."

"But why you?"

Rudra shifts his gaze from the door to Kshitip and says firmly, "Because I am the descendant of Arjuna."

"What are you talking about? How is it even possible? And when did you start believing all this stuff?" Kshitip stands up while talking.

"Now, I understand everything. Earlier, I thought I had special knowledge because of which I was kidnapped and kept under all this strict surveillance, but all these people know about this stuff. I am alive because I am meant to end this world," Rudra replies, almost blabbering, without even looking at Kshitip.

"If this is the case, you can deny. OK, my sentence makes this seem like a democratic process, but I mean we can do something so that you don't have to lift Gandeev. We can run away. You know very well that if it is true that you are the descendant of Arjuna and the weapon is what they think it is, and you can launch it, everything will end. Everything. If nothing works out and I have to kill you to stop this, I will not hesitate," Kshitip states very bluntly.

Rudra looks at Kshitip with a sad smile and whispers, "I know."

"At least tell me the riddle," says Kshitip in frustration. Rudra puts his hand in his pocket and takes out the red cloth. He throws it to Kshitip, who manages to catch it.

"Come on," Kshitip says angrily. He unwraps the piece and inspects it for the riddle. It is like a fishtail with an intricate hair-like design. When he looks carefully, he finds something written in those lines:

setemelti rudraksha awataranam

"Sir, they just read the riddle. Please focus on the video," says one of the guys sitting with the man.

"I can hear everything," he replies while pointing at his ears.

"I don't know what it is about, but wait… why did you give it to me? Now they also know the riddle," says Kshitip, panicking.

Rudra leans towards Kshitip and whispers, "The weapon can only be destroyed once assembled."

"What did he whisper? Fill it, and make sure they don't talk anymore. Anyway, now we know our destination," says the man in the Armani suit.

Suddenly, smoke starts to fill the container from vents. Rudra and Kshitip cover their noses and mouths but fall unconscious on their berths in less than a minute.

35

The Last Nail in the Coffin

Rudra opens his eyes and finds Kshitip already awake and sitting upright on his berth. Rudra also puts his feet on the floor and sits directly facing Kshitip. Kshitip's facial expressions are pretty clear; he is still angry.

"Kshitip, let's be practical. We are their captives. No matter what, they would have forced us to share the location, had they resorted to violence. I just did that to save time," Rudra says unapologetically.

"Save time? That's your excuse?" Kshitip barks at Rudra. Rudra doesn't like the way Kshitip shouts at him; he looks at Kshitip sharply. "We are dealing with an end-of-the-world scenario. Every minute of delay takes a minute away from billions of people."

"Then why did you read that loudly? You could have whispered or kept that to yourself only," says Rudra, controlling his anger. Kshitip opens his mouth to shout again, but stops.

He answers calmly, "You could have hinted, Rudra. I know it is my mistake. I am angry at myself more than I am at you."

"You remember what I whispered before passing out, right. Just keep that in mind and don't blame yourself. The container is not moving, which means they have solved the riddle for us, and we are already at our destination," says Rudra.

As soon as he finishes, the door of the container opens.

"Come out," comes a voice from outside.

They stand up and move towards the door. Rudra comes out of the container first, without any signs of fear. It is not very bright, so it must be either early morning or evening. He fails to understand. Kshitip also comes out, a little scared and a lot confused. He looks in all directions and finds a familiar stone structure. He elbows Rudra and points towards that structure with his eyes. A huge round stone is perched on a smooth slope.

"Mahabalipuram?" says Rudra, and the colour of his face suddenly turns pale yellow. Kshitip notices this change in Rudra but fails to understand why.

He repeats, "Mahabalipuram, Mahabalipuram, Mahabalipuram, Arjuna's penance. Yes, Mahabalipuram is famous for Arjuna's penance," and his face also turns pale yellow.

They look at each other, and Rudra says, "So is it true?"

"No, it can't be. Those are just stories. No, no, it can't be true," Kshitip behaves cynically.

"When Amatya Baahudhwaj said about annihilation, I never took it literally. But it is true," Rudra is in incredulity.

"No, no, Rudra. Yugas are mythology, not reality. These people deciphered the riddle incorrectly."

"When Marco Polo visited Santhome, which is now in present-day Tamil Nadu, he was regaled with the stories of the seven temples of Mahabalipuram. His descriptions found their way into the Catalan Atlas of the fourteenth century, which was put together by a Catalan Jew named Abraham Cresques. This map mentions Mahabalipuram as Setemelti, which is assumed to be an erroneous version of Sette Templi or seven temples. So, we are not incorrect. We are where the riddle wanted us to be," says the man in the Armani suit.

"Twenty-seven, you need to understand, your master is not looking for a weapon which will make him powerful again. It is a weapon which can destroy the whole world and no soul on Earth will be left to rule," Rudra screams.

"You have no idea about anything. You both are just pawns," says Twenty-seven.

"*You* are a pawn, Twenty-seven. You know about a map made by somebody in the fourteenth century. Don't you know about Arjuna's penance and the weapon associated with it?" Rudra shouts.

"Obviously, I know about Arjuna's penance and the weapon that he received."

"And you still believe your master simply wants to get his kingdom back?" Rudra gets angrier with every passing second due to Twenty-seven's ignorance.

"Don't shout, Rudra. You need to be calm. Our master will intimidate the world leaders with it, and eventually they will accept him as the supreme leader of the world."

"Come on, Twenty-seven. You are a knowledgeable and logical man; how can you even believe this? Do you think today's generation will even take it seriously? It's not just the younger generation, but older people too. There are other religions also, and they comprise a larger population than Hindus. Do you think they will ever believe that a bow and arrow can end the world? Everything is in your hands. Let's find the last piece and destroy it rather than handing it over to your master," Rudra pleads.

"Hahaha. You don't know my master. Just a glimpse of him will make people believe whatever he says." Twenty-seven remains stubbornly obedient to his master.

Rudra shakes his head in disbelief.

Twenty-seven says, "Let's not waste time. Start finding it."

"Twenty-seven, we are talking about the Pashupatastra here. It is the mightiest and most catastrophic weapon in Hindu mythology. Lord Shiva gave Arjuna this weapon after seeing his pure penance, but don't forget that it is the same weapon that Lord Shiva himself uses to end a yuga," Kshitip says, trying to convince him.

"You are the one who believes in gods, right? You should be more terrified in that case," Twenty-seven chuckles and jokes after seeing a dog nearby, "I hope this is not Lord Shiva."

"How dare you disrespect Shiva?" Kshitip plunges towards Twenty-seven, but two people catch him.

"I am referring to the story, you idiot. Let's go and find the piece. We don't have time anymore," says Twenty-seven and moves in the opposite direction of Krishna's butter ball.

"Which story?" asks the man holding Kshitip.

"Really?" says Kshitip.

"It is related to how Lord Shiva gave his Pashupatastra to Arjuna," answers Twenty-seven. "When Pandavas were in exile, their well-wishers suggested they use this time to please the gods to get more weapons for the war, which was inevitable. On the suggestion of Lord Krishna, Arjuna started worshipping Lord Shiva. After knowing this, Duryodhana sent a demon to distract Arjuna. The demon took the form of a wild boar and left for where Arjuna was.

"Lord Shiva saw all this, and he took the form of a hunter and left to save Arjuna from the demon's attack. When the demon approached, Arjuna shot an arrow and killed the demon. At the same time, Lord Shiva, as a hunter, also shot the boar. When both reached near the body of the boar, a fight broke out between them about who had killed the boar. Arjuna was no match for Lord Shiva, but he didn't give up easily and kept fighting.

"After a while, he realised the person with whom he was fighting was not a normal hunter but Lord Shiva himself, and he surrendered. Lord Shiva was moved by his gesture as Arjuna kept aside his ego and accepted the fact that a normal hunter was a better warrior than he was. He blessed him with the Pashupatastra, a weapon which cannot be launched on a weak opponent."

They all keep walking towards Arjuna's penance, the world's biggest open-air relief. Twenty-seven leads the pack, right behind him is Rudra with two large men on both sides, and Kshitip following them with two men in the same formation and one man in the back.

"Why are we going in this direction? Isn't the main temple complex in the opposite direction?" Kshitip asks.

"Do you remember what the riddle was? Setemelti rudraksha awataranam, right? And do you know what rudraksha means in this?"

Just for the sake of conversation, Kshitip prompts, "What?"

Twenty-seven narrates the story that comes from the Panchatantra.

There was a partridge who lived in a safe and warm hollow under a tree. Unfortunately, there was no proper source of food available near his home. So, he decided to go out in search of one. He soon found a field with an ample supply of food, so he did not return to his home for a few days and ate to his heart's content every day.

While the partridge was enjoying himself in the field, a hare happened to see the partridge's old home. He liked it and started living there.

One fine day, the partridge decided to return to his old home again. He was now very fat because of consuming a heavy diet.

When he saw the hare comfortably living in his home, he asked him to move out immediately. They had a long verbal argument but could not arrive at any decision. So, one day, they decided to approach someone else who could solve their problem.

They travelled far and wide, finally reaching the banks of the Ganges. There at a distance, they saw a tomcat. However, they were scared to approach him. The cat was very wicked. He quickly closed his eyes and stood on his hind legs, and started praying at the top of his voice. The partridge and hare were surprised as they saw a holy cat for the first time. They decided that he would be a good judge for their dispute.

When they approached him, he decided to take advantage of the situation.

He had slyly said, "My dear friends, I am so sorry, I am old and hard of hearing. Both of you come close to me and tell me your problem. I will do my level best to help you out." As soon as the partridge and the hare came near the wicked cat, he killed them both and had a lavish meal.

"The cat is called Rudraksha, a word which mocks such fraud holy men," explains Twenty-seven.

"What is the relation of this story to the riddle here, except the word 'rudraksha'?" Kshitip taunts him.

By this time, they have walked hundreds of metres in the dark, crossing walls and gates. Twenty-seven switches on a torch, flashes it on a massive rock in front of them, and says, "This rock is the finest example of the artistry of ancient India. It is called the 'Descent of the Ganges.' The artists who worked on this rock converted its defect into its highlight. Do you see this crack in the rock? It has been designed as the Ganges descending from heaven, and all the gods, demigods, sages, and animals are praying around it. Awataranam."

Kshitip nods his head as it definitely means the 'awataranam' word from the riddle, but the rudraksha part is still not clear. Twenty-seven flashes the torch at the bottom of the rock, just above the ground. On the lowest level, a cat stands on one foot with folded hands towards the sky.

Words automatically come out of Kshitip's mouth, "Rudraksha." Twenty-seven nods with a winning smile on his face.

"So, what next?" Twenty-seven asks, tapping his right foot. "Now, we know we are at the right place, but what are the next steps? How will the piece present itself to us?"

He looks at Rudra, who shakes his head, signing, *I don't know.* Kshitip expects Twenty-seven to ask him, too, but he doesn't even look at him. Twenty-seven moves towards the rock relief, calculating his steps and with utmost care touches the hands of the cat, Rudraksha, with his right hand, but nothing happens.

Twenty-seven turns back, hearing someone's soft laugh; it is Kshitip.

"Lakhs of people must have touched the hands of that cat by now. Had touching the hand been the way to find the piece, it would have been found the very next day," says Kshitip.

Twenty-seven comes closer, glaring at him to intimidate him and says calmly, "I know. Now you tell me how it works."

"There is no standard way of cracking the riddle; every time it's different. Mostly 'when' and 'what' were part of the riddle, but in this case, it is not clear, like the Lepakshi temple riddle. In that case, the riddle only led to the temple, and we had to find the 'what' ourselves," answers Kshitip.

"Try to find an abnormality. Something which is not common," Rudra adds.

"That cat is abnormal, don't you think?" asks one of the men.

"Yes, it is. But find more such things. Later, we will try to find which one we are looking for," says Rudra, moving towards the structure. One of the men tries to stop him, but Twenty-seven waves his hand to dismiss him. Kshitip also follows Rudra, and so do the rest of them.

36

And the Search Continues

"Half-human half-snakes, humans with lion's head, deer sitting like humans, people flying, dogs resembling lions, everything is abnormal here," Twenty-seven shouts. "We have been searching for the last 10-11 hours to gain nothing, absolutely nothing." For the first time, his men see him frustrated and get scared to their cores.

"Did you find anything?" Rudra whispers to Kshitip.

"No. You?" Kshitip shakes his head. "What are we missing here? I don't know why; something doesn't seem right with the cat."

"What do you mean?"

"I don't know, it seems like rudraksha means something else, other than the cat."

"Rudra means the sun, aksha means axis, right?" Rudra mumbles, and suddenly his eyes lit up. "Does it mean that the piece will present itself at a specific time of the day?"

"I don't know whether it will present itself or not, but something will happen at a specific time which will lead us to the piece. Stop talking and just keep your eyes focused the whole day. Let's not miss anything."

They wait for the sun to rise.

"Go see if there is coffee available somewhere. I need it badly," Twenty-seven orders one of his men and walks back to a wall nearby to sit against it. Rudra and Kshitip, along with the rest of the men, join him. Rudra and Kshitip face in the direction of the relief to ensure they don't miss anything when the sun rises.

The sky starts to light up and changes colour slowly. The first rays of the sun fall on the stone boulders. Kshitip and Rudra stand up in excitement, expecting something to happen. Twenty-seven notices their behaviour and gets intrigued. They move closer to the relief. The sunrays fall from the top to the bottom of the relief—the rays touch the tip of Arjuna's hands; nothing happens, then they illuminate the whole body of Arjuna; still nothing, then it goes down to the next row of designs and finally it touches the cat, Rudraksha, and yet nothing happens. With every passing moment, their hope starts to die down. They sit down again in dismay once the sunrays cover the whole relief. Twenty-seven also takes his seat.

"Where is the coffee? It has been more than an hour," asks Twenty-seven, looking for the man who went to get it.

After a while, that man returns with big packets in his hands. Before anybody can ask anything, he pours coffee into the cups and opens the other bag of freshly fried medu vadas. They all start having breakfast, but Rudra and Kshitip remain lost in their thoughts.

37

The Beginning of the End

It is about noon; the sun is shining overhead. Rudra, Kshitip and Twenty-seven stand just 5-6 feet from the rock. The rest stand a little far away, keeping an eye in all directions, but they are not vigilant enough as the tiredness has started showing its effects.

Even Rudra is having difficulty keeping his eyes open. He turns and goes to one of the men who has a bottle of water in his hand. He takes the bottle from his hand and starts washing his face. Twenty-seven also moves to that man to do the same. Kshitip sits with his hands wrapped around his knees, facing the rock. In frustration and dismay, he notices Rudra and Twenty-seven washing their faces, and he also stands up to go there.

While standing up, still looking at the rock, the moment his eyes come to the level of Rudraksha's head, he notices that its hand is shining. His tired mind dismisses it because the sun is exactly in the centre of the sky. The moment he is about to turn his head away, he observes something bizarre from the corner of his eye. The hands of one of the carvings on the relief glitter unrealistically—there can't be such coincidences; it must mean something. He starts going away from the rock and jumps.

Rudra notices it and walks briskly towards Kshitip, and Twenty-seven follows them.

"You noticed something?" Rudra whispers in Kshitip's ears.

"I think I know," says Kshitip, looking at the idol of a man in the middle of the rock, on the right side of the symbolic Ganga crack.

Twenty-seven comes closer to Rudra and Kshitip, "What is it?"

"Shhhhh," Rudra shushes Twenty-seven and pretends to stare at the relief. Twenty seven is taken aback by this. He quietly takes two steps back and looks at his men.

Kshitip whispers in the faintest voice, "Distract them. This is the time. We have only a few seconds."

After hearing this, Rudra turns to the rest of them with a plan in mind, but before he can do anything, a loud noise of whirring blades of a helicopter fills the atmosphere. All those men put their hands in their overcoats to grab their weapons and look up. Twenty-seven signals his men to lie down under nearby trees, facing the sky.

Kshitip and Rudra grab this opportunity with both hands.

"You see, at this particular time of the day, the hands of these three particular carvings are shining, that cat's, that man beside the symbolic Ganga and Bhagirath's. Now, we must decode it before the sun changes its position," says Kshitip, pointing at the three carvings.

"Touching all three simultaneously at this particular moment can be the key," Rudra almost immediately says.

"But, one person cannot touch all three points, Bhagirath is too far away," Kshitip mumbles, lost in his thoughts.

Rudra sits down near the cat, closes one eye to focus, looking towards Bhagirath's carving, and says, "All these points are collinear, but what are they pointing at?"

He keeps looking above Bhagirath's carving, but there is nothing peculiar. Kshitip also tries to find some abnormality on that side of the rock. Rudra thinks of going closer to Bhagirath's carving and tries to stand up. He puts his right hand on the ground for support, but his hands slip and he falls. He realises his fingers are inside something.

He turns his head and notices two small slots at the bottom of the rock. They are big enough to fit a man's palms. Something comes to his mind, and he looks downwards from the second carving's hand towards Rudraksha's hand and freezes in excitement—one of the slots is collinear too.

Rudra almost runs to Kshitip, grabs his hands and says, "What we are looking for is not above, it's beneath the rock," pointing at the slots.

"What are we supposed to do with those?"

"I think it is for lifting the rock," Rudra says hesitantly, not believing his own words.

"OK, let's do it. We don't have time anyway, the light on the hands is fading." Kshitip agrees without thinking who will do this impossible job of lifting a thousand-ton heavy rock.

He puts his hands in the slots and gathers all his strength to lift it. Rudra stands behind him, not waiting for the rock to tilt but thinking of a real solution.

He hears a roaring sound, turns towards Kshitip, and cannot believe what he is witnessing; a major part of that rock has slid open like a mystery door, and Kshitip is standing in front of it, blocking the view.

He immediately pushes Kshitip to see what is inside. It's dark, but it looks like a stairwell. Twenty-seven also hears the roaring sound and finds the scene unbelievable. He asks his men to follow Rudra and Kshitip. They all run towards the open door. Rudra and Kshitip enter, so do three of Twenty-seven's men, but before he can enter, the rock slides back to its original position.

38

The One Who Wants You Dead

Vahanus runs uncomfortably and breathlessly in that extremely cold, dark, endless alley. With that massive hump on his back, why wouldn't he be breathless? The distance that he needs to cover in that tunnel is about 250-300 metres. It is so narrow that even two people can't walk shoulder to shoulder. To add to the misery, it is lit by the frail light of oil lamps, fixed several metres apart. Vahanus stops at one of the lamps, perhaps to catch his breath. He smiles as he moves forward.

He turns to the wall where the oil lamp is mounted. It seems like there's a doorknob on the wall. It is impossible to say confidently in that darkness.

Vahanus says with a grin, "Finally, this dungeon will be used after 5000 years," and he resumes his uncomfortable run.

"Master, they have opened the gate," Vahanus says, his eyes fixed on the ground.

"Hmm, finally.".

"I have started the preparations," Vahanus says with excitement in his voice.

"What preparations? No preparation is required. Are you arranging the pyre for the dead? The whole world is going to become a giant pyre today," the master says with an eerie calmness in his voice, looking towards one of the walls of his gigantic room. "You have served well, Vahanus. We are just moments away from the end. Go, do what pleases you."

"Oh, my master, from the day I was born till today, I have only enjoyed one thing, serving you. That is the only objective of my life, the only thing that gives me pleasure," Vahanus says with trembling lips. Suddenly, he clenches his fist, and his pitch increases in anger. "I was born to witness this very day. How many Vahanus before me died with the hope in their hearts to see this day and take this revenge, which we have been waiting for, for 5000 years. No, I am not going anywhere, please allow me to stay with you, grant me this honour to die beside you, please, please," Vahanus pleads with his bowed head.

The master comes closer to him and touches his head. "Awashya, Vahanus. Awashya."

"Did you notice?" Rudra asks.

"What?" Kshitip questions back.

"Suddenly, the air has turned cold," says Rudra, and Kshitip nods. The three mercenaries, who are walking behind, also sense this sudden shift in temperature.

"We must have been walking for at least thirty minutes. How long will your lights last?" Kshitip asks one of the mercenaries about the torches on their automatic rifles.

"Very long. Keep moving," says one of them and pushes Kshitip.

All of them are extremely exhausted due to the lack of rest and continuous journey, but sleep is miles away from their eyes because of the circumstances. They continue walking in that cold, dark, endless alley. The tunnel is immeasurably long and so narrow that even two people can't walk shoulder to shoulder. It is lit by the frail light of oil lamps, fixed several metres apart.

"Every time we reach a temple, the piece presents itself after finding the solution to the riddle. Where is the piece? Are you thinking the same thing that I am thinking?" Rudra asks nervously, adjusting the bag on his back.

"I also think, today is the day," Kshitip replies.

The first guy, leading the group, stops abruptly and sets the brightness and range of his rifle's torch. After 20-30 seconds, he says what they all have already guessed by now. "The tunnel ends in another 300 metres tops."

The sudden rush of terror in their veins makes their heart beat so loud that in that dark and silent tunnel, the heart beats can be heard like ticking clocks. The first guy proceeds further, and the rest follow. The fear of the unknown forces them to take longer to cover these 300 metres.

When they reach the end of the tunnel, towards their right, a huge gate awaits. Before they can think of how to open the gate, it opens on its own.

The gate leads to a humongous room which is ornamented like a palace. The whole room's floor is covered with an expensive red carpet so thick that it feels like walking on a bed of roses. The walls have big paintings, weapons, and exquisitely carved animal heads. Several decked-out mannequins are covered in armour, with various weapons in hand. The room is filled with pillars everywhere.

They all walk carefully forward, and suddenly the man leading the pack falls flat on his stomach. Rudra thinks that something hit the man, so he ducks down instinctively.

"Master, I didn't do it on purpose. I looked at you by mistake. Forgive me, forgive me," pleads the man.

Rudra opens his eyes and lifts his head after hearing the man plead. The man is begging with his face on the ground and both hands stretched out towards one of the pillars. Rudra turns his head towards the pillar and finds a man's bare feet behind it. Rudra looks up to see his face, but due to the lighting in the room, he cannot see him. He notices the man is wearing a white dhoti and is incredibly tall, at least eight feet.

The tall man moves towards the man lying on the floor and sits near his head, putting his right hand on it. He says, "Stand up. You didn't do it willingly. Go watch the gate." The man immediately stands up and, without looking anywhere, goes directly to the gate.

When the tall man sits near the pleading man, that is the perfect moment for Rudra to look at the man's face. At that moment, the master is sitting face-to-face with Rudra, and while instructing that man, he looks into Rudra's eyes, and Rudra stares back at him in utter fear.

Fear, because he thinks he knows who the master is. But it can't be, because that person is just a mythological character, not a real human being. Everything is so distinctly and excruciatingly like him, though. He is taller than eight feet, at least 9-10 feet, with the body of a warrior and that famous blood stream from the forehead. It can't be anybody other than Ashwatthama. But nobody can live for 5000 years. A curse by Krishna and a head jewel like the third eye—all this cannot be true. It's illogical.

"Greetings, Rudra," the master articulates.

Rudra wants to ask how he knows his name, but his mouth goes dry. It feels like he doesn't have control over his body—his mouth is wide open, and he is not sitting but almost lying on the floor. Kshitip has been watching this from two metres; he is shell-shocked too.

The master stands up and wipes his forehead with a cloth kept nearby on a table. He turns to Kshitip, "You are the other guy, huh? Put him in the ekank kaksha."

Vahanus appears out of nowhere. He asks one of the mercenaries to hold Kshitip, and leads the way. "I need him, I need him," Rudra keeps pleading, but Vahanus doesn't flinch, and they drag Kshitip out of the room.

"Are you going to kill him?" Rudra asks the master, point blank.

The master doesn't expect this question, but he answers, "Quite contrary. He is going to be put in the safest room in this whole world. No catastrophe can enter that room. When we end this world, he will be the last one to die." The master has no emotions on his face.

Rudra sits on the floor like a dead duck, his bag by his side. He remains there for quite some time, and then Vahanus comes back with the mercenary. Kshitip is nowhere to be seen.

The master waves towards the bag, and Vahanus gets it. Rudra doesn't even notice. Vahanus sits closer to Rudra and says, "Don't stress. Everything is going to end. Everything, you know." He says it slowly, almost like poetry.

"What did you do with Kshitip? Where is he?" Rudra demands loudly.

"He is safe. He is in the safest place on Earth today. Now you stand up and finish the work," replies Vahanus, grabbing Rudra by his arm.

"Vahanus," the master says softly but with a warning. "Show some respect."

Vahanus leaves Rudra's arm and says, "My master is still talking about showing respect to you, whose ancestors killed my master's father dubiously. They took away his mind jewel, and cursed him to live till eternity with a bleeding head. He will avenge everything today. Stand up and assemble the weapon!"

"I can't."

"You can't or you won't?" Vahanus asks in anger.

"Believe me, I want to. I need to destroy it. But I don't know how to assemble it," Rudra barks like a dog in rage, staring into Vahanus's eyes. Vahanus becomes red in fury and lifts his hand to hit Rudra, but stops on Ashwatthama's signal.

"Take everything out of the bag," Ashwatthama orders Vahanus. And they start emptying the bag.

First comes out the hard hat with torch, then pulleys and string, followed by the teeth of lions from the Kailash temple, rods from the Samod and Sun temples, and the brick from Harishchandragad. They segregate everything and keep the parts of the weapon in one place.

"Now assemble," says Vahanus, throwing the brick on the ground. It breaks, and a shiny metallic crescent moon comes out of it.

"But I don't know how to," says Rudra in frustration. "Please bring Kshitip. We have been able to do things only because of our synergy. I beg you, bring him, please." Vahanus looks at Ashwatthama in confusion, who gives him a nod.

Vahanus leaves the room and after a few moments, returns with Kshitip. Rudra tries to go closer to Kshitip, but one of the mercenaries stops him.

"Help me assemble the weapon," Rudra requests.

Kshitip looks at Rudra and asks, "Have you lost your marbles? How can you even think of assembling the weapon?"

Rudra goes closer to Kshitip's ears and whispers, "The weapon can only be destroyed once it is assembled."

"Says who?" Kshitip retorts. Vahanus tries to get closer to them as he cannot hear anything, but Ashwatthama asks him not to.

"The man in the temple. I told you this," Rudra responds.

"What makes you think he was not with these guys?"

"Trust me, Kshitip, he told me how to destroy it. If we don't do it now, this fear will hover over humanity's head for thousands of years. This is the time," Rudra pleads.

"Did he tell you how to destroy it?" Kshitip asks with a glimmer of hope in his eyes.

"Yes, Kshitip, yes!"

"How?"

"Enough!" shouts Ashwatthama, "Assemble it. I don't have patience left for this chit chat." His booming voice echoes in the hall. When a ten-foot-tall, 5000 years old, mythical man with bleeding head shouts, you don't shout back. But Kshitip cannot control his anger for long and stares back at Ashwatthama with that enviably brave expression in his eyes.

Ashwatthama notices his gaze and starts approaching Kshitip. Rudra realises it and forcefully turns Kshitip's head to the bag and asks, "How to proceed?"

Rudra feels a soft fabric brushing on his left hand's finger. Ashwatthama is standing right behind him, looking at Kshitip from almost twice his height. Rudra clutches Kshitip's hand, asking him to calm down and focus on the job at hand.

"Do you think, uhh, keeping them one after the other will assemble it?" Rudra says innocently, just to start assembling the weapon and avoid Ashwatthama's fury.

Kshitip looks up at Rudra and says, "And, where do you think these teeth would fit?"

He is right, they have various pieces—one crescent moon, two rods, a fish tail. The fish tail is obviously the rear end of the arrow, the two-foot-long rod is the middle, and the crescent moon is probably the head. That's what they have seen on television, but what about those lion teeth and the ball from the Kailash temple's lion?

"Do you think chanting a specific mantra can be a solution?" Rudra thinks out loud. Vahanus' eyes light up.

Kshitip questions, "Which mantra? Isn't it too vague?"

Vahanus nods his head in the distance.

Rudra pushes his theory, "What about any mantra or shloka that mentions the Pashupatastra or the end of yugas?"

"There are plenty," answers Kshitip, but after a pause, corrects himself, "Don't know about the Pashupatastra, but about the end of times and civilisation, there are many shlokas."

Rudra thinks for a while and then says, "Do you know the mantra which Ravana chanted to please Shiva when he went to Kailash? I mean, I am talking about that Kailash shaking episode."

"Rudrashtakam," says Ashwatthama.

"Oh, yes," says Rudra spontaneously, "I should have asked you; weren't you born in the very image of Lord Shiva himself?"

Ashwatthama looks at him, surprised. "Do you know this?"

"Everyone who has read or watched the Mahabharata knows this," says Rudra. Ashwatthama nods and turns away.

After a few seconds, Ashwatthama suggests, "I don't think it is about any mantra. There must be some kind of blueprint to assemble the weapon."

"But, if it so, where can we find a blueprint?" Rudra murmurs. "On any of the clue parchments?"

Kshitip jumps in excitement, "Where is the bag?"

"Everything from the bag is already on the floor, in front of you."

"Not everything, tell me where the damn bag is!" Kshitip shouts in desperation.

Vahanus throws the bag towards Kshitip.

Kshitip says to Rudra, catching the bag, "Do you remember the print of the pillar's bottom from the Lepakshi temple? It had random shapes on it, in addition to the clue. What if that's the blueprint?"

Ashwatthama looks towards Vahanus, who bows his head in a last goodbye.

Kshitip takes out the paper and unfolds it, in proper light near a lamp. They can clearly see the shapes, such as teeth, a tail and other parts. Rudra and Kshitip start placing the pieces on the paper.

Kshitip whispers as quietly as humanly possible, while arranging the pieces, without looking at Rudra, "The weapon is almost assembled, all hopes are on you, Rudra."

Rudra whispers back, "No matter what, don't wield the Pashupatastra."

"You are going to wield Gandeev, Rudra, not me. You are the descendant of Arjuna," Kshitip hisses again.

The parts lying on the paper start glowing. Kshitip looks at Rudra finally. Rudra lifts his head and says, "You go to that jail silently." He finishes the rest of the sentence in his head, *I will find a way to destroy it or die. This weapon will never be launched.*

Every eye in the room is fixated on the weapon, except the confused eyes of Kshitip and the determined ones of Rudra.

The intensity of light increases to such a level in a fraction of a second that nobody can keep their eyes open. With a thundering sound, the light mellows down, allowing people to reopen their eyes.

First, Rudra opens his eyes and sees the weapon—an arrow with a crescent moon as its head and attached to that crescent head are two bent metals whose other ends are attached to each other, forming a V shape and their common end is connected with a long, straight rod which has a fishtail in the end. The weapon is levitating and glowing. The paper below is completely blank now.

Kshitip notices that the ball from the Kailash temple is still in his hands. He thinks, *Is it not part of the weapon?*

Vahanus comes running with two guards. He cries, "Catch him and put him in the ekank kaksha," pointing at Kshitip.

"No, Vahanus, no," says Ashwatthama, shaking his head, and Rudra's heart starts thumping like a tornado. Vahanus looks at Ashwatthama, confused. Ashwatthama looks at Rudra resolutely and says, "I must appreciate Vishnugupta for such an elaborate planning. Wow!"

He looks at Kshitip and says, "Oh, you are not aware? That's the best thing about good plans, even the key members don't know everything about it." He turns to Rudra and continues, "But you know. Did you know from the beginning? I don't think so, if the descendant doesn't know, how would you?"

Kshitip is dumbstruck.

Ashwatthama comes close to Kshitip and says, "You know, it was all planned in such a way that only a descendant of Arjuna could get all the pieces. Only a descendant could press the eyes of the snake in the Kailash temple, put the Shiva linga in the void in the Harishchandragad temple, see the shining part on the relief or lift it in Mahabalipuram. Most importantly, only a descendant could read the messages on the pieces. Only the descendant could assemble the weapon." All the events start flashing in front of Kshitip's eyes, and he starts thinking, *In the Lepakshi temple, Rudra could not read the clue on the paper. Yes, it was I who pushed the eye of* the *snake. I read all the clues.*

He remembers Rudra throwing the last piece to him in the armoured van to read the inscriptions. He sees the lights; he lifts the rock. His head starts spinning because it's Rudra who knows how to destroy the weapon, not him. And there is no chance that they are going to let them talk.

Rudra has a knife in his hands. He plunges at Ashwatthama, but now there are too many suspicious people around to allow something so obvious. Ashwatthama stands tall, without any iota of distress in his eyes. Two of the guards intercept Rudra at the time the knife is only a few millimetres from Ashwatthama's chest.

Ashwatthama looks into Rudra's eyes and turns.

He walks a few steps towards the wall and says, "I was cursed by Krishna to live until the end of Kali yuga. I have spent 5000 years on Earth with this bleeding head and wounds on my body, which do not heal. I have seen the worst of this world—diseases, wars, crusades, erupting volcanoes, tsunamis," with every word, the pitch of his voice is increasing, "And you are trying to kill me with a knife? I have lost count of the calamities that I have planned to end this world so that I could find peace. I plagued this world with the same disease that I have, and I transmitted it to humans; hundreds of thousands of people died. There were dead bodies everywhere, and it seemed like the end of the world, but these humans survived. We helped Oppenheimer in creating atomic bombs, and all he remembered was कालोऽस्मि लोकक्षयकृत्प्रवृद्धो. And what did they do with a weapon so mighty?

"They just bombed two cities and signed a peace treaty after that. I showed these scientists the path to the creation of the God particle and even funded the Large Hadron Collider project, but it was shut down before they could intensify the trials. These are just the smallest examples. I tried to get my redemption and die, but every time, I failed." Ashwatthama turns towards Rudra. "And you know, who didn't let me succeed? Your Vishnugupta. But finally, he is dead. Now, there is nobody to stop me," he sighs with a sense of victory and relief.

Rudra and Kshitip look at each other with helplessness in their eyes. Each of them tries to find any emotions for Vishnugupta in the other's eyes, but they don't have any. They don't even know who he was.

Ashwatthama says after a pause, "And you are trying to kill me with a knife."

"You will not succeed. You know that already," says Rudra with a firm voice. Vahanus jumps in, slaps him, and orders his men to take him to jail. Two men hold and drag him out of the hall.

Rudra keeps on shouting, "You will not succeed. I know, you will fail. The weapon will not launch. Kshitip, no matter what, the weapon must not be launched." Kshitip stands as if his soul has left his body already.

39

This Is the End, Your Only Friend

Vahanus has come back after putting Rudra in the ekank kaksha. He gasps and sweats profusely, which clearly shows that Rudra has not allowed them to put him behind bars easily. He catches his breath and orders two of his men to bring Kshitip towards one of the walls.

Kshitip has been in trance all this while, but now he fights back to gain control of his body. Two men hold him and drag him to the wall. Near the wall is a grand table with a shiny red cloth spread on it. The table is at least ten metres long and five metres wide. Its height is about five feet. And why won't it be? It is Ashwatthama's table. Kshitip stands beside that table with his knees bent, head hanging low, and two men holding his arms. He notices the huge table, but due to his posture, he is unable to see what is on it. He gets on his feet, straightens his knees and lifts his head to see the thing kept on the table—a massive bow with many strings.

"Pick it up," Vahanus commands, but it seems Kshitip can't even hear him. "I said, pick the damn bow," Vahanus shouts. Kshitip doesn't flinch.

Ashwatthama rushes to lift the bow and forcefully puts it in Kshitip's hands. The bow must be at least five feet, a foot less than Kshitip's height.

"Fix it," orders Ashwatthama.

Kshitip lifts his head and looks at Ashwatthama, but there is no hate or anger in his eyes, just plain and confused eyes. Surprisingly, he starts fixing the strings on the bow. He does it effortlessly. The bow is ready.

"Wield the Pashupatastra," Ashwatthama says with hope in his voice. Vahanus pushes Kshitip towards the levitating Pashupatastra. Kshitip behaves like someone who doesn't have control over his body. He stretches his hand to lift the Pashupatastra. He holds it and puts it on the strings.

Vahanus folds his hands, bows his head and starts praying. All the guards fall on their knees and mumble something, but Ashwatthama stands tall, bare-chested, right in front of Kshitip. Kshitip stretches the strings with the Pashupatashtra on it. The Pashupatastra glows even more.

"Hit me," shouts Ashwatthama.

Kshitip turns towards Ashwatthama to aim. The moment he takes aim at Ashwatthama, the Pashupatastra stops glowing and starts getting heavier. In just a few seconds, it gets too heavy for Kshitip and falls to the ground. Ashwatthama witnesses everything anxiously. The Pashupatastra doesn't even bounce; it just falls flat. The moment it falls, Kshitip fails to control his hands, and his grip loosens on the strings.

Gandeev, which is known for its mighty power, is launched. It causes a deafening noise with volcanic vibrations around. The ground starts to shake, the paintings start falling, followed by the roof and the walls.

Kshitip looks around and finds Ashwatthama standing in front of him, staring at him, but nobody else can be seen. A massive piece of the roof is about to fall on Kshitip, but he escapes his death and hides underneath the table. Ashwatthama still stands the same.

"What have I done?" Kshitip curses himself. "I caused the destruction, what was I thinking?"

A cloud of dust covers everything around. Kshitip removes his shirt and ties it around his face to avoid inhaling dust. The dust and darkness engulf everything in that cave.

40

Friend or Foe?

Kshitip fights for his life. He doesn't get sufficient air as huge boulders have cut him off from the outside. The ancient table underneath which Kshitip has taken shelter is still intact, but from all four sides, stones have entered. The space is not even sufficient for him to sit. The sound of everything falling and breaking has stopped.

He pushes the boulders, but they are too big. He tries with all his might, but fails. He is filled with guilt for killing millions of people. Ultimately, he sits down in that cramped space, puts his head between his knees and starts crying.

All the memories of his life flash in front of his eyes; memories that don't matter. Fake parents, fake friends, fake education, fake life, no love, no care, nothing. And then he realises he is not afraid of losing his life as there is nothing meaningful in his life anymore. He has failed miserably to fulfil the sole aim of his life. He cries as millions are dying because of him. He feels the oxygen scarcity, starts gasping and falls on the floor.

Kshitip opens his tired eyes, tries to push some stones, vainly, and closes his eyes again. He reopens his eyes after hearing the sound of falling stones. The space for him is shrinking further, and he closes his eyes, thinking about this destitute end of his life.

A big stone of at least ten kilograms hits his right knee, and Kshitip screams in pain. He sits on stones with folded feet, knees almost touching his forehead with an arched back, curled like a ball. The space further reduces. He prays to God, with closed eyes, in his last minutes, but suddenly, his lungs feel alive as he inhales sufficient oxygen. There is a hole in the heap of stone debris, and a hand reaches out to him.

"Kshitip, Kshitip, are you alright?" Rudra asks, touching Kshitip's head. There is no movement, but Kshitip's lungs are getting much-needed oxygen. Rudra pulls out his hand and starts removing the debris like a madman.

In less than a minute, he removes sufficient stone to make space to pull Kshitip out of it. He uses all the energy he has and gets Kshitip out. Rudra notices that Kshitip's chest is heaving. He sits down near his body to catch his breath.

Rudra hears some stones rumbling nearby. He lifts his head and sees some movement through the dim light coming from the hole in the roof. The stones are falling outwards. Rudra shivers in fear, realising what is about to come out of that heap. Even in that dim light, identifying Ashwatthama's body is no brainer.

"You idiots, you wasted my only opportunity of salvation." Ashwatthama is devastated. "Living with a bleeding head, scorching pain, blisters on the body for 5000 years is not just a curse but the biggest punishment anybody has ever received in the history of mankind. Yes, I made a terrible mistake by killing their unborn child. They could have killed me or punished me in any other way, but Krishna had to curse me with this brutality.

I was a god-fearing man, a worshipper of Shiva and practitioner of dharma.

"They killed my great father and their own teacher with cunningness, and they became the rulers of the land. When I took revenge for my father's death with the same astuteness, I was cursed by a god. Every person I ever loved died thousands of years ago. The last person I knew in this world died today." He lifts his head and looks at Rudra with rage in his eyes.

He has dust all over his face and body, blood flowing from his head and red eyes. He looks like a pure demon. He stands up and strides towards Rudra. Before Rudra can stand, Ashwatthama clutches Rudra's neck and lifts him in the air. Rudra throws his hands and feet towards Ashwatthama to hit him. Though he is six feet tall, his limbs are no match for Ashwatthama's. Slowly, his movements die down.

Kshitip opens his eyes and takes a few seconds to adjust, but he doesn't have time. He notices the scene around him, picks up a big stone, and hits Ashwatthama's toes. Ashwatthama seethes in pain and throws Rudra about ten feet away. He goes on to hold Kshitip by his neck. Kshitip has already been suffering from a lack of oxygen. He doesn't have the strength in his body to retaliate.

Rudra stands up and starts throwing rocks at Ashwatthama—at his body, face, everywhere. It irritates Ashwatthama, and he leaves Kshitip to protect his face with his hands while trying to get hold of Rudra. Rudra keeps running away from Ashwatthama while hitting him with stones. By this time, Kshitip also stands up and starts doing the same.

Ashwatthama gets attacked by two sides. The hits are not life-threatening, but any stone that hits his face is painful as hell.

Ashwatthama shouts, "You insects are not worth hitting, but you have forced me to do this." He picks up a huge boulder and throws it at Kshitip. It hits him on his head, and Kshitip falls flat.

"Kshitip," shouts Rudra, but he can't do anything except keep throwing the stones as Ashwatthama is standing between him and an injured Kshitip. Rudra picks up a stone, but before he can throw it, he realises it is vibrating in his hand. He turns his head towards the stone in his hand and notices it is the round-shaped stone from the Kailash temple.

Ashwatthama clasps Rudra by surprise and lifts him in the air. The stone in his hand shines and vibrates more and more, attracting Ashwatthama's attention. Rudra moves the stone towards Ashwatthama's head.

Ashwatthama looks into Rudra's eyes. Rudra blinks and says, "Yes, you are right."

Ashwatthama lets Rudra touch his forehead, and the moment the stone touches Ashwatthama's head, its outer shell disappears, and a shining red stone emerges. It automatically fits in his forehead in the same spot, which is bleeding.

All the blisters and the blood on his body disappear. The muscles on his face, arms, legs, chest, and back start healing themselves. Just in a few seconds, instead of a weathered warrior, a prince stands in front of Rudra.

The prince is no longer in the mood for combat; he is grateful. He folds his hands and says with tears, "Thank you. Thank you. Thank you."

Rudra looks at him in bewilderment with his mouth open. Ashwatthama turns to Kshitip, lifts him on his shoulders and asks Rudra, "Please take the Pashupatastra. We must leave or else he will die."

Rudra picks up the Pashupatastra, wraps it with Kshitip's shirt, ties his own shirt on its end, and puts it on his back like a sling bag. He starts following Ashwatthama, but suddenly stops. "What about Gandeev?"

"Oh, yes." Ashwatthama picks up Gandeev and walks towards the corridor.

Rudra warns, "That whole corridor has been destroyed. We should walk to the top from where the light is coming. We will manage Gandeev. I don't think there is even a walkable path in that direction."

Ashwatthama smiles at his naivety and says, "Two weapons that together destroy the world *must* not be close to each other. Anyway, we are not going to the corridor."

Though the roof has fallen off in places, the pillars are still standing tall. Ashwatthama stops near one of the pillars and does something, and the pillar splits open. He puts Gandeev in the pillar and turns to Rudra. By the time he turns, the pillar returns to its original state.

Ashwatthama climbs the stones to reach the roof effortlessly as if he is strolling in a park, but Rudra struggles to jump from one stone to another. Just after reaching the hole in the roof, Ashwatthama jumps out with Kshitip on his shoulders and disappears.

When Rudra reaches there, he realises he can't even get to the edge of the opening in the roof. He tries multiple times, but the edge is completely out of his reach, and there is no sign of Ashwatthama. He starts panicking. *Did I trust the wrong person?* The rock he is standing on is also shaking; it can't take more hits. Rudra has only one attempt left with the heavy Pashupatastra on his back.

He gathers all his leftover energy and jumps with all his might, but that gap is too big for him. After reaching the maximum possible point, he starts going down. At that time, a hand comes down and holds him.

"Sorry, sorry, I didn't realise that the gap was so big for you," says Ashwatthama, apologetically, pulling Rudra.

Rudra comes up and lies down on his back, breathing violently with closed eyes. Ashwatthama watches him with admiration in his eyes.

"Who is your father, Rudra?" Ashwatthama asks suddenly.

Rudra opens his eyes immediately. "I don't know, actually," he says blankly, trying to understand Ashwatthama's expressions.

"Hmm, I guessed so," says Ashwatthama with an expression which cannot be explained.

Rudra asks spontaneously, "Do you know?"

Ashwatthama replies immediately, "No, no, how would I know?"

"I think you do."

"I look like someone who knows everything, Pra..." he stops abruptly without finishing his sentence and instead says, "We need to hurry, else he will not live."

Ashwatthama stands up quickly and walks in a narrow walkway. Rudra is still trying to process what happened, but he starts following him silently.

They continue on the walkway for some time, and then Rudra notices the end of the tunnel. Ashwatthama keeps walking, about ten metres ahead of Rudra. As the tunnel is sufficiently lit, Rudra can see no alternate path at the end, but he trusts Ashwatthama now. After reaching the end, Ashwatthama pushes the wall, and it opens like a hinged door, and they get out into the open.

Rudra hears the temple bell. He turns around and realises that they have come out through the rear wall of a temple. *But why the hell is it so cold? It's summertime, and when we entered the tunnel today, even the morning sun was scorching hot.*

There are trees everywhere, and the sky also doesn't seem right.

"Where are we?" Rudra asks. Ashwatthama doesn't reply. "Please tell me where we are?"

"You will find out. You have only a few moments left with me, people are not accustomed to seeing a ten-foot-tall human," answers Ashwatthama, walking ahead cautiously.

Rudra is perplexed. He wants an answer, but he doesn't pry on it. "Where should I take Kshitip for treatment?"

Ashwatthama looks at him strangely, "You just saved the whole world, and you are asking where you should take him for treatment? I will leave you on the road, from there you will find many people to help you. After all, it is the land of the Gods."

Rudra hears his last sentence but avoids asking the same question again. He instead asks, "How am I supposed to destroy this weapon, the Pashupatastra?"

Ashwatthama stops and turns his head to look at Rudra's face. After a few seconds, he starts walking again, and Rudra gets irritated.

Rudra asks again, this time firmly, "Tell me something, I need to get done with it and go back to my life."

Ashwatthama doesn't stop this time and says while walking, "You have lived your life, now it is not yours anymore. In fact, you never had a life..." His sentence is cut short by the horn of a vehicle. There is a road nearby, hardly 100-150 metres from them.

With every step towards the road, Rudra's heart races as he knows the only person who can help him can leave anytime and before he leaves, he wants something out of him. Rudra stops and shouts, "Please help me, I am tired, I need your help. Tell me where I should go to destroy this weapon?"

Ashwatthama comes to Rudra, puts his hand on Rudra's shoulder and says, "I have always targeted to find this weapon and never thought of destroying it, but..." Rudra lifts his head in hope after hearing the word 'but'. Ashwatthama is nowhere to be seen, but there is an echo, "Antah asti prarambha, prarambhah asti antah."

Rudra stands up and looks everywhere frantically, but Ashwatthama has left already, and Kshitip is lying on the grass. The sun has gone down, and darkness is already replacing the light. He lifts Kshitip on his shoulders and walks the last fifty metres.

There are some people walking on the road who come running to Rudra after noticing a body on his shoulders. Rudra just sits down as he doesn't have any strength at all. He explains to them that Kshitip needs medical attention. He doesn't allow his mind and body to faint as he has a weapon of mass destruction to take care of.

Somehow, these kind-hearted people take them to a small hospital, and the doctors start their treatment urgently.

Rudra is on the hospital bed with drips on his wrists, but he is still holding the wrapped weapon. Sometime in the night, after all the struggle, his body gives up and falls asleep. But before falling asleep, he notices the name of the hospital on the bed tags, they are in Dehradun.

41

One More Riddle to Solve

Rudra opens his eyes; the sun is shining bright outside the window of his hospital room, and Kshitip is nowhere to be seen. Before he passed out, Kshitip was sleeping on the adjacent bed. Rudra still has drips in his hand, and the moment he thinks of removing them, a male nurse enters.

"Finally, you are awake," says the nurse.

"Where is Kshitip? I mean the guy who was on this bed," Rudra says, pointing towards the bed.

"I know who Kshitip is, the whole hospital knows. He woke up yesterday evening. He has gone for a walk," the nurse replies casually, checking the bottle on the stand.

"He woke up yesterday. How long have I been sleeping?"

"Today is the third day. I personally thought you would be the first casualty of this hospital," he answers, deadpanned and then bursts into laughter after noticing the expression on Rudra's face. "Lots of people have died here. You wouldn't have been the first. It's a bad joke, but I loved your face. Anyway, I will send food for you," says the nurse and leaves the room.

Rudra waits for Kshitip to return and starts thinking about what Ashwatthama has said, *Antah asti prarambha, prarambhah asti antah. So, do we need to put the weapon in* the *Saraswati* Koop *in Allahabad? Everything started from there.*

Kshitip enters and comes running to Rudra after seeing him awake. "How are you?" He asks, hugging him.

"I am feeling better, you look good too."

Kshitip sits near Rudra's feet and says, "I woke up yesterday evening and was getting bored, so I went to explore the neighbourhood. How did we come to Dehradun, and how did it all end? I am so happy that I am alive, and this world is safe."

"I will tell you everything in detail, but first we need to destroy this weapon, and for that we need to know where to go and what to do," says Rudra restlessly.

"I thought that's why you came to Dehradun," he says and tries to read Rudra's face. "Aren't we going to the Bheem bridge?"

"Bheem bridge?"

"Yes. Logically, it fits. This is the location where the Saraswati disappears. It is also mentioned in the Mahabharata that this is the place from where Pandavas started their journey to heaven. At this place, when Draupadi could not cross the river, Bheem lifted a huge rock and placed it there. It is now known as the Bheem pul or Bheem bridge. The cave in which Ved Vyas wrote the Mahabharata is also on the banks of the river," shares Kshitip, expecting a compliment from Rudra.

Rudra thinks about Ashwatthama's words, and his facial expressions change. "Genius, bro. Genius. Let's leave," Rudra says and starts getting off the bed.

"You are still very weak. Let's spend some time here and leave when we are healthy," Kshitip says out of concern.

"I cannot rest until I destroy this weapon," says Rudra, carefully removing the drip from his wrist. He puts on his shoes, puts the bag and weapon on his shoulders, and walks towards the door. "What about the bill?"

"These people say, we are their guests, and they are not charging anything."

"Wow. Come, let's go," says Rudra and gets out the door.

After a while, he realises that Kshitip is still inside the room. He turns back and goes to the door. Kshitip is still sitting on the bed. "Hurry up, bro, let's go."

"I am not coming, Rudra," says Kshitip, looking out of the window on the opposite side. Rudra cannot believe his words.

"What do you mean, you are not coming? This is what we are supposed to do."

Kshitip continues to look outside the window and says, "This is what you are supposed to do. My role is over. I was supposed to wield Gandeev."

Rudra enters the room hurriedly, "No, no, no, no, no. We are a team, and that's how they have planned things. You cannot leave me now."

Kshitip stands up and comes closer to Rudra. "Rudra, I am done, and I don't care about them and us anymore. I need peace. After experiencing everything, all I need is peace. I don't expect anyone else to understand but you," says Kshitip, hugging Rudra.

"I do, bro, I do," Rudra says and his throat chokes. "Where will you go?"

"To someplace peaceful," says Kshitip, smiling, but fails to hide the tears in his eyes. After a long, awkward silence, they both leave the hospital.

"Where will you go after destroying the Pashupatastra?" Kshitip asks while walking on the deserted road.

Rudra puts his right hand in his trouser pocket, where he has permanently sewn the artefact. He wants to tell Kshitip about it, but he is hesitant. Kshitip understands his reluctance, puts his hand on Rudra's shoulder and says, "It's OK. You are doing the right thing by not sharing."

"It's not that I don't trust you, but somebody died just to ensure that I have the key. I have to honour his death."

Kshitip pats Rudra's back and says, "You don't have to explain anything, Rudra. You are doing the right thing. Let's walk, we have a long way to go. You didn't tell me what happened after I fell unconscious, and to be very frank, I don't care now. But if ever our paths cross, tell me that story." Kshitip hugs Rudra again and immediately starts walking in the opposite direction.

Due to the lockdown, there are no passenger vehicles on the road. In the thirty minutes that Rudra has walked on the road, not even a commercial vehicle has passed. Rudra gets restless to see the artefact—the key that the old man has given him.

He finds a secluded place, a few metres from the road. He puts his hand in his pocket and grabs the piece. It is heavy and probably conical in shape. He tears the pocket and takes it out. It's a smooth metal piece, hefty for its size, and hardly two inches tall, pyramidic in shape.

"My worst nightmare became true."

42

The Last Ascent

"Are you Tata or Birla? Why do you give him free food? He is just some maniac with no responsibilities," says an angry woman to his shopkeeper husband.

"Have you ever heard of anybody climbing this unscalable mountain? I don't know who he is, but he has covered almost all the mountain twice and doesn't even have any fancy equipment. He has a replica of the mountain in his hand, made of some precious metal. He is not a normal man," the shopkeeper says in awe of the man.

"Have you seen his attire? He looks like a beggar. He has not taken a bath in at least fifteen days. He stinks so bad that when he eats here in our stall, others don't come. You are losing business because of him, Shankar," the woman yells.

"My love, this place is the land of Shiva, his own house, his abode. Let's have a bigger heart. And let me tell you, he is not a maniac; the way he talks clearly shows he is an educated and intelligent man. And, you already know the kind of things that happen to people who try to climb this sacred mountain, but he seems untouched by all that. Kindness never goes to waste, my love. Om namah Shivaay," Shankar replies and starts preparing tea.

The man, who is wrapped in a dirty shawl, turns and comes closer to Shankar's stall. He has long, dirty hair and an even dirtier beard. He is wearing torn shoes, and only God knows how he is surviving in such terrain and climate. He sits on a bench in the stall and starts tying his shoelaces.

"Are you going to climb the mountain again, sir?" Shankar asks. And he just nods in response.

"Ok, I will pack you something to eat," Shankar says, starting to pack something while his wife gives him a cold stare. "Take care, sir." Shankar gives the bag to him.

He bows down and touches Shankar's feet. Shankar is hardly five years older than him. Shankar is taken aback and gets teary-eyed. The man leaves.

"He is not coming back; I could see it in his eyes," Shankar says, getting busy with his daily chores.

"Where should I go, Lord Shiva? Show me some light, show me a path, please. I don't have the strength left now. Today, either I will find the door or die!" he shouts, starting his last ascent on Mount Kailash.

He starts climbing the mountain around 9 a.m., and now it is about 2 p.m. He has not found anything different from what he saw in his last two climbs.

Suddenly, the ice under his left foot caves in, and he falls. Luckily, his fall lasts for only 10-15 feet, but his head hits an ice boulder, and he starts bleeding. He stands up, angrily removes the metal piece from his pocket, and lifts his arm to throw it on the ground.

The sun is shining bright in the sky, for the first time since he arrived in Tibet. While throwing the piece on the ground, he notices an extremely fine ray of sunlight passing through it when it comes between his eye and the sun. His arm is already in motion, and he throws the piece on ice between his feet. It makes a hole in the ice and is not visible at all.

What just happened? he thinks, digging the ice with his bare hands. The ice is very hard, but he knows this is the clue he is looking for and can't let it go.

Finally, after great effort, he recovers the piece and immediately looks for that small hole. The light passes again at a certain angle, through a small hole. He understands that this hole is the location of the door, but he soon realises that there must be two holes in the piece for the light to pass through, which means two potential locations of the door.

He turns the piece 180 degrees to find the other hole, but the light is not passing through. He tries from multiple angles but fails to see the other end of the tunnel through which light is passing. As an engineer, he knows that there must be two ends in a straight line to allow light to pass, but how come the light is visible from one end and not from the other? After failing to find the other end, he gives up, praising the engineering.

By this time, he is fully aware of the geometry of Mount Kailash and that piece. His heart sinks after realising the side on which the hole is. It's the north face of the mountain, which is utterly unclimbable. He starts going towards the north face, but he has to climb down by a few hundred feet to reach a point from where he can start a fresh ascent.

It takes him about an hour to get to that point, but he still can't find any possible way to climb this side. And now he realises why it is called unclimbable. The inclination is about seventy degrees, and after a certain height, it progresses outwards. This is where the hole on the piece is; reaching that point is impossible. No one in the universe has ever climbed this mountain.

The sun has almost gone down, and in the excitement of uncovering the location of the door, he doesn't realise that in the next few minutes, he won't have any source of light in the most dangerous terrain in the world. He realises that he has run out of food and water. He has only one shawl, no torch, or any source of light.

The biggest problem of all is his lack of a source of light, and it becomes almost fatal for him when he puts his foot on a loose rock, which fails to withstand his weight and gives way. He falls from hundreds of feet. After rolling for about a minute, his head hits a tree stem, and he passes out.

He feels in his dizzy state that somebody lifts him and puts him on their shoulders. He tries to open his eyes, but direct light on his eyes does not let him. He realises there is blood all over his face. Suddenly, his body freezes in fear after realising something—the man is wearing an impeccable suit with brown leather boots.

The man in the Armani suit puts him on the ground, near the source of light.

"No, no, I am very close to finding something extraordinary, you can't kill me now. I can't afford to die now," Rudra pleads, his eyes are still shut. He is not fully conscious.

"I have not come to kill you; I have come to repent for everything that I have done. Tell me where you need to go, I will take you there," says the man in the Armani suit, sitting very close to his face.

Rudra is partially conscious and has no control over his actions; he just wants to go to that door so badly that he doesn't process whatever is happening around him. He shows him the location on the north wall and points at it. The man lifts him and opens the door of the light source, putting Rudra in.

"It's the same craft," he says. The craft takes off.

He can hear mild groans of the man. The whimpering increases as they reach closer to the point.

Rudra asks, "Who are you?"

The man doesn't reply as he is in extreme pain. After reaching closer to the point, the man just pushes him out, and he falls on the ice. The moment he falls, the craft falls like a dead bird. From the point where he is, he fails to see what happened to the craft, but the way it is falling, he knows the outcome. He hears a sound of something hitting the ice.

He is so cold that his hand can't differentiate between his body and ice. He can't even walk or crawl. His hands are so stiff that he cannot even fold them. He is so close yet so far.

He thinks of his father, who is not even his actual father, but who has always loved him and sacrificed his life to save him. He thinks of his mother, the most amazing, loving and caring mother, even though not his real mother. Then he thinks of the girl, their fights, scooter rides, the hug on his roof and her at her window in her white nightdress, waving at him.

"Sorry, I am sorry." He passes out.

A door opens, and two huge, hairy hands take Rudra in.

Epilogue

"Arjun Bhaiya, Arjun Bhaiya," a twelve-year-old boy runs on rocky ground. It's a black ground with an ancient temple in the background. He runs towards the cave, which has a huge Shiva linga, half-submerged in water.

"Arjun Bhaiya, somebody asked me to give you this," he says when a well-built man in his early thirties comes out of one of the caves.

"Take a breath, Murugan. Who gave you what?" Kshitip asks.

Murugan puts his hand in his pocket, takes out an envelope, and hands it over to Kshitip.

Kshitip opens the letter:

"The Guruputras are not what we thought they were. The world is in danger, and I need you. Meet me at 36."

Coda

This is the year 2071; a man is standing at the entrance of a cul-de-sac. The street and houses are in ruins. It's evening and there are no streetlights on. Some poor kids are playing or may be running after stealing something.

The man stops one of them. "Does anyone live here?" he asks.

The boy tries to run away, but the man holds his arm.

"I asked if anyone lives here?"

The boy is terrified and tries to free his arm, but he gives up after realising he won't be able to. "Yes, that old crazy woman. Except her, nobody else," he says, pointing at a ruin with a window towards the street. The man lets him go.

He enters through the door of the house, which doesn't even have a latch. There is a candle burning inside, and an old and fragile woman is lying on her bed, groaning loudly.

"Who is there? This house has nothing for you," she says in a broken voice.

The man stands in the dark without speaking a single word. After a while, he says with a lump in his throat, "Roshani."

The old woman is taken aback and tries lifting her head to see him.

"Rudra? Is that you?"

"Oh my god, Roshani. I am sorry for everything," Rudra breaks down.

"You better be, you moron," the woman says, trying hard to lift her head but failing to.

"No, no, Roshani," says Rudra and runs to her bed. He puts her head on his thighs and starts crying.

"I knew you were alive. People said you killed your parents and ran off, but I never believed them. I knew you would come for me," she says with an indescribable pain in her voice. Rudra keeps on crying.

"Don't cry. My condition is my choice. Mummy and Papa died trying to make my life happy. They wanted me to marry, but how could I? My answer was 'yes,'" she says with a tired smile. Rudra's pain increases with every single word she speaks. She touches Rudra's face with her wrinkled hands. "How come you have not aged. Your skin still feels like you are in your thirties or forties, but what happened to your fingers?"

"It's a long story," replies Rudra in pain.

"Time is all I have," she says with that same sad smile. "Tell me."

Rudra starts telling her about his life, and somewhere in the middle, he feels that she has stopped listening and her chest has stopped rising. He cries for hours.

He comes out of the house and leaves, burning two houses behind him.

Acknowledgements

This list has to start with my mother and grandmothers, people who ensured I slept with a story in mind. A big thanks to my brother who bought books, comics and novels with his pocket money, the sources that ignited the fervour in me to become an author. To my sisters for being amazing listeners and storytellers.

A big thanks to my publisher, Om Books International and its editor in chief, the very dynamic Shantanu Ray Chaudhuri, for the guidance and for believing in my story. A big shoutout to my vivacious and energetic literary agent, Suhail Mathur, for representing my story and all the encouragement and guidance. To the team at the book bakers for designing a captivating cover. A sincere thanks to the editor of the book, Kalpita Ratnashree, for the spot-on suggestions and corrections.

Special thanks to my friends Arvind, Sachin, Deepak, Anurag, Lalit, and Gaurav for the storytelling nights at HBTU during power cuts. Thanks to Satya, Ali, Alisha, Veena, Prashanna, Shardha, Shubhra, Tarun, Harish, Paras, Aman, Akash, Mayur, Ila—the cheeky monkey guys for their encouragement.

Thanks to my adorable daughters, Aadu and Cuckoo, for forcing me to tell two very, very, very new stories every night. Their cute questions make me close potential loopholes in my stories. And finally, thanks to my wife Dipti for motivating me to start putting my idea on paper. A huge thanks to her for being my only test audience and confidante; without her motivation and support, this story wouldn't have seen the light of day.